THE LOGIC OF FLESH AND OTHER STORIES

THE LOGIC OF FLESH AND OTHER STORIES

Norval Rindfleisch

AUTHORS CHOICE PRESS

iUniverse, Inc.
Bloomington

THE LOGIC OF FLESH AND OTHER STORIES

All Rights Reserved © 2000, 2012 by Norval Rindfleisch.

No part of this book may be reproduced or transmitted in any form or by any means, graphic, electronic, or mechanical, including photocopying, recording, taping, or by any information storage or retrieval system, without the written permission of the publisher.

This is a work of fiction. All of the characters, names, incidents, organizations, and dialogue in this novel are either the products of the author's imagination or are used fictitiously.

AUTHORS CHOICE PRESS

Published by iUniverse, Inc.

For information address:
iUniverse
1663 Liberty Drive
Bloomington, IN 47403
www.iuniverse.com
1-800-Authors (1-800-288-4677)

Originally published by Xlibris Corporation

Because of the dynamic nature of the Internet, any Web addresses or links contained in this book may have changed since publication and may no longer be valid.

The views expressed in this work are solely those of the author and do not necessarily reflect the views of the publisher, and the publisher hereby disclaims any responsibility for them.

Any people depicted in stock imagery provided by Thinkstock are models, and such images are being used for illustrative purposes only.
Certain stock imagery © Thinkstock.

ISBN: 978-1-4759-2712-2 (sc)

Printed in the United States of America

iUniverse rev. date: 05/30/2012

CONTENTS

PROLOGUE 9

IN AUTUMN 13

EVERYTHING ALWAYS COMES
   UP ROSES IN MIDDLE AMERICA 21

FIRST HUNT 35

A CHILDREN'S PLAY 45

ELEGY 56

AGON 63

THE TRAGIC FLAW OF TOM CASSIDY, Jr. 70

THE LOGIC OF FLESH 80

CAREER MAN 89

NOVAK ON FEEGAN 97

THE TOLL OF SPRING 105

MY HERITAGE 115

THE GOOD BOWLER 129

Grateful acknowledgment is made to the publications in which some of these stories first appeared:

To the *Yale Literary Magazine* for "The Logic of Flesh" and "Novak on Feegan"

To the *Northern New England Review* for "Agon," "Everything Always Come Up Roses in Middle America," The Toll of Spring," and "My Heritage" (Originally entitled "The Irish Woodpile.")

To Ithaca House for "A Children's Play" and "First Hunt" in the collection *In Loveless Clarity*.

To the Foundation Workshop, Theater by the Sea in Portsmouth, New Hampshire for the Concert Performance of the play version of "The Good Bowler" and to the production staff and the actors who participated. Dec. 1983

PROLOGUE

In the beginning there was James J. Hill and he stood alone on the edge of space and time, looking westward and northward with ambition and greed, and he saw further and dreamed larger than other men of his time and so that historical moment became his. As he stood looking, he saw an Empire of land, staggering in its expanse and wildness, majesty and loneliness, and he said:"Let there be a railroad to bind this land and make it whole and subject unto me."

When that had been accomplished with cheap imported oriental labor, James J. Hill looked at what he had wrought and saw that it was good, but he was not yet satisfied. He said: "Let us people the land with Swedes and Danes, Germans and Irish, Finns and Norwegians, and anyone who was strong enough and energetic enough and ignorant enough to endure the long cold prairie winters by the ice bound rivers and lakes."

Then he sent his agents as missionaries into foreign lands and they spread the gospel of innocence and purity (and economic opportunity) in the Virgin Land (for James J. Hill still believed as late as the 1880s in the faith of de Crevecoeur and Jefferson). And the peasants, the farmers and craftsmen, came out in thousands from the lands of corruption and limited opportunity to people his land and break his soil and produce crops for his profit and consume products also for his profits. And James J. Hill, the Scotsman, looked at what he had wrought and saw that it was good. Then to make his profits flow more abundantly and rapidly he said:"Let us offer them the gift of credit. Let them borrow money to buy tools and machines so that historians will be more kind to us than to the other railroads which preceded us and got the lion's share of the graft and thievery." And when the humanitarian old Jim Hill (who did not abandon his people on the prairie because it would not have been profitable) looked at what they had wrought at his bidding and encouragement, he was pleased and saw that it was good.

Then he said, so long as he was playing god and needed to curse his people with some kind of original sin less they grow proud and complacent: "Let them buy in a closed market and sell in an open market so that they will forever be in bondage and pay homage to their benefactor who has delivered them from corruption and brought them forth into the Promised Land."

This then became the first curse: the profits of the free and open market went not to those who worked the land but to those who bought and sold on margins and shortages and futures and who never saw or touched the grain and livestock they traded. But this was all good, even sacred, because this was laissez faire. When the people bought tools or seed on credit, they bought at the price determined by the railroad or her agents without competition and not in the open marketplace. This too was good because the more victims one held in bondage the greater the glory in a world which admired ruthless power. Thus, the Empire Builder's fame grew until he became that magnificent full-blossomed rose for which the weaker buds had been pruned.

Now out of all of this came the railroad culture, which grew rapidly and culminated briefly in a fullness in which the climactic moment for most of the people of the upper plains was the joy or the sorrow of the coming and going of trains. Villages, towns, cities proliferated along the rails at the junctions (in those alternate sections of land owned by the railroads—gratuitously given to them by the state legislature which had already been bought.) The junctions were trade centers and the middlemen gathered there to share with the railroad in the profits of others' labors. And James J. Hill saw in his enlightened self-interest that to share a small portion of his wealth with those who could be easily bought was good for J. J. Hill and thus good for his Empire. So grain elevators rose, owned or controlled by the railroads, and great stockyards spread to feed the packing plants that were built on driven timbers in the low areas along the rivers. The products of new industries—barbed wire, pitch forks, shovels, milk pails—were retailed in the railroad stores at the railroad prices—on credit of course—to clod-hopping, slow-thinking farmers in coveralls whose hesitation in the face of the slick-talking salesmen was not a sign of caution and wisdom, but a mask of fear and uncertainty. And all of this seemed wondrous and good, but the railroad culture was doomed, and just when it seemed most opulent when those magnificently decorated and furnished executive railroad cars had become the epitome of luxury, its fall was most imminent, for great highways and tractor trailers and trucks and cars had already begun to transform the world he had created.

As he reaped the fruits of others' labor, so the others inherited the legacy of his recklessness, for they were all trapped by the curse of nature which was unimagined abundance which sprung from the deep, rich, black earth and glutted the markets in cycles, in unpredictable fits and starts but ultimately in a gradual spiral of increasing surpluses and declining prices.

So the two curses, James J. Hill and Nature, defeated the people in time. They were slow to articulate their grievances. They thought it was the lack of paper money or silver that was the cause. They found their spokesman in the Boy Orator who promised James J. Hill that the people would not be crucified on a Cross of Gold, manufactured by J. P. Morgan and shipped and rebated by Jim Hill. There were Grangers and Greenbackers, Populists and Progressives, Farmers and Laborers and whether it was Munn vs. Illinois, or the U. S. vs. Northern Securities, it was always the People vs. the Railroads, the People vs. Old Jim Hill.

The People won the political and legal battles, but it was all too late. The people triumphed in time, but the glory belonged to James J. Hill and the price was paid by the people. They had come to the land in droves to settle the last frontier, but the land could not support them—not because the crops had failed (although that was true of the farmers west of the twenty-inch rain belt) but because they produced too abundantly: the supply was always greater than the demand. The Great Depression just made official for everyone an economic condition that had been true for the farmers for years. The farms had to become larger. They left the land and took refuge in the city—in Chicago, Minneapolis and Kansas City—where they were exploited by others more adapted to the techniques of industrial and urban thievery (which was also good because it, too, was laissez faire and survival of the fittest.) Thus the farm houses were abandoned and small villages depopulated. Villages and towns whose Saturday night lights once dazzled the eyes of children who had never dreamed of such splendor became virtual ghost towns. Only widows who could no longer stay alone on the farms, employees of the elevators or lumber yards, and the operators of pool halls and grocery stores now lived in the villages. Then paved highways proliferated and new trade centers (not owned or controlled by the railroads) based upon automobiles, trucks and buses developed.

The railroads petitioned for the withdrawal of the passenger service and abandoned the towns they had created. Now the people have inherited his Empire and their politicians indict him for his sins, but Jim Hill knew that history is written not about the good or the bad but about the creative. The railroad has lost its power, but the monuments of his schemes are everywhere. Now though the people have seized his power, they live in the shadow of his tomb, on the other side of his historical moment. Everywhere, his work (the very names and locations of villages and towns, counties and cities) pervades the Empire he won and lost. In his largest cities you will see his greatest mausoleums, train depots, huge, stone caverns of emptiness, the boldest artifacts of the departed spirit of the Empire Builder and his wildest dreams. The people live now in anticlimax and decline—in the winter and the night of time at the other end of deserted rails.

IN AUTUMN

The boy shuffled his feet and squirmed on the wooden seat. His eyes wandered out the open windows and he gazed, filling his eyes with the flood of sunlight that, after two days of rain, had restored the summer green and deepened the autumn bronze. The subdued voice of the teacher murmured above the sounds of shuffling feet and squeaking desks as she spoke to two girls at her desk. He turned his eyes back to the geography book on his desk and read in the chapter on Argentina about the Gauchos on the pampas, the vast treeless plains like the prairies he lived on, and where there still survived a vestige of the cowboy and horse culture similar to the Old West in America. He did not read so much as he looked at the pictures accompanying the text. He read: "The seasons in Argentina are the opposite of those in the northern hemisphere. When it is summer there, it is winter here."

The boy thought of Charlie and the horse. He was not conscious of chalk markings on the blackboard though he appeared to contemplate them with an almost mystical intensity. He looked out the window again. In the schoolyard a stockade of bush spears surrounded the privy and glinted in the sun. The cottonwoods beyond the playground cast long shadows back across the grass that had been almost grey a week before. To the north of the trees ran the road to Miller and beyond that were the fields—brown, even black—and the pastures with their stolen greenness, filling in the irregular spaces between the harvested and already plowed crop fields. He had seen the horse still grazing in one of those pastures.

He could accept his confinement if it weren't for the weather.

He didn't mind the classroom when it was cold or snowing and the trees and earth had hardened down, but it had suddenly turned to summer again. The turf had softened and began to ooze like sap. During the noon hour he had seen Nels Jensen and his wife leave the village in their car toward Miller. He knew where Charlie would be when school was out. He thought of Charlie, the horse, and the summer days when Nels was on the other side of his land cultivating and the horse was alone in a pasture adjacent to his father's crop fields.

He heard the sound of books closing, and bodies moving when the bell rang. His eyes surveyed the floor for paper before the teacher's voice could remind them of their daily closing chores. She inspected the floor and nodded dismissal, and the classroom emptied in an whirlwind of motion.

He was running before he was out of the door. He went down the path past the school buses and onto the gravel road that led to the crossroads where a paved county road and a state highway intersected. The sounds of the other children's shouting were lost in the noise of the crunch of his steps as he ran along the edge of the gravel. Near the crossroads were a Mobil station, Clarence Johnson's grocery store, Evy's Cafe and Helmut's Pool Room—vestiges of an idea of civilization that prepared for the main line of a railroad that never materialized—only a spur to a grain elevator that had already been abandoned, its rails harvested as scrap metal and its creosote soaked cross ties sold to landscape architects and golf course designers. The state highway to Miller came later and maintained truck service to the elevator. After a time, the crossroads became incorporated into a small town with the name Amberg in honor of the first family in the area from Norway who had broken the prairie sod for farming.

Widows who could not afford Florida or California retired from isolated farm houses, which were soon abandoned, to mobile homes or small frame bungalows on main street between the school house and the crossroads. Three school teachers and two ministers and their families comprised the professional population.

Most of the other residents of under two hundred persons commuted to jobs in larger towns or worked the land of abandoned farms for cash crops.

A farm machinery sales company had flourished for a while and still survived in a diminished condition on the edge of town, dilapidated and rusting farm implements like artifacts of a prehistoric culture dominating the new machinery in the yard. The hardware and seed store had stabilized the village economy and sustained the population over the years.

He crossed the road by the gas station and ran past the American Legion Hall and the cafe to the pool hall and climbed the three stairs to the open porch that served as a kind of sidewalk along the front of a cluster of stores. He stopped at the front door and tried to peer through the screen, but he could not see inside. He turned around and walked to the end of the porch and looked around for Charlie's old Ford. He saw it parked in the shade along the side of the building.

He could not see into the darkness back by the tables even though a lighted clock advertising Grain Belt beer hung on the wall above, its light softly reflecting on the markers above the tables that players slid back and forth with the tips of their cues to mark score. To his left behind the bar near the tobacco counter and the cash register a huge bulk of white and pinked moved.

"Did you see Charlie, Mr. Helmut?"

The mound of flesh moved to wipe a fly.

"Ain't seen 'em—lookin' at 'em." He breathed asthmatically.

Toward the end of the bar the boy's eyes caught the shadowy outline of an indistinct form, obscured not because it was dark but because it was hidden behind a mist of cigarette smoke that the boy had just smelled. Charlie sat at the end of the bar.

Charlie could have been anything in his day. There were rumors that he had been a cowboy, a carnival barker, a rich rancher who had lost a fortune gambling. Because of his way with horses, some speculated that he was part Indian, and that he preferred a miserable life of poverty to returning to a reservation. He just dropped into the crossroads one day at the beginning of the war and never left.

He was old now and lame. He lived in a shack that he had built out of old lumber from abandoned farm houses on public property along a hardtop county road just east of town. The County Commissioner's office had sent him an official warning to tear the building down, but no-one had enforced the order. Once they had done their official duty, the commissioners decided it would be just as well, and a lot easier, to wait for him to die when the problem would resolve itself.

He did odd jobs over the years—helped farmers with the harvest or pumped gas. He drove a tractor most of the past summer for the boy's father who had taken a full time job at the new 3M plant and now farmed only part time. Charlie didn't mind tractor work but he couldn't handle hard physical labor anymore. He lived mostly off food stamps and charity the rest of the year and spent most of his time sitting in Helmut's pool room drinking spiked beer—"to keep the bugs away" he said, and his eyes would twinkle if he had not been drinking for too long. It was his eyes that one noticed—clear, blue beacons, signaling intelligence from a craggy mass. His coat was a long, khaki army surplus, and around his shoes a torn pair of rubbers had been fastened by inner-tube binders. On his head was the drooping black remnants of a once smart rancher's hat.

The boy approached him and whispered, "Nels is gone to town—once more, Charlie, before winter . . ."

Charlie's eyes stopped the boy. They seemed glazed and uncomprehending. Charlie was not just feeling good as on those summer days when the boy stole his rides on Nels Jensen's big stallion that loved only Charlie or his smell or his voice. Charlie was drunk.

Charlie tried to speak. The boy tugged his arm and whispered again. Charlie moved and then answered loudly.

"Boy, you tell yer old man that old Charlie ain't gonna help with the corn. I told him before. Charlie will work anything but shelling corn."

The boy smiled. Good old Charlie had responded. And then the boy pleaded out loud how his father was working long hours now in the city and didn't have time and for Charlie to come, but Charlie refused. Shelling corn was something he could no longer do. But Charlie had little heart for their game. His tongue became thick. He lost the sense of his words and soon the words themselves became muffled efforts—grunts in his throat.

That summer the boy would take the lunch his mother had made for Charlie, along with the rope halter, bit, and reins, and drive the small Ford tractor to the field where Charlie was working with the Farmall. After Charlie had finished his lunch, they drove the small tractor along the fence to where the horse was grazing in Nels' pasture. They stopped and the boy ran ahead and slipped under the lowest strand in the barbed wire and then held the strands apart for Charlie to get through. All the boy had to do was get Charlie close enough for the horse to smell him or hear his voice so the animal would calm down and approach them. Then the boy could ride him after Charlie had fitted the tack and lifted him onto the bare back. At first Charlie held the halter and walked the horse in tight circles while explaining how to handle the reins. When the horse became accustomed to someone other than Charlie on his back, Charlie let them go alone, and in time the boy handled the horse by himself, moving about the pasture in measured gaits until he felt confident enough to let the horse gallop as he pleased.

Jensen would have nothing to do with the horse since he had been thrown. He let the animal run free with the cattle until it had almost turned wild again. Charlie asked Nels if he couldn't try his hand with the horse, and in a short time brought the stallion under control. Since then Jensen let him take the horse on trail rides with the Amberg Riders, providing he didn't drink and was clean shaven and dressed up. In a borrowed cowboy outfit he and the horse had twice led the Riders in the Homecoming parade at the State University. Except for Charlie no-one rode him. No-one dared until the boy had begged Charlie to let him try.

After a few minutes Charlie finished off his beer and settled himself slowly to the floor and walked up the bar, bumping the stools as he went. The boy ran ahead and opened the screen door. As he passed Mr..Helmut, Charlie hinted with his head and put a finger up. Mr. Helmut handed him a half-pint—shook his head against more—and before Charlie had left, Mr. Helmut had marked the sale down in his account book. Charlie's credit was good. He worked enough to pay his bills. When he was drunk, Mr..Helmut cheated him so if Charlie were to die and never pay him, Mr. Helmut would not lose much.

Outside, Charlie lifted his hand before his eyes in a gesture that seemed to beg forbearance from the glare of the sun, though the sun had already sunk low in the sky and the air had already cooled. The boy led him for a while and then ran ahead excitedly to the old Ford parked on the side of the pool hall and then back to Charlie who had lost his way and almost fell off the porch. In the shade the boy felt a sudden chill.

The car was covered with mud. The upholstery was ripped and the inside smelled of manure and whiskey. Charlie leaned against the hood without getting in. His face seemed frozen. It was covered by red and purple patches and two days growth of gray prickly beard. His watery eyes did not seem to see. The boy pleaded with Charlie. Then he opened the car door and began moving Charlie back around the door to the driver's seat. He pulled Charlie's arm back and then twisted his body. Then he pushed him against the rear door, pulled an arm, twisted, bent him and finally leaned against him until he fell through the space of the open door toward the seat. Charlie bounced a little and made a slight effort not to slide off the seat onto the floor. He lay, face down on the seat, his feet still touching the ground. Outside the car, the boy tried but couldn't lift his feet off the ground. He ran around the car, opened the other door and tried to pull Charlie through. A button on Charlie's coat caught on a spring protruding from the worn seat fabric.

He whispered into Charlie's ear. "C'mon, Charlie, get up, get up."

There was no movement. Charlie's breathing was deep and steady. He had passed out into a drunken sleep. The boy sat down on the running board. He was sweating and breathing heavily. The sun was now entirely blocked by the buildings, and the shaded area had grown to cover the entire parking lot and the lower half of the white clapboard building beyond. He sat for what seemed a long time though it perhaps only a few minutes. He heard Charlie groan and the springs of the seat squeak. He stood up on the running board and looked in at Charlie who had twisted inward so that he faced the back of the seat. He was breathing quietly. The boy reached down and shook him gently and hopelessly.

By the time he reached the railbed that ended near the abandoned loading platforms behind the grain elevator, he looked back to see that the street lamps were already shedding cones of light at corners throughout the village. The sun had settled below the trees and buildings, but he could see streaks of light radiating skyward.

He began his trek homeward along the railbed, through the edge of a wildlife marsh and lake a mile from town and then east through the crop field where his father had left a half mile strip of corn stalks for the pheasants' winter feeding. Soon when the snow cover became permanent, he would ride the school bus.

Two summers before he had walked out to the railbed to watch the crew of college students, shirtless and in shorts, rip up the rails and ties and load them on flat cars to haul back to the rail yard in a distant city. Each morning an engine arrived at the end of the line with two flat cars and the crew, rumored to be recruited from the state university football team. They had begun at the end of the line in Amberg and each day the line grew shorter as the rails and ties were stripped and loaded and hauled away, the rails to be re-smelted and the ties sold to lumber yards. It was a memory that had already begun to fade. It seemed to be so long ago that he couldn't remember there ever having been rails and ties. Walking along the marsh, he watched the huge bank of snows and blues that covered the far side of the lake. Every few minutes a small flock took flight and headed south while another small flock circled in from the north and joined the larger gathering feeding and resting.

As he cut down the railbed embankment and entered the footpath he had made himself during the spring and summer and which he would have to recreate in the coming spring, the long shadow from the setting sun spread across the land. It seemed so long ago that he had been in school, so long ago he had tried to awaken Charlie for another chance at summer, so long ago that he had ridden the horse bareback across Jens' pasture. The moments of this day seemed to have already blended into events of weeks, months even years before in an immense, indistinguishable landscape of memories like the cemeteries where he went with his parents to visit the old fashioned and weather beaten headstones of generations long dead along side recent graves garnished with fading blooms on barren mounds of freshly shoveled earth..

He saw the yard light glowing in the distance as he slipped under the barbed wire. He entered the middle row of the several rows of unharvested corn along the edge of the crop field. He walked slowly and quietly. He stopped briefly every few minutes and listened to the rustling of leaves as the pheasants plunged ahead of him in fear. Near the end of the strip as he approached the gravel road leading from the highway to the barnyard and home, the pheasants in a wild fury of fluttering wings, suddenly rose above the corn stalks, gathered height and wheeled back over his head toward the distant marshland where they would hide in safety for the night. He turned and watched them glide above the stalks and then gain height and glide again. Above the fading rim of light on the horizon, a layer of blue turning to purple melded into the darkening sky.

EVERYTHING ALWAYS COMES UP ROSES IN MIDDLE AMERICA

Protected by childhood innocence during The Great Depression (and safely sheltered until the last years of World War II when I gradually became aware of a world gone mad) I believe I can look back with some objectivity and assert that our trials and tribulations during those years of economic despair were not really as traumatic as my parents claimed them to be. In fact, judging from what I remember of the relative comfort and security that was our way of life back then, I might never have known that there was world-wide hunger and unemployment had I not been constantly reminded of this grim fact by the daily conversations of my mother and father, who, I suspect now, tried to unburden with words of concern some of the guilt they must have felt for not being as badly off as others.

In retrospect, though I respect them for the compassionate guilt they expressed at the time, the truth is that in my middle-middle class family we didn't have it so bad. My parents often gave voice to emotions not entirely justified by our particular circumstances, and on one occasion at least my mother resorted to an unwarranted and consequently foredoomed regimen of retrenchment that brought her to the edge of despair and us, my older brother Hank and me, to the brink of open revolt.

One evening in early June, perhaps three months after my father, at that time a wholesale beer distributor, went broke and after all other courses of action had been tried or rejected, Mother gathered the family in the living room, and we discovered that we were going to live according to a strict budget. She had worked it out on paper and was going to read the budget aloud to the entire family so that we all understood what sacrifices were expected. She hoped to avoid the necessity of discussing the specific points of it one by one as each point arose. It was better to get it all over at once, she said, and save her the anguish of separate decisions.

She began with the most difficult decision first.

"There will be no more Saturday matinees."

Hank, who was my spokesman, objected immediately.

"Geez, Ma, it's only a lousy dime each."

"Every lousy little penny counts," she answered. "Money doesn't grow on trees, you know. You can begin with a little self-sacrifice."

"But Kit Carson just went into this cave that's a gold mine, trying to rescue this pretty girl the crooks have tied up in there, and they've lighted this long fuse to these barrels of dynamite stacked up just inside the entrance to the mine, and if that goes off... Wham!!!! There's the end of Kit. He'll be trapped in there for sure."

"I am certain he will survive. He has escaped worse hazards than that for eight weeks now and the serial has seven more to go. You can rest assured that he will survive for at least six more."

"But we'll miss them. We won't know how they'll all turn out."

"You can ask one of your friends. Next item."

She cut the gas money for the car to a dollar a week. But Father proceeded to show that, bankrupt failure or not, he knew what finances were all about. "It will be rather difficult," he interrupted mildly, "to look for a job with only a dollar gas money."

She hadn't thought of that. She established a special emergency gasoline fund for job hunting only and Father commented that she was showing true capitalistic spirit: you have to spend money to make money.

She allotted so much money for food, so much for clothes, gas, light. She projected our savings over a six-month period before Father reminded her of five or six items she had overlooked. When he had finished his list of her omissions, Hank protested once again but with waning fervor,

"We're giving up a lot, but what sacrifices are they going to make?" He pointed to our younger brother and sister.

"Why, they're only babies, Hank," Mother answered. "They don't go to movies and they don't eat any more than birds."

"Yah, well he," Hank said, pointing at our little bird brother, "eats like a vulture."

"Each according to his needs," she answered in what I now realize was the spirit of true Christian socialism.

"O.K.," said Hank, who was something of a budding economist himself, "we'll divide the food in direct proportion to weight." He laughed and rubbed his plump hands in gluttonous anticipation of the more substantial portions he was certain to receive as the only member of the family who was at that time in his "fat phase" of physical development.

II

That we arrived at that evening gathering at all requires an explanation or at least some recapitulation of the history of my family, for any form of planned economy was improbable for two reasons: first, my mother had been raised with certain social and economic advantages and had never experienced the need to sacrifice and, second, to speak bluntly, she was incompetent in practical matters.

Although my father had little formal education, he was able to achieve a pretense to status by becoming an accountant and bookkeeper. He had apprenticed in a bank, withdrawn to the inner vaults, and emerged five years later a respected manipulator of money and books. When he courted my mother, he was a rising young banker, and, therefore, not entirely objectionable to my mother's parents, though Grandmother often said that she thought Mother could have done better. Though they were relatively uneducated themselves, they expected a college graduate for their daughter who had been liberated by the two years of finishing school that they had purchased, cash on the line according to Grandfather, out of their then substantial wealth.

My father was already a vice president (then as now, a position rendered meaningless by redundancy) when in 1932 his bank collapsed. His unemployment became a social as well as a financial problem because Grandfather and Grandmother, having lived long and conspicuously in retirement, had died within three years of each other leaving little more than the house. And the house was badly in need of repair and remodeling.

He soon had opportunities, but Mother rejected them all because they represented a level to which she would not stoop.

"You can't do just anything for a living," she argued. "There is a dignity to be maintained even in adversity." And so he did nothing for a year.

To serve his time of disgrace and failure, Father began two hobbies—reading philosophy and raising flowers. He read Plato and Marcus Aurelius long into each night, awoke early to tend his flowers planted around the house, and then read and napped in the afternoon before supper. The beginning of those two hobbies was the beginning of his gradual detachment from the family. He grew vague and disconnected over the years, and to talk to him eventually became a chore. It seemed as though he never understood you directly, as if everything said had to be translated by some mysterious spiritual mediator who alone held discourse with him in the ethereal regions of his absent-mindedness. But his total absorption in philosophy and flowers came later. During the first year of unemployment, they were only hobbies, harmless substitutes for the professional duties and dignity of which he had been deprived by the Great Depression.

When Prohibition was repealed, Mother finally agreed to his

taking a job as auditor and accountant for a large whisky and beer distributor—a mean and vulgar occupation some would say but founded and directed by some of the best families in town who condoned the vulgarity of the new business because of its grand scale of operation. As they saw it, they dispensed massive dosages of alcoholic euphoria to a poverty-stricken and depressed world. Except that the profits were exorbitant, the services rendered might have been considered public spirited if not downright Christian.

A year later my father, encouraged by his contribution to the firm's success, decided that he was ready to go into business for himself. He negotiated a franchise contract for a national beer, rented a warehouse, and went into partnership with his younger brother, a skilled mechanic who had flourished during the days of prohibition as a twenty-four hour "on call" emergency truck mechanic for a bootlegger.

But, alas, after a short healthy spurt, their business began to decline and finally collapsed. Once again he found himself unemployed, and once again mother was embarrassed by the social condition that unemployment symbolized. And once again, Father eagerly returned to reading the Stoics and tending flowers as the central occupations of his unemployment.

We escaped starvation because Father had kept twenty per cent of his assets in cash in a safe deposit box. He tried to explain his failure. Apparently the law of double causation with reciprocal effect (or something like that) had been at work: cash is static; invested, it is dynamic. You have to spend money to make money. If you save it in hard cash, your business may go under, but then you will always have money with high purchasing power. He did not convince Mother that whatever he had done, or not done, was all for the best any way you looked at it. To tide us over until he could secure a new job and because he had so obviously failed, Mother decided that it was her turn to mismanage things.

Not unexpectedly, she did a poor job with the budget from the very beginning. Her attempts at economy often cost her more than she would have spent before she started the budget. She wasted money on "sale" foods such as prunes or spinach or macaroni that we refused to eat and which had to be thrown out after it had been placed before us in various exotic disguises two or three times and picked at grudgingly. She had forgotten the ice man, and since it was an unseasonably hot week, she had to borrow two dollars from some other entry or from the week ahead. She was two-thirds through her second week's budget before the end of the first week. All of this resulted in mismanaged meals, something she never did in the days of carefree spending in the open marketplace.

Once about a week into the budget, for unknown reasons, we had an elaborate roast beef dinner that was virtually a banquet. It was followed by three days of tasteless penances, as if we were to pay for the unfortunate consequences of fate, bad national planning, and her incompetence as a home economist by eating purposely distasteful meals. Then, a week later perhaps out of guilt for the punitive meals, she surprised us with steak and French fries and an unlimited supply of catsup which Hank and I greedily poured over our potatoes and meat and mopped up later with bread for dessert. Hank and I were allowed a sip of wine each, and we extended the spirit of the meal by reeling about the house in imitation of the drunks we had seen in movies.

III

Two days before the Fourth of July, in one of her punitive, austerity moods, Mother stated, and without any provocation on our part, that there was no money in the budget for fireworks. "We don't have money to burn," she announced in a futile attempt to avoid the issue before it had been broached. All she managed to do was to begin forty-eight hours of sullen murmurs and innuendos, of vague griping and bickering—all thinly masking the real source of disappointment.

The day before the Fourth came and went without any signs of weakening. We had hovered around the house, observing her for some evidence of affection or humor which would be a prelude to surrender. Hank was especially kind, leading the rest of us in a campaign of cajolery, but she remained tenaciously aloof and indifferent to our manipulation.

That evening before we went to bed, we somehow convinced ourselves that she would weaken, that after we had gone to sleep she would buy the fireworks and surprise us in the morning. So we went to bed with a feeling of happy and nervous anticipation. And as we spoke quietly before sleep, we worked out in detail the order, the program of our fiery display: a barrage of Roman candles and whirling pinwheels, of exploding sky rockets, and three-inch salutes.

There were no fireworks the next morning. Distant explosions, echoing the pleasure and fulfillment of others' dreams, some near and some far, mockingly beckoned us, but when we went to watch, it became too painful to witness others' delights and we returned home depressed and sullen. After lunch we ventured up the alley to watch some older boys who were exploding empty baby food cans fifty feet into the air with cherry bombs. They placed the little red bomb with its green wick protruding under the can, lit the fuse, then ran back. The smoke raced into the can, disappeared, and then for a tense second all seemed quiet. When the bomb exploded, the can shot into the air high above the silhouette of trees and then dropped in a wobbling arc like a wounded bird, and we all raced to see the damage and stood admiring the force that had twisted the can so grotesquely.

In the early evening the younger families up and down the street began their celebrations. We walked across lawns and jumped hedges and stood casually in the background as fathers instructed their children how to hold the Roman candle or how to use a punk cautiously from behind to launch a sky rocket.

"Geez, a three year old kid." Hank cringed in disgust. And

we moved on to another yard in whose confines another ritual was reaching orgiastic intensity.

As it grew dark we withdrew to the front porch and watched dejectedly the last sputtering of joy in the distance. Mother, who had complained of a headache from all the noise, had gone to her room for a rest after supper, and Father, who had tried to salvage some part of the day by taking the younger children of the neighborhood wading in the city pond, now spoke to us from the far end of the porch, indirectly and philosophically. His words were cryptic and obscure, but he seemed to be making an appeal to our compassion. We were assured that there were more important things in life than fireworks and he implied that this situation, like all situations, would soon pass away.

IV

And he was right in his ethereal way.

At nine o'clock Mother came downstairs and out onto the porch. Her hair was combed neatly and she had put on fresh lipstick. A sweater draped loosely over her shoulders, and she carried a purse dangling from one arm.

"I'm going to the store for a loaf of bread and some milk," she said.

"You'd better take the boys with you to help carry the groceries, unless you want me to drive you."

"No, I'll walk. The boys may come if they wish."

It was four blocks to Gilbert's Confectionery Store, the only store open at that hour of the day. The sounds of celebration had dwindled to infrequent and distant echoes. A few families were indoors, though, and we could hear voices from behind darkened porch screens and bursts of laughter. An occasional cigarette glowed and went out, and where there were lights, bugs seeking the inside banged against screens.

Mr. Gilbert's confectionery was a one-floor, wooden frame

building neatly divided into two halves. On the right side was a long counter stacked with bread and pastry and behind this, in shelves to the ceiling, were canned goods. It was on this side he sat on evenings, holidays, and Sundays, because his business then was based on last minute purchases of items that had been forgotten by families during their bigger shopping sprees.

But on the other side of the store was the real source of Mr. Gilbert's wealth. Glass candy cases four feet high, crammed with malted milk balls, strawberry jaw-breakers, and candy bars, were arranged as counters on top of which were brilliantly decorated penny punch boards. Behind, stacked on shelves to the ceiling, were model airplanes and ships.

Mr. Gilbert extended credit to any boy who wanted it, and he kept a large ledger with each boy's name listed and the charges entered. Few parents ever heard of the ledger, for the boys were terrified to let it be known that they had a charge account for a punch board. But none could resist the chance of winning and all were intimidated to pay sooner or later by the fear that Mr. Gilbert would expose their gambling accounts.

His profits were gleaned penny by penny. He never burned more than one light in the evening, so it was difficult to tell whether he was open or not. In the winter the store was barely warmer than the outside, and Mr. Gilbert sat in a heavy coat by a stove fire hardly worth tending. He always grumbled or threatened, moaned or complained, but boys were drawn by those colorful punch boards and the rare possibilities they offered. He told slightly off-color stories to the older boys, and laughed and winked and insinuated himself into their confidence.

When we first entered, we saw the fireworks display on top of the candy case and on the floor in front. It was decorated with red, white, and blue crepe paper streamers. Mother picked out a loaf of bread and sent Hank to the back of the store to the wooden and glass cooler to get two quarts of milk. Mr. Gilbert was sitting to the right, his white head camouflaged by the remaining loaves of bread on the wire stack that rested on the counter.

"You have a great deal of fireworks left over. Has business been bad?" Mother asked.

"Yes, indeed, Mam. You can see for yourself." He got up from his chair and stood there half stooped for a moment. "Every other year my supply was all gone before the Fourth, but not this year." He spread his palms on the counter. "This year people are afraid to spend and it's my theory that's why things are so bad. You can't sit on your money. Spending keeps it in circulation, but everyone's afraid—that's the cause—everyone's afraid to spend.". Mother cut him off.

"I expect you will take a big loss on the fireworks. People won't buy them tomorrow," she said as she turned, selected a Roman candle from the display counter, and examined it at arm's length.

"Well, that's true. But I can save most of them for next year." He came from behind the counter and stood next to the display.

"But you have spent good money for them, and now your profits will be tied up in the surplus. Isn't that correct, Mr. Gilbert? Isn't that the way business works?" She unsnapped her pocketbook and began rummaging for her coin purse. "You, as a seller, have to keep your money working, just as I, the purchaser, must keep spending. Goodness knows, I don't know much about it, but my husband, who is an accountant, you know, has explained some to me," she said taking out money to pay for the groceries.

"You are right. Money has to keep working." He spoke to Mother out of the side of his mouth over his shoulder. "Why, if I could sell the rest of these fireworks, I could buy other things and sell them; for example, if you were to buy these fireworks, then in no time with your spending and my money working, there wouldn't be a depression." He began to stack the fireworks neatly.

"Won't it be dangerous to store those fireworks for a year? Won't there be danger of spontaneous combustion? And if you store them in a damp place, you might ruin everything." She turned her back on the display.

"Why, yes," he said. "You have a very keen sense of business.

You are able to look at it from the small businessman's point of view. Not many understand my problems."

Then she began to bargain, first article by article, and then lot by lot, at prices well below retail. They agreed on so many Roman candles, and so many sky rockets, and the larger the number the lower the price per article until we had three large sacks full at about half the regular price. Mr. Gilbert was smiling and full of compliments. As we left, he said that if everyone understood business as well as Mother did, there would be no Depression.

When we arrived home, Hank whooped into the house looking for empty bottles as sky rocket launches. And Father, when he understood what had happened, woke my younger brother and sister and brought them down to the front porch. Hank and I began the festivities with a three-inch salute, which announced to our startled neighbors that a fireworks display of major importance was about to take place.

Hank stuck sparklers in the lawn and lit them one at a time until the whole yard was a blaze of light. Then we arranged ten sky rockets in bottles and fired them successively. They shot out of the bottles and into the sky, exploding in kaleidoscopic patterns of red and white and blue. Hank and I had Roman candles in each hand, and we sent the fiery balls shooting over the distant trees while Father nailed the pinwheels onto the trunks of the maples in the side yard and set them whirling in colorful arcs in different directions.

V

Now generally speaking, prosperity is always just around the corner in America. Contrary to Mother's admonishments, and figuratively speaking of course, money does grow on trees and we do have an apparently endless supply of disposable income to burn in the waste of fireworks and conspicuous consumption.

The Mr. Gilberts always get rid of their surpluses and die rich and the rest of us are carried along by their success.

The Great Depression was more an emotional than an economic depression in our family. For a while it shook my parents' faith in the old economic gods, but there was never any doubt that they would inherit sooner or later the legacy of prosperity that was the birthright of every American. And they were correct. Ultimately, even a two-time loser like my father managed to hold on to something.

Even our deepest tragedies are somehow incredibly superficial as if it all could have been avoided had we saved our money for a rainy day. The intensity of our suffering has always been mitigated by the certain knowledge that things are always getting better. We have survived our panics and we have won our wars. And this was the truth of the times in the days of my youth.

The budget, of course, went up in smoke and flames out there on the front lawn in less than an hour. Financial responsibility was returned to Father the following morning. Gradually over the next few years and because of the war our family's economic fortunes began to improve.

Father finally found a respectable job as an accountant with a commercial airline that, because of its maintenance facilities, was awarded huge contracts for the remodification of bombers from the North African to the European theater of operations. He was frozen in his job for the duration. Mother liked to pretend that he could do much better, but she was secretly pleased. The job was stable, firmly propped by government spending, and it was romantic and progressive. She used to say, "Oh, yes, Rudy's been with the airline now for several years."

She had some problems during the war because of rationing. A planned economy was forced upon her and she had trouble managing the stamps and tokens. But if she did a poor job, she had a built-in excuse—the war. When we didn't have meat because she had wasted or misplaced the red stamps, we were being patriotic and there was nothing she could do about it. Rationing was much easier for her to handle than her budget because rationing was an externally imposed discipline with all incompetence sublimated to the level of national loyalty. She was caught unexpectedly by the sudden demise of OPA with a Mason jar full of change tokens which she had somehow managed to save for a rainy day.

After the war Father stayed with the airline and when the materials restricted for war use were released, we began the repairs on the house. We redecorated each room one at a time. We renovated the kitchen completely, put in a false ceiling, ripped out the old wooden cupboards and replaced them with slick white metal ones. Hank and I helped paint and paper the living room and dining room. We bought new furniture, modern in design, and Mother gave our old furniture to the Salvation Army or the Goodwill Industries a piece at a time as it was replaced. We painted the house and bought multi-colored striped canvas awnings to decorate, to embellish the old fashioned, sharp-peaked Victorian design. We even placed a black wrought-iron lamp post on the lawn near the first landing of steps on the way up from the sidewalk.

Although we had made a decent recovery, it was a relative accomplishment. As we recouped the old, the world around us grew affluent beyond the expectations of even those dreamers nurtured on the wild optimism of the Roaring Twenties. The post-war building boom brought with it new designs and styles. Homes were rising in almost every vacant lot in our neighborhood, almost every one larger, more dramatic and imaginative than ours. All of our renewal efforts were ornamental, thinly disguising an outmoded and outgrown social order. What had been the affectations of upper class pretenders thirty years before, in the days of my mother's free and prosperous childhood, had become broadly middle-class commonplaces in the post World War II abundance society.

Yet there were consolations. Mother grew complacent, even pleased with a rejuvenated status vicariously achieved through our newly affluent neighbors. And the old house, redecorated and surrounded with flowers from April through October, became a stabilizing influence of the past on the fluid and free flowing homes of recent construction and families of recent wealth.

FIRST HUNT

A week before Christmas vacation, their friendship quickened. They began to meet even at school during recesses and noon hours in secret liaison. When friends came near them, they stopped talking and David, the older boy, quickly shuffled into his pocket a worn and folded piece of paper which the two had been conspicuously and ceremoniously marking and examining, remarking and re-examining since the first permanent snow covering in the middle of December.

After school they went off alone to an elevated point behind David's house. They carried with them a pair of field binoculars that belonged to Will's father, a former artillery officer in the army. The binoculars, his old uniform that hung in the basement stairway, and an artillery company flag that stretched under a glass on his father's desk were sacred emblems of his short lived glory. Whenever Will let David peer down into the deep ravine which cut through the hills toward the river, he did so with a reluctance and brooding anxiety, bred of a fear of his father's discipline if he were to bring them home wet, or if, God forbid, the lens were scratched by the needles or branches of the clump of white pine which was their reconnaissance shelter.

The ravine they peered into and then mapped from memory the next day at school was covered with oaks, scrub maples, pines and cedars. In the pine the ruffed grouse slept in the highest branches, or else at the foot of the root trunk they buried themselves in the deep snow that had blown and drifted under the lowest boughs. The cedars stood as minarets of protection, impenetrable barriers against the plunging red-tailed hawk, and close to the cedars, darkly grotesque and brittle, were the wild cherry, the bark of which became in the winter after the grass was gone the main food of the rabbits. At the very bottom was a stream bed that carried water only when the snow melted in March and April and was covered with willow and alder thicket.

There were clumps of laurel dispersed on the far side of the ravine under the oaks and maples and through the binoculars the boys, undetected, could examine the sumac and juniper which they had read was a food supply for wild life.

They made mental notes of points of natural coverage and tracks in the snow. They hurried to their reconnaissance point after a new snowfall and scanned the places where they had recorded tracks previously. They had marked on their map the results of their observations and the dates. Patterns began to form and as more detail—of coverage, dead logs, and tracks—was etched, they began to draw conclusions. The rabbits had betrayed their warren and feeding habits, the patterns of their natural adaptation.

II

They had finished, in the jargon of their primary source material, the "preliminary reconnaissance." They had mapped the spatial distribution of the rabbits' way of life. Next would come the time evaluation, which could only be done after the Christmas holidays had begun. Their chief source book was "The Young Sportsman's Guide to Hunting" by Col. Arthur Dennis, U.S. Army, Retired. The book was a combination of the systematic application of military methods to the hunting of small game and the detailed and accumulative scientific observation of the field conservationist. The book promised the young sportsman and hunter the same effects that might be achieved by an Indian scout. Col. Dennis guaranteed his reader that the application of his military and scientific methods would achieve results "approximating the empirical certainty that the aboriginal hunters must surely have developed in solving their fundamental logistics problems."

As they cautiously gathered their evidence and completed their map, their faith in Col. Dennis grew. They began to speak the codified and ritualistic language of the Colonel, and their friendship, that had been spasmodic and uneven, became welded by secret liaison and military routine. They distributed responsibility. Will, because of the binoculars, was in charge of logistics, reconnaissance, and supply, while David, because of his pump air rifle, was in charge of deployment and attack. The divisive forces of their friendship, that David was an insuperable two years older—a disparity entrenched and institutionalized at school—and that Will's family, because of a knotty pine basement recreation room with a fieldstone fireplace complete with caribou head, was ever so subtly better than David's, were forgotten in the wake of Col. Dennis' triumphant rhetoric and the evidence they had gathered.

They retained, however, for all of the Colonel's military persuasion, a feeling for the original impulse that made them want to hunt. They were still Natty Bumppo and Chingachgook, the Deerslayer and his trusted Indian, conquerors of the wilderness and symbols of natural truth and justice. Their sense of adventure had not been diminished by the Colonel's military and scientific methods, and they went forth each day after school as if they were the first to survey a virgin forest in an inaccessible valley full of mystery and wonder and promise.

III

There were too many unknowns in their pursuit of the true sportsman formula for successful hunting. They had yet to discover the times during daylight that the rabbits fed. When vacation came, they planned to spend different hours of the first four days watching from a distance the places they had selected of highest probability. They had to map the route to the point of cover that they had decided would be the best shooting position. But there were, for all their planning, eventualities that were beyond their control, elements that depended entirely upon the caprice of others. There was always the possibility once vacation began that their careful preparation would come to nothing, that those painfully detailed patterns would be disrupted by careless hunters wandering aimlessly through the ravine. The one flaw in Col. Dennis' method was that it assumed an abundant prey in an isolated and undefiled wilderness, or, perhaps, it wasn't so much an error in method as his beginning with a first premise that verged upon audacious presumption.

When vacation began, they set to work the first day at daybreak and within half an hour three rabbits appeared, and then intermittently for a period of an hour they caught glimpses through the binoculars of several rabbits. They spent most of the day going back and forth between Will's knotty pine basement and their reconnaissance post. Although they saw an occasional rabbit throughout the day, it appeared that early morning just after daybreak was the moment, according to Col. Dennis, of "maximum opportunity."

They were anxious to verify the results of the first day, but a cold wave with high winds and snow arrived, and so they spent the next day under the caribou head before a fire, transferring the accumulated evidence of their tattered map onto a larger sheet of paper and correcting their original errors of proportion an scale. Then they began a journal, in diary form recommended by Col. Dennis, of all of their outings and the evidence gathered so that the journal in narrative form corresponded precisely to the map. It was, perhaps, their most pleasant day since they had begun, and they imagined themselves to be in some remote cabin in the august presence of the Colonel making the final logistic preparations before the big hunt.

The next morning, although still cold, the wind had subsided and just after daylight, they plunged through the drifts to the pine clump and saw again the rabbits feeding. Their faith in the Colonel was unbounded. It was perfect. They could get to their shooting position under the cover of darkness and be ready, "deployed in attack positions" before daylight.

IV

The day before Christmas they were drawn into family circles. The temperature was still close to zero. They could not hunt until after Christmas Day and the chances that their hunting area would be disturbed were unlikely because of the weather. They made a final check on Christmas Eve just before sunset and saw the rabbit tracks still undefiled by human footprints, and then withdrew each to his own home to pleasures and promises somehow intensified by the secret dreams of expectation and fulfillment for which they had prepared so faithfully.

After Christmas dinner the next day, Will's father gave the boys a lesson in manual arms drill. He showed them present arms, order arms, port arms, and the finest of all, inspection arms, which the boys took turns practicing and then performing at each other's commands. Then Will's father took them outside into the back yard and demonstrated the power of the gun. He loaded the rifle and then began to plunge the pump rod under the barrel up and down until he could compress no more air into the chamber. He had pumped the rod twelve times. He took the top of the garbage can off, propped it into the snow twenty-five feet away, and shot a hold through the galvanized steel.

They gathered tin cans and took them out to a small washout declivity on the ridge of the ravine just below their lookout post. They practiced their accuracy from the prone, kneeling, and standing positions, all recommended by the Colonel, and decided that if at all possible, they would shoot from the prone position. Although they could not pump the gun more than six times, there was enough power to puncture a hole in a tin can at fifty feet.

V

They practiced again after dinner and then walked up to their reconnaissance post for another look. Across the ravine less than a hundred yards from their hunting area was a party of tobogganers. They watched as the group, some riding and some pulling, cut across the middles of their preserve on the way to the river hills.

They ran home to get the binoculars so that they could get a closer look. When they returned to the lookout, Will focused sharply on the footprints and the flat tracks of the toboggans. Someone in the party had noticed the tracks and had followed them for about twenty feet to the edge of a thicket of laurel and then the tracks widely separated slanted back down the small hill and merged again with the other tracks.

There was little they could do. The damage had been done and might mean they would have to start all over, but it began to snow again before dark and during the night the wind whipped the fresh snow into peaked ridges and plateaus. When they looked again the next morning, most of the footprints had been covered and the rabbits had again timidly and cautiously ventured in quest of food into the open spaces between cover.

VI

Before daylight the next morning they met at the observation post and began their hike down the near side of the ravine. They ran from point of cover to point of cover and dropped to their stomachs and waited silently for the noise of movement to subside. When they reached the bottom of the ravine, they walked slowly with crouched bodies along the stream bed under the cover of the alder thicket until they reached a point just below the blue spruce under which they planned to hide. They knelt and David loaded the gun and then, leaning with his full weight, pumped the rod with the butt in the snow. He carefully put the safety on. They crawled the last thirty yards over the snow and then slipped quietly under the boughs and covered themselves with snow. The lower boughs of the trees were weighted with snow and bent to the drifts, so they cautiously shook the branches until they sprang higher, revealing a clear shot at the open space they had charted. Just above them, not twenty yards over the snow, was the low bush out of which the rabbits would certainly appear.

The night sky was clear when they left, but now with the coming of dawn snow clouds hung low and dark. The wind began to blow in short thrusts whirling the dry snow in spirals. They had dressed well, according to the Colonel's recommendations, but they had not camouflaged their clothing for it was really unnecessary given their natural blind.

The first rabbit they saw bolted so quickly across open area that they didn't have time to aim. David released the safety and began to swivel the end-sight across the target area using his left elbow as a fulcrum. On his extreme right he sighted on some black sumac seeds that hung about a foot above the snow. He moved across the open space to his extreme left and then slowly and systematically back to the sumac seeds. High above them they could hear the wind in the top branches of the oak.

Another rabbit appeared. It hopped cautiously along the edge of the brush still not distinctly silhouetted against the snow because of its color. The rabbit hopped once into the open area clear of the brush and David aimed as carefully as he could in his excitement just above the left front leg. As he was about the squeeze the trigger, the rabbit pushed suddenly with its hind legs, and David, fearing it would bound away, fired. The rabbit sprang into the air and dropped into the snow whirling in circles toward the brush.

"We got him," Will yelled and they squirmed from under the boughs and ran across the snow.

The rabbit had been shot in the left rear leg and in his urgency to escape had spun in the snow leaving wheels of blood where his shattered leg had dropped helplessly.

"Don't let him get into the brush," David shouted, and Will ran around and the kicked the rabbit back into the open area with a spongy "whump" and the metallic ring of his overshoe buckles.

The blood congealed quickly in the cold air, and David gently pressed his foot on the rabbit holding it firmly against the snow. The rabbit squirmed and struggled, its eyes almost exploded out of its head, and it began to cry, wailing and whimpering. They were startled for they had never heard a rabbit make a noise.

"What do we do now?" Will asked, and before David could answer, he lost his balance on the struggling rabbit which had broken through the crust into the fine powder. The rabbit in crippled hops tried to escape again into the brush and David fell forward into the snow. Will kicked it back again, but this time he was sickened by the spongy, bruising sound.

"You should have shot him in the head or heart," Will yelled. "Now we have to kill it."

In his fall, David's air rifle had plunged into a drift, scooping snow into the barrel. David was wiping the rifle on his coat and trying to shake the snow out of the end. The rabbit lay quietly in the snow, too weak and full of pain to struggle continuously.

"We have to kill it now," Will said. "We have to kill it now."

"We'll shoot it in the head at close range," David said. He loaded the gun and the two of them began to pump, Will underneath and David leaning his body on top. They managed to pump seven strokes with their combined weight. Then David said,

"Hold him still while I shoot."

" I won't touch him."

"Hold him down with your foot or get a stick so that I can get a steady shot."

"I wish he would quit crying."

Will placed his foot across the rabbit and pressed down. He

could feel even through his overshoe the bones and softly resilient organs that gave way under the pressure.

David placed the end of the rifle into the cavity of its ear and against the skull and pulled the trigger. The rabbit's head jerked violently and rivulets of blood appeared in the snow. The shot had veered off the skull and split its ear. They pumped again and then again but the shots simply wouldn't penetrate the skull. In frustration David tried to choke it with the rifle butt, but the snow was soft and shifting and the butt rolled and slipped off the loose fur of the neck. Then he began to swing the rifle wildly at the rabbit's head, cracking the cartilage of the nose and the fine bones of the jaw when he landed a blow, but just as often chopping viciously and harmlessly into the snow.

The rabbit was still alive, quivering spasmodically and with sudden bursts trying to crawl for cover in the brush. Its eyes bulged and it whined once again.

"We have to crush its head somehow," David shouted. Then he began to run down the hill toward the stream bed. "Kick it down here . We'll get a rock."

Will began to kick it through the snow. He pressed his toe under the animal and then flung it into the air and it tumbled two or three feet at a time until it dropped over a sharp embankment into the stream bed onto an area that had been swept clear by the wind. David had dislodged a boulder and pushed the quivering body until it lay on a flat stone. He raised the boulder in both hands, squared his widely spread feet, and brought it down with the full weight of his body. But the angle was wrong and the jagged edge of the boulder scraped an eye from its socket onto the frozen gravel bed. He raised the boulder again and brought it down this time unerringly. Its hind leg quivered for several seconds and then it lay still as the yellow urine of death grew into a pool on the frozen ground.

They covered the body with small stones they could kick loose and then broke branches from a nearby alder and laid them flatly over the remains. They brought snow in armfuls from a drift further up the stream bed and covered the alder and then packed it hard by stamping. They felt hot and tired. Their skin was wet under their heavy clothes and Will loosened the top button on his coat and pulled out his scarf to let in the cold air. David began to clean the fragments of flesh and blood from the butt end of the rifle by rubbing it back and forth in the snow and then against his coat.

As they turned to go home it was snowing. It had been snowing lightly for some time but they had not noticed. It would be a general snow covering three states as it moved eastward. It would fall all day and into the night and probably into another day. It would fill and level the tracks of desperation and slaughter. It would cover the bright red wheels of blood, blotted and frozen in the crust of broken drifts.

A CHILDREN'S PLAY

Although his oldest child is almost nine, he has not yet told his children that they are human—that they are mortal. He lies to them as often as he must. They still believe that they are more closely related to fairies or angels than to the one-flesh that is his wife and he. They can still see over their shoulders the wispy jetstreams of their shooting star souls, the intimations of their immortality, and although he has long since lost that vision, he does not begrudge them theirs.

It is a rainy cold-fact Saturday afternoon. His wife has gone shopping with friends to a distant city and left him in charge. The children have coaxed him once again, despite his vows to the contrary, to witness their play. He rocks impatiently, stretching to keep in touch with the floor. This white, wicker rocker is too stable; it seeks the shortest arc and he is mildly annoyed by the effort required to sustain its motion. He stares into the empty space of floor which will soon be transformed into a stage.

"Who knows," he says to himself, "who knows whether the trauma of disillusionment is worse than the certain knowledge from an early age that the world is nothing but facts—the trauma of no-disillusionment?"

He has turned the rocker around in the middle of the room. He tries to forget that behind him is the television set and that he and it are immersed in a sea of impulses which is the Game of the Week. Alas, so near and yet so far.

The children are rehearsing in the bedroom and soon they will come down the hallway chattering with excitement and anticipation. Stage fright. They will hush each other and announce the first act. There will be plenty of exposition, complication, and resolution—there will be too much resolution. He will be part of the drama too. He plays the role of the audience so he must applaud and shout approval, and they will flush in triumph and giggle at his praise. He will lie an incubator world where fantasy grows as if there were no end to things, for he too on this cooling, sputtering globe is trapped somewhere between Aspiration and Fact.

He had tried to talk them out of it. He had said,

"'All the world's a stage'. What do you want a play for?"

And his oldest daughter, Annie, answered,

"But you promised. You said you'd do what we wanted and all you have to do is be the audience."

"You don't seem to realize that, philosophically speaking, a play is a very unsubstantial reality," he explained.

"I don't understand you." She stamped her foot. "Why don't you speak American?"

"Well, if it's American you want, how about watching the baseball game? Cincinnati's playing the Giants. Good game. Pitching versus hitting. The classic formula."

"I don't like baseball," she said. "Besides, it's raining."

"Not in San Francisco," he answered.

"We don't want to watch baseball," she argued. "We're girls, you know."

"All right, all right." He acquiesced. "I'll be the audience but I don't want any arguing like the last time with the circus and who was going to be the high wire star."

"We won't argue," she answered confidently and turned happily to the bedroom. "I'm the director."

"Did you know," he shouted after her, "that Plato banished playwrights, directors, and actresses from the Republic?"

She stopped and turned with a puzzled air.

"No, I didn't, but I don't care."

"Well, I just wanted you to know."

"Well, I don't care," she said decisively.

"I know you don't. I just thought I'd tell you," he shrugged.

"Who's Plato anyways?" she asked over her shoulder and he knew she didn't expect an answer.

He can hear the rustle of costumes along the floor and a suppressed giggle or two. He readjusts his position in the chair and stiffens himself into attention. They stop just out of sight and then Annie peeks shyly around the corner and asks,

"Are you ready?"

"Are you ready," he flings back at her.

"Oh, we're ready. Are you?"

"Yes. Yes. On with the show," he says and wishes to be delivered from this artifice, theirs and his. But he adds a flourish of the trumpets to prove he is enthusiastic.

"Da-Da-Dee-Dum-Dee-Dum."

Annie steps around the corner and into the area they have agreed will be the stage. She wears a bathrobe to the floor and carries a wand with the star of dreamdust scotch taped to the end. She dances forth on her toes and does a pirouette, a stumbling whirl, and a grand, unbalanced curtsy. Her eyes are cast downward in conscientious avoidance of his gaze. Then she states with deliberate calm, her voice a delicately feminine and compassionate falsetto faintly reminiscent of the Fairy Godmother's voice in the movie version of Cinderella.

"The name of the play is 'The Three Wishes Come True' or 'The Princess's Happy Birthday'. The first scene takes place the day before the Princess's birthday party."

She dances on her toes offstage to the bedroom hallway. Immediately upon her disappearance two obviously royal personages enter stage left. They, too, wear long and regal bathrobes and on their heads are paper crowns. One, a neighbor's child, is two feet taller than his littlest girl whose every line will be delivered with a happy rush and grin.

"Good Morrow, Good Queen," the taller child stiffly blurts in another artificially high-pitched voice.

There is no response. Little Rachel has forgotten her lines. A voice hisses from offstage. Already he senses in this urging, scolding voice a straining of this make believe.

"Good morrow, Good Princess," Annie prompts.

"Oh, yes," Rachel burbles. "Good morrow, Good Princess." Pause. "I forgot the rest, Annie," she shouts offstage to the prompter.

Time out is called for a conference. He crosses his fingers to represent suspended time. The Good Fairy-prompter-director-playwright takes angry steps upon the stage. The willing suspension of disbelief is willingly unsuspended.

"Tomorrow is your birthday, Good Princess. Who would you like to invite to your party?" Annie says emphatically as if she can't believe anyone could be so stupid.

As Rachel repeats the lines word by word, it occurs to him that the Queen is two feet shorter than the Princess and at least three years younger. He is mildly disappointed when he realizes that because the other child is a guest, she has been given the starring role. He chides himself that he has taught his children so much decency they cannot properly cast a play. The fault is his, no doubt. He ought to be more hard line, reality is reality. You cannot have a Princess twice the size of the Queen. He reminds himself to take a harder line in the future. A spade is a spade in this dog-eat-dog world, no doubt about it.

"Tomorrow is your birthday, Good Princess. Who would you like to invite to your party?" Rachel says echoing the sweet falsetto of the older girls. The action has resumed.

The Princess has her back to the audience but she upstages only herself, for the Queen cannot stand still. She keeps a fluid stage, back and forth, and seems as much a spectator as he.

"I would like to invite the Good Fairy, the Prince, and all the Fair Children of our Realm," the Princess delivers with mechanical intensity and is glad to have it out and done. The Queen stands a moment, uncertain, waiting for the prompter or a cue.

"Very well, Good Princess. Tomorrow at two o'clock," whispers the prompter impatiently.

The Queen repeats the lines and then they hurry off the stage. He claps and shouts, "Hooray," but Annie, offended, steps upon the stage.

"You're not supposed to clap yet, Daddy. It's not over. Wait 'til the end."

"How many acts are there?"

"At least four or five."

"Can't I clap any time before the end? What if there is a showstopper/"

"What's that?" she says.

"That's a scene that's so good the audience can't stop from clapping."

"Oh, that's all right, but I don't think there'll be too many of them," she says.

He has been duly admonished, and he should have known better. Restraint, restraint he scolds. He must not overact his role. The burden of the proof is his. He thinks of Hamlet and the play within a play. HE couldn't keep his big mouth shut either. He thinks of Claudius' or was it Gertrude's sound advice. Be reasonable, they instructed. All children must follow their parents into the dust. It is the way of man. So what if the funeral meats are put forth coldly at the wedding feast. The Good Fairy enters, pirouettes again, and waves her magic wand.

"It is now the next day. The birthday party has begun."

Her eyes are downcast and she seems to be inducing his belief with a blessing of the wand. As she exits, he prepares himself for the instantaneous passage of a day and thinks that they will not throw such time away when they are older.

Hard upon the Fairy's exit, the Princess and the Queen enter, chit-chatting as they stroll about the stage.

"It is a wonderful birthday party, Good Queen, and I thank you from the bottom of my heart, but where is the Good Fairy?" says the Princess.

The Good Fairy enters dancing on her toes with her arms and wand a slowly dying swan.

"Here she comes now," says the Queen who cannot miss this line.

"I am the Good Fairy and I have come to grant you three birthday wishes," she says.

"For my first wish," says the Princess, "I wish to marry the Prince."

The Good Fairy drops to her heels and scolds again.

"No. No. No. We changed that. You are supposed to say 'I will save the wishes and use them for the good of the kingdom'."

"I forgot. You changed so much I can't remember everything, you know," the Princess says in anger and repeats the lines correctly in a huff.

"Very well," says the Good Fairy on the verge of tears. "When you make your wish just call on me."

They exit all in haste. Clothes rustle. Someone runs down the hallway and slides into a door. She scrambles back just out of sight. He hears whirling, a mild debate, agreement, and silence. A dramatic pause ensures. Annie enters bent double, all in black with a hump on her back and a broomstick between her legs. She carries a kettle and sets it on the floor. A cauldron. She wears a paper Pilgrim's hat, a relic from the Thanksgiving party in the second grade. Beneath the fringe of her black cape shows the Good Fairy's bathrobe. She stumbles with a grotesque limp and cries,

"Hee, hee, hee. I am the Wicked Witch of the West. Cackle. Cackle."

"Hiss, boo, hiss," he shouts and rages disapproval. He cannot overact this role.

"Hee, hee, hee. Cackle, cackle," she repeats and parades in little meaningless circles, round and round the cauldron. She looks at him, a crooked, suppressed smile.

"Hiss, villain, boo," again he shouts (and to himself–monster, symbol of Age and Degeneration and Death, Pestilence, Famine, and War, Suffering, Disease; Spirit of Original Sin, Depravity, Injustice, foul fiend impinging on this child's world). He is carried away almost genuinely by this digression

After the curse has been properly wound, the Wicked Witch stops by the cauldron and spreads her arms and chants. He can almost see the smoke or steam.

> Bubble, bubble, boil and toil
> The Princess's birthday I will spoil.
> Around, around my pot of stew
> We will make an evil brew.
> We'll throw the stew into the air
> And ruin the Princess's birthday fair
> Since even before I was born
> Let there be the biggest storm.
> (Cackle, Cackle).

The Wicked Witch picks up her cauldron and limps off stage. Before she is out of sight, she extends the kettle to an outstretched hand. Almost immediately, there is a banging of kettles. He sits bewildered for a moment, then realizes the cauldron has become the thunder of the ensuing scene.

The Princess enters pressing the palms of her hands against her temples in anguish.

"This is a terrible storm. I hope the lightning doesn't strike the castle towers," she cries and raises her arms in supplication and despair.

"Wish! Wish! Wish!" shouts the prompter.

"Oh, yes. I wish the lightning doesn't strike the castle towers."

He notes they have made a refined distinction here. There is a difference between hope and wish. Hope is but an emotion; wish has efficacy. It abides in faith and can move mountains or save the castle walls. He is impressed by the meaning in this scene.

The Good Fairy bounds upon the stage and announces dramatically and with the cadence of a spell unbound,

"Thy wish is granted."

The kettles are still banging away. The Good Fairy looks over her shoulder and repeats her incantation in a tone of harsh command.

"Thy wish is granted."

Now the thunder stops as Rachel hears her cue. A momentary pause and the Queen enters majestically and proclaims,

"The Storm hath ceased."

As they rush offstage to prepare the next scene, he is tempted. Should he tell them now that the castle towers make excellent lightning rods and that a simple wish or prayer will not suspend nature's wildest laws? He wonders should he stop the play and quietly lead them to Mithridate's banquet feast, there to imbibe, bit by bit, an immunity to our blemished unwish world. Perhaps he should have started with their pretty, white, blue-eyed kitten, a rarity, flattened beneath his wheels. He should have brought them out to see before he scooped it into the cardboard box...

The play continues much more smoothly now. There is a Flood, an aftermath of Storm. It is wished away. The Good Fairy again enters and announces with the cadence of a spell unbound,

"Thy wish is granted."

And the Queen, who has stopped imitating the sounds of a flood, rushes on to the stage and proclaims with much happy enthusiasm,

"The Flood hath ceased."

Next a Famine, an aftermath of Flood. There is unquestionably a logic here, a thread, a weave of natural law. The Famine is wished away. The Princess cries, "I wish there wasn't a Famine," and the Good Fairy announces, "Thy wish is granted," and the Queen proclaims, "The Famine hath ceased."

The earth abounds in fruit and as a just reward, a bonus, the Princess is promised the Prince's hand. Oh, happy, happy resolution. Exit all in triumphant procession led by the Good Fairy.

The end... the end... the end...

He sits momentarily stunned by this sudden, crashing conclusion. But he recovers quickly, knowing that he must prepare his deception. He reviews the better features of the play. It wasn't so bad. Well structured. Nice clean exposition, convincing force of evil in the complication. It really wasn't so bad, he repeats to himself. Worse plays than that have received serious critical attention, he argues. Why, even "Hickory, Dickory, Dock" has an Aristotelian plot—rising and falling action. Peripety without discovery.

"Well done!" he shouts and applauds when they return for a curtain call. They curtsy together and he says,

"A pretty little play and you all did fine, just fine."

"All except for Rachel. She couldn't remember her lines," Annie says.

"But she did a good job with the thunder," he argues, knowing that she knows the flaws.

"But she didn't stop on time," Annie persists.

"I couldn't hear you, Annie," Rachel says, defending herself as best she can.

"Sure," he says, "in big plays on Broadway they have a stage manager running around telling everybody what to do and when to do it. You did a good job considering you didn't have a stage manager.:

"I guess it wasn't too bad," Annie finally concedes. She brightens now. "It wasn't too bad considering we didn't have a stage or a stage manager," she says convinced.

"You didn't have any scenery or lighting either." He pursues his logic toward total probability. "And that part about the three wishes, the storm, the flood, and the famine following each other was very convincing."

"I thought of that myself," she says all smiles.

"I liked the witch's chant, too," he says.

"I didn't do that myself," she admits. "I borrowed some from THE WIZARD OF OZ.".

"'Somewhere Over the Rainbow'," Rachel sings. "I could just cry every time I hear it."

"You borrowed some from MACBETH too," he adds, disregarding the interruption.

"Oh, I didn't know about that." She forgets the train of thought. They skip off now with his praise still echoing in their footfalls.

"And Polly did a great job as the Princess. It must have been very difficult to learn all those lines," he shouts after them as the finishing touch to his duplicity.

They return immediately without costumes for another curtain call.

"In case you didn't know who was acting in the parts, I would like to introduce the cast. Polly played the Princess. Rachel played the Queen and the Thunder and I was the Good Fairy and the Wicked Witch of the West. We made it up ourselves."

"I'm glad you told me," he says, "because there wasn't any program."

Annie has a new idea.

"Let's make programs for our play."

They run back to their room without a hint they know of his deceit. He wonders why she clarified the roles. Was his acting job so good? He speculates that Annie wants to be applauded for her naked, unmasked self. She has a foot in either world.

Now he is rescued utterly from his fraud. The Princess's real mother calls to invite the children for an early supper. When he hangs up, he calls the children from the bedroom and quickly packs them off in raincoats into the wind and storm. He limps back into the living room, rubbing his hands together in villainous satisfaction and laughs, "Hee, hee. Cackle, cackle."

He spins the rocker about and faces it squarely in line with the television set. He springs across the empty space, pinches the button, and in the proper electronic time adjusts the picture. He settles in his chair and rocks to the ritual of men at play. It is the sixth inning and the Giants are leading three to one. During the inning break, he hurries to the kitchen, opens a can of beer, and returns to sit once again in his chair.

But for all his efforts to escape into this world of factual play, the subjunctive mood descends. He cannot keep his mind on the game. Twice he looks over his shoulder at the empty stage. He cannot shake the memory of his children's play.

He is moved by it all, not by the play but by their futile impulse to create a land of wish-come-true. He is moved by the pathos of his oldest child who labors so hard to contrive. She senses the artifice of her childhood is cracked and she plots to patch the ruin of her dreams. The play is flawed, is twice removed—an image of an image of a thing. She is barely holding on.

He is moved also to wish a thousand, thousand done and undone things. He wishes the fruit of his lust spared the plight of man—the sin, the labor, and the end. And if not that, at least that their lives might be a pleasant, happy dream or a play which resounds in every act the triumph of the gentle and the good, and death but the awakening from that dream or play to a truth or beauty thinly shadowed and foreshadowed in their sweetest schemes. Ah, could he but lose all Father now.

He wishes undone a thousand, thousand things: Adam's rebellious fingers gently stayed, that innocent Maid (for his daughters' sake) spared the fiery stake, Socrates delivered from his hemlock couch, and Christ, Lamb of God for the sins of man, uncrucified.

ELEGY

Musty asked for it. She didn't know half of what was going on and Freddy Klinebauer, whose ma used to be a teacher and made him do his homework, knew more about every subject than she did. She tried to fake around that, but whenever we asked something we figured she didn't know, she pretended that she knew but she wanted the answer to come from one of the class. She always called on Freddy or one of her pets, mostly girls, but Sparrow Kiernan told the girls and Freddy to keep their mouths shut, and even though Freddy was kind of a suck, he wasn't going to cross Sparrow. Nobody crossed Sparrow. He was our ring leader along with Canary Gagnon whose old man was a cop.

Freddy said he didn't know, and then she tried some of the girls and they didn't know, so she just stood up there looking stupid with the black hair on her upper lip all quivering with little sweat drops.

When school started, she tried to be friendly with everybody. She used to come around to the desks and try to suck up to us, but you could smell this perfume that was sickening and underneath that you could smell the sweat. She had B.O. and a big wart under her ear on her neck and when she leaned over to give us "individual attention" all you could see was that wart and all you could smell was sweaty perfume and that was why we called her Musty. Her real name was Miss Ardsley. Harold Herbert, who was kind of queer always playing with the girls got sick on the desk one day when she was leaning over him and he said it was her musty smell. The next day she wore her hair to cover the wart and there was no more individual attention.

You got to give her some credit, though, because she figured out right away that Sparrow was our leader. Sparrow was three years older than the rest of us and about two feet taller because he had flunked two or three times. He was skinny and already getting kind of bald and he had a pigeon chest he showed us once in the toilet. He wasn't going to go to high school. He was just waiting around for his sixteenth birthday so he could quit school and get a job setting pins nights in the bowling alley or full-time in the packing plants.

Anyway, he had Canary, who was a good drawer, make this picture of this naked woman laying on her back with her legs spread out. This naked woman had a big wart on her neck and a moustache on her upper lip and hair all over her legs and this woman was saying, "Hold your nose and come and get me, I'm hot." We were passing it around and laughing when Musty got hold of it and did she ever get mad! She figured right away that Sparrow must of done it, so she hauled him out of the class and took him and the picture to the principal, Miss Kaufman..

She is really tough. Even Sparrow is afraid of her. She is crosseyed and can stand in the middle of the hallway and look both ways at once, and she's got whammy power in them cross eyes and she is mean. Sparrow went to her office with Musty . Sparrow claimed he was innocent and offered to take a lie detector test. Then they called us in one at a time and we all swore that Sparrow didn't do it, and we weren't going to rat on who did. Miss Kaufman finally decided that Sparrow didn't do it.

Later when Sparrow came back, he was a hero and he told us about Musty crying and being hysterical. During afternoon recess Miss Kaufman called us boys into her office and she really called us names, sewer minds, vulgar, cruel, and things like that, but we didn't pay any attention to her because there was a school board rule that she couldn't hit kids anymore.

Musty gave up the friendly approach. Every time a pencil dropped on the floor she had somebody standing in the corner. One time after about ten pencils drop most of the boys are standing all around the room against the blackboard with our hands over our heads and Miss Kaufman comes by and asks what's happening. Musty turns red and explains about the pencils dropping. The old bird has us all sit down and takes Musty out into the hall and we can hear her tell Musty that school ain't no concentration camp and that Musty doesn't understand what is meant by discipline.

By November it was getting pretty cold and things were dull in the classroom. Musty wouldn't talk to anybody except to ask questions or to drill us. Sparrow figured it was time to move against her again. It was during recess and it was really cold, and the steam radiators were sizzling. We couldn't go outside so we had recess in the hall. Musty was in charge of the lavatories and she was supposed to keep an eye on the boys' toilet so we wouldn't steal or deface anything. We sent Harold Herbert out to ask her a question and Sparrow has Canary and a couple of the other boys leak on the radiator. Well, steam comes off that really stinks and we get out of there fast and before long the whole hallway smells something terrible and they have to evacuate the classrooms and hallways.

Musty was called into Miss Kaufman's office to explain how it all happened and she was gone for a long time. We were sent downstairs while the janitor aired the hall out and when we came back, Musty returns and she had been crying. Sparrow gave a big wink and we all laugh. Then he raised his hand and Musty called on him and he asked her if she could explain that terrible smell 'cause we were all wondering what it was. She told him to sit down and shut up, and we all snickered like everything. Sparrow had a lot of good ideas to bug Musty.

There were these two guys named Riley and Gallagher in our class, and they were the dumbest two guys I every met. They were always asking her stupid questions. Riley was tall and thin and had tight curly hair. His eyelids always drooped half closed and his face looked like he was half dead or asleep all the time. Gallagher was a little shrimp with one buck tooth out in front.

Musty doesn't let them sit near each other. She has Gallagher sit in the left front desk by the window, right in front of her, and Riley sits in the last seat in the first row on the other side of the room. Gallagher and Riley are always playing cowboy, running around slapping their behinds like horses and having gun fights. Sparrow gets them at recess one day and tells them he knows a good game they can play on Musty.

We all come in from recess and Musty was explaining something on the board and all of a sudden Gallagher stands up and turns around at his desk and yells, "Riley, you're a varmint." And Riley stands up and says, "Gallagher, you're a varmint." And then they both yell "Draw" and each pretends he was pulling a gun from a holster and making his hand into what looks like a six shooter. They were both faster than lightening and shot from the hips. "Bang," says Riley. "Bang," says Gallagher. Then they began to stagger around holding their chests. "You got me, Gallagher," says Riley. "You got me, Riley," says Gallagher and then they both fell down on the floor.

We were all laughing like crazy and Musty is standing up there with her mouth hanging open. They both laid on the floor like they were dead and finally Musty says, "All right boys, your little game is over. Now, get back in your seats or I'll take you both to the principal." She really tried to play it cool, but they both kept laying there not moving a muscle. Pretty soon Gallagher begins to move and gets back in his desk and we all give him a big cheer, but Riley doesn't move a muscle. Musty was still in control of herself and she says, "All right, Riley, I will count to ten. 1—2—3—4-" She counts to ten and Riley doesn't move at all. One of the girls looks at him and says, "Miss Ard sley, Riley doesn't look well." Musty goes over to Riley and we all get up and crowd around. He was out like a light. He had hit his head when he fell and was lying there looking greenish-white and half dead. One of the girls screams, "I don't think he is breathing," and Musty really gets panicked and she yells "Artificial respiration." She dumps Riley over on his stomach and puts his head on his arm and climbs on his back. She yells at the girls to get Miss Kaufman and the school nurse.

By the time Miss Kaufman arrives, Riley has come around. Musty is still on top of him and he is yelling, "Get off of me, ya old bag. You're killing me, get off." Well, Musty really does get hysterical this time, and they have to take her down to the nurse's office with Riley and give her a sedative before she can come back.

While she is gone, we are left alone and so Sparrow takes over the class and imitates Musty's way of talking. He stands up in front and says,

"Mr. Canary Gagnon. What is artificial insemination?"

"No fun, " says Canary.

"Correct," says Sparrow. "Miss Darlene Love, spell the word fornication."

There ain't no Darlene Love in class, of course, so Gallagher stands up and in a high-pitched voice he says,

"Fornication. S-c-r-e-w. Fornication." And then he sits down.

"Sparrow says, "That is correct, Miss Love. You may take the rest of the day off for being so smart."

Just then Musty comes back, and Sparrow says to her that he has been keeping order for her because he figured he was the logical choice since nobody could beat him up.

Musty's end came in the middle of January. We didn't do anything direct to get rid of her, but Sparrow has to be given credit for getting her to the last straw and the end of the rope where she hung herself. She said something in class once that maybe the nuns in the Catholic school could do better with the likes of Gallagher and Riley. It got all twisted by the time it got to the parents and the school board.. Somebody said that what she said was that Irish Catholics didn't have any right to go to a public school and that they ought to be sent to St. Leo's. Musty wouldn't have said anything if she knew that Gallagher and Riley had already been kicked out of St. Leo's.

I guess she, being a public servant, wasn't supposed to say anything like that because it wasn't professional. The parents and the school board got all steamed up and called Musty before a public hearing to show cause why she shouldn't be fired.

None of us could go, but we pieced everything together that happened from what he heard our parents talking about and what we read in the paper. It went something like this. She was called before an open hearing and asked to resign, but she refused. She said she didn't want a black mark against her so early in her career and that the charges against her weren't true. You have to admit she had spunk. Then this lawyer gave the parent's side against her. He said she wasn't very clean and didn't take very many baths and that she accused us of things we didn't do. He said she made us stand up for a long time with our arms out for only dropping a pencil and that she couldn't keep order anywhere and that once because she wasn't doing her job, somebody set a stink bomb off in the boys' toilet. He said nobody in the class was learning anything and those comments about Gallagher and Riley going to St. Leo's was undemocratic and against the code of ethics or something like that.

Musty tried to defend herself but everything she said came out wrong and went against her. She said that it wasn't any stink bomb set off but boys urinating (that's just a big word for peeing) on the hot radiator and nobody believed their children would do that at all. She said she was on duty but too embarrassed to stand way inside and watch the boys go to the toilet. She could tell nobody was believing a word she said and she began to get hysterical.

Then that old bird, Miss Kaufman, tried to defend her and queer everything. She said that the charges were overstated and not exactly true. She said that the wild element in the class had gotten the upper hand and that Musty might do much better in one of the lower grades and that if the Board was willing, she would arrange to change her teachers around a bit and keep Musty on 'til the end of the year. But everything Miss Kaufman did for her, Musty undone when she started raving about how most of us children got cesspool minds and are vicious little beasts.

The Board decided in five minutes and said that they had all voted to fire Miss Musty and that anyone who believed that children were vicious little beasts with cesspool minds was not fit to teach, and then Musty answered them right there and said that anyone who didn't believe that about children would never be able to teach, but she was booed by everyone and almost run out of town that night because she had her share of brazen nerve, somebody said.

She is gone now and good riddance. She asked for it and she got it. We got a substitute teacher for the rest of the year. He had been in the army and he told us all about it. He said damn and hell every once in a while and the girls thought he was good looking. He coached us in baseball that spring. He was real smart because he got Sparrow on his side right away and every time he wanted something done, Sparrow gave us the word and we all did it because nobody was going to cross Sparrow.

They say Musty left town the next day after she was fired and went back home somewheres and nobody has seen her since.

AGON

Though the light is shaded, I still must squint as I stare down the sheet of green. The light hums. The net stretches tightly across at regulation height. I have measured it in the middle and on each side to assure myself that the enemy will not exploit even the slightest advantage. There is nothing I can do about the playing surface. It is heavily scarred on both ends, especially along the edges where losers have hacked in rage and frustration and winners in exultation and triumph. Bad hops are an uncontrollable variable, but they should work out with some statistical equality unless I continue to have the bad luck that has plagued me in all our confrontations.

Beyond the trapezoid of fluorescent light that floods the playing surface, all is darkened. He is upstairs finishing a cigarette, an endemic weakness of his generation and a vulnerability I have calculated in my game plan. He expects another routine victory. He has failed to detect my emerging will to win. I have discovered that he has stood triumphant these many years not by virtue of his strength but as a consequence of my weakness.

I have resolved to put an end to his domination. For two weeks before vacation began, I challenged the best Chinese and Rumanian students at the Foreign Student Center. I have not had a beer in a week, pot for two. I have prepared my mind with hard study in my courses and daily sessions of Transcendental Meditation. I have limited the frequency, intensity, and duration of my erotic fantasies. I am pure, disciplined, clarified.

I hear him stirring about upstairs. Soon you will perceive that the differences between our styles of play are symbolic of that vast philosophic and political gulf that separates our generations. I am an idealist, a progressive. I want to win by superior skill, by pure shotmaking, by taking risks. My game is offensive. I want to win points not capitalize on mistakes. His game is deliberate, defensive, steady. He is a pragmatist and a conservative. (He is all compromise. I am purity.) He takes up a position two or three paces from the table and lays back, keeping the ball in play until I in my impatience try to put it away. He plays my weaknesses, e.g., deep to my backhand, or he sets me up with purposely lazy lobs, knowing that I cannot resist slamming it usually into the net or off the end. His game strategy follows from his point strategy. He plays safely at the beginning, building up an early lead and forcing me to press and make mistakes.

I hear his footfall now upon the stairs. I quickly go over in my mind the basic principles of my game plan. (I speak to myself in the second person singular for purposes of objectivity.) (1) Keep the ball in play.(2) A corollary of (1): Resist the urge to slam unless the height of the ball and your position are perfect. (3) When serving, get the ball into play. No sneaky quick ones that end up in the net. If the ball doesn't get into play, you can't possibly win the point. (4) Increase the tempo of the game. Don't give him a chance to rest. He uses the breaks in action, e.g., when you retrieve an errant slam, to rest. (5) Keep alert. He is cagey. (6) Think pure thoughts. (7) Hustle at all times.

He comes casually down the stairs, his self-confidence verging upon arrogance. I know that resisting the slam is going to be difficult. It is the most emotionally satisfying part of the game. A smash executed with an upward thrust of the arm, behind which is delivered the full force of the body is purifying, vindictive, cathartic. I want to stick the ball in his ear.

We flip for ends. I am lucky. I will defend the open end toward the washtubs. His forehand will be cramped from behind by the stairs. Because I have won the open end, he has first choice of paddles. He pretends to choose indifferently as though there is more in the man than the paddle. He chooses the green rubber, his favorite, every time.

While I run in place to loosen up, do six or seven deep-knee bends, and roll my head in loose arcs, he sucks on his cigarette. He takes several quick drags and flips the butt into the washtub. It sizzles briefly. I dangle my hands loosely and shake them as I run in place. I suggest that I have inexhaustible energy. He pretends indifference.

He tosses the ball casually across the net to begin our warmup. I lay it back cleanly though I could have slammed it. I must establish the pattern and discipline of my strategy now. We exchange shots. I keep the ball in play. He pretends he is forced to lob. I return a straight but hard volley. He tries to cut the ball. It is caught in the net. He throws it into play again. I lay six successive shots to his backhand before crossing over to his forehand. I hit one off the end, but I am pleased. I feel loose. He is panting already.

"Ready to volley for serve?" I ask.

"What's your hurry?" he says. "I'm just beginning to loosen up. Don't rush me."

"After I beat the hell out of you, I just don't want you to have any excuse that we volleyed too long and you were tired."

"Don't count your chickens before they hatch."

I do not respond to the chicken metaphor. Like his political philosophy or his style of play, his language is hackneyed and atavistic. I continue to lay the ball back with surprising consistency and I can see him working to keep it in play.

We volley for serve. I stay close to my end and drive the ball deep to his forehand. He backs off, giving way as we exchange shots. I talk to myself out loud. I say "nice shot" or "keep it in play." He catches the tip of his paddle on the edge of a step and, his timing disrupted, hits the ball into the net. My serve. I pretend his mistake is the result of my brilliant play. I congratulate myself out loud. "Atta boy. ATTA BOY. Way to go. WAY TO GO."

"Let's volley again," he says. "I hit my paddle on the step."

"Tough shit," I say, preparing to serve.

He doesn't argue. It is his own local ground rule that any point lost when the paddle hits any obstacle—a post, the neon light fixture or the steps, or the wall, or the washtubs—is not replayable. When he first invoked it on me, he called it the "toughshit" rule. He said then, "Tough shit. Quit crying. Play ping-pong."

I hit the first serve low and fast. It hits on his end line, catches a hack mark and shoots deep and flat toward the stairwell—a bad bounce. He jumps back, not having expected the shot to be so low, and in his haste lunges at the ball. His paddle hits the stair and clatters to the floor. He picks it up, slams the step twice with his paddle.

I serve the ball up again deep to his forehand. As we exchange several shots, I can tell he doesn't have his old zip. He seems to be hesitating slightly on his back swing. He loses two points into the net. I notice he has shifted slightly to his right in anticipation of my forehand volley. I serve again and return suddenly to his backhand and catch him off balance. I clean the first five points.

He is behind now and forcing his serve. He loses two off the end, takes one point with a chop and tries to tempt me with a defensive lob, but he lays it up too high and I slam it. It caroms off the table and hits him in the nose.

"For Christ sake," he yells, "you don't hafta hit it so goddamn hard." He finds the ball under the stairs and throws it angrily across the net.

"Sorry, Pa," I say. "I'll angle the next one so you won't get hurt." I toss the ball back to him. "It's still your serve. 1-8." I dance on my toes, do a deep-knee bend, and assume a balanced crouch, ready to receive his next offering. I take the next point and announce the score: "9-1, Mr. Bauman, fils."

I serve quickly now, giving him no rest between points. Now after each point I win, I pretend I am a TV announcer. I interpret my game strategy. I shout excitedly. I say things like "Holy Cow, what a shot!" or "Holy Mackerel. He did it." (I refer to myself in the third person for purposes of objectivity.)

Falling behind 11-3, he says, "Why don't you shut up and just play ping-pong?" In the next point he lays up another lazy lob. I wind up to slam. He retreats to the stairs. I suddenly unwind and dunk the ball just over the net. He smashes his paddle on the table trying to get to it.

Now, I restrain myself, play steady, exchange points, wipe him out with my serve 21-12. As we change ends, he lights a cigarette. I am ready to go. I push him. "Your serve." I swerve in my receiving crouch.

"You don't mind if I take a short break?" he says.

"You tired, Pa?" I ask. "Want to call it quits for the night?" I put my paddle down. "Maybe you'd like to take a nap between games." I look at my watch. "It's only ten o'clock. We got all night."

He takes another long drag, blows out the smoke, then two short quick ones and flips it into the washtub and prepares to serve. I resume my stance and begin to sway. In the second game, I stay close to the end of the table and clear of the stairs. I take his shots on the short hop, defensively. I flick my wrist upward in a quasi-slam motion and drive the ball to his backhand two or three times, then cross over quickly down the outer edges of the forehand court. I set a fast pace in my serves, resist the slam, keep the ball in play. I am nimble, quick. He begins to lunge in desperation. I can hear him gulping air. I get the game quickly in hand and apply steady pressure. He deteriorates completely when the score is 15-7.

In the last game, because I have already won the rubber, I play with wild abandon. I cash in on fore and backhand slams, dunks and chop shots, cut serves, top spin volleys. He is sullen, defeated. He complains about the stairs, the lighting, the weight of the paddle. Once he accuses me of an illegal hand-cover serve. I concede the point. Once he claims I moved the table with my body on a slam follow-through. I concede the point. He wants to argue, but I won't let him. My sportsmanship is infuriating. I win 21-7.

He sits down, exhausted and dejected, on the stairs. I push by him and up the stairs to the kitchen where I turn on the tap and wait for the water to cool.

"Hey, Ted," he shouts up the stairwell. "Get a couple of cold beers from the ice box and open them, will ya? I'm too tired to climb the stairs."

"What do you want two beers for?"

"One for me and one for you."

"For me?"

"Why not? You're old enough now that they dropped the age to eighteen. Besides, isn't that about all you college kids do now is drink beer or smoke marijuana? I haven't had any evidence of much studying. You might as well drink in front of me instead of behind my back."

I drink two glasses of water quickly. "No thanks," I yell. "I can't stand the stuff, but I'll bring you one."

I get a beer, open it, and descend the stairs. He is smoking again. I hand him the beer. He tilts it back and drains half in one guzzle. He belches. I cross the floor and lean against a post and stretch. He drains the bottle.

"You know, I was just thinking," he says. "I was just thinking that I might be able to get you a job at the airport this summer. I heard they were going to take on some college kids and though I'm no top executive, I've got twenty-five years of seniority and some influence."

I slide down the post and sit cross-legged on the floor. I pretend indifference. He continues.

"You'd have to work the swing and midnight shifts, for a while, but the job pays $3.25 an hour and you get to learn a lot about servicing jets. Could begin a career right there this summer. Then when you finish college in a few years, you could move right into the company. I can't see what you're studying is going to prepare you for anything anyhow. Get me another beer. I'm still pooped."

I walk grudgingly up the stairs to the kitchen, open a bottle, and return. A casual insolence pervades my slouching gait. Still sitting on a lower step, he gulps a third of the bottle. It fills with foam. I resume my seat in the center of the floor, my back leaning against the post.

"Anyhow, I was thinking that if you got a job this summer, you'd be an employee and qualified for the company ping-pong ladder. We could be partners in doubles. With my steady play and your slams we could go right to the top. There's some bastards in the Sales Division I'd like to beat the hell out of. Besides, you could make some money and help pay for some of the goddamn tuition that fancy college charges for turning you into a smart ass."

I turn a deaf ear to his materialistic cant. I assume the classic lotus position. I perceive a small crack in the cement, shaped like a spermatozoa. I concentrate. I lose myself in cosmic reflection.

THE TRAGIC FLAW OF TOM CASSIDY, JR.

A Fable for Critics in which the Contradictory World Views of
Marx and Freud Are Perfectly Reconciled

as delivered during the early
morning slack hours to the assembled
young Smartass Yardhands of the
Night Shift. Hogside Chutehouse, Union
Stockyards, February, 1955.

Voice
BIG LOUIE
Chute Counter and Folk Philosopher

I tell this story fairly without prejudice, rancor, or pity. I leave the pity if there is any to you. It is a story of the common man, a laborer at first in the packing plants and later here in the stockyards, and though I too am a common man and for thirty years a union member, I tell this story fairly and objectively and I leave the pity if there is any to you. It all started in a joke and the joke became rumor and rumor became accepted opinion and opinion became myth and then the myth became confused with the truth and he stood in defiance and lost everything.

Now, I don't plan to tell this from the very beginning because there isn't any beginning that any living man can remember. It started when the first man looked at the first woman, way back there with Adam and Eve (so far as you ignoramuses are concerned that was just before old George Washington was born). I'll just begin with old Tom Cassidy because he is as far back as I want to go and I figure that's far enough so long as I'm the one telling this.

First of all I'm not going to tell you about old Tom's brothers and sisters and uncles and aunts and their families that have been running the junk yard down by the city dump since before there was one, and brothers marrying sisters for about three generations and not one of them knew it was against the law until the social workers went in and broke it all up. I know you're all itching to hear about them, but I'm going to tell you about young Tom of the respectable Cassidy's.

Now you can quit shaking your heads and raising your eyebrows as if there wasn't any such thing as a respectable Cassidy. I admit old Tom was a Cassidy, but his missus wasn't and just because he married someone other than his sister or his cousin or his niece is enough to ameliorate any Cassidy. Besides, his missus was a good woman to boot which is real cream on the pudding in any man's language though I admit she did have a mite too much hair on her upper lip for my taste.

Anyhow, I worked nights with old Tom for years but I don't claim I ever knew him. But then I guess nobody knew him as a man that is, until, after he had spent five silent years here yarding, he got sick one night and didn't show up and Fred Cosgrove had to load six double decks of sheep by himself in the rain. Some said he wasn't sick at all, that he stayed home on purpose because finally after five years he thought it was time to be noticed, but I personally can't accept that explanation because its just too philosophical for old Tom. I just can't believe he figured he could predicate his existence, antithetically, out of its own negation.

Now I can see you don't even know what I'm talking about so I better give you Playboys some straight advice right now: You better start reading something other than Poontang Westerns and Manhood Magazines if you plan to stay up with Big Louis. Because Fred called him every name under the sun that month, we began to pay special attention to old Tom. Oh, we always knew that he was different from the fence posts because he could move and we knew he wasn't a hog or a sheep because he could stand up, but we suddenly realized that nobody knew him as a man even though he had worked here for over five years. With old Fred leading the way, we tried out names on him to show old Tom how much we appreciated his contributions to the fellowship of the night crew yardmen over the years. We tried Thing and Chimp and Grunt and Monk, but nothing stuck very long except we all agreed that, generically speaking, he was probably more closely related to our cousins in the ape family than to the human race.

It wasn't long before some of Mrs. Cassidy's friends and relatives took offense that we thought old Tom wasn't human like a monkey or chimpanzee. They figured it was a bad reflection on her and they claimed old Tom was more of a man than the rest of us rolled together because he had twelve children, mostly boys and they said that's still about three times more than any of the rest of us had. They granted that he probably didn't even know there was a depression and kept on having kids right through the years he was laid off, but they said if that was stupidity then it was stupidity of heroic proportions.

After that argument old Tom seemed to grow in dignity and stature. We figured anybody who was laid off for as long as he was and could fling five children straight into the teeth of history when he was unemployed had genuine intestinal fortitude, and, besides, he wasn't completely irresponsible. The missus made him round up at least six of those strapping sons of his and off they went to the county warehouse to carry away the lion's share of every surplus commodity shipment. No one begrudged them their share, but as we watched old Tom herding his sons back and forth between the warehouse and home all loaded with sacks of flour and cereal, crates of oranges and apples, and sides of beef and pork, we kind of felt that subsistence was their right, but conspicuous consumption on relief was another matter. You don't know what conspicuous consumption is, do you? Well, I'll tell you: Conspicuous consumption is like making water bombs out of Trojans. I figure *you* know what *that* means unless, of course, the pea-brains who dropped them from the second deck on Squeaky and Highpockets the other night don't know a balloon from a Peacock.

Anyhow, Ed Ruckman took care of the argument that claimed old Tom was more of a man than the rest of us because he had so many kids. Ed could see deeper than the rest of us and that's why there was speculation when he died of a brain hemorrhage that it was from using his head too much. But then there were others who said it wasn't *how much* you used your brain but *what kind* of ideas you have that counts. They figured Ed's death was a kind of moral retribution.

Be that as it may, old Ed put old Tom back in his place when he said that three, four, five, even six or seven kids might make old Tom a man, but fourteen was more like a mink or a rabbit and that there was something missing in each of those boys so that if you rolled all of them up into one person you might end up with one normal human being and since old Tom never did anything else to prove he was human let alone a man, although we laughed (even though it was kind of a joke), we believed old Ed's version was closer to the truth because there wasn't any other proof.

I can see you are all snickering and I suppose you might as well laugh at what you can figure out now, because there will be damn little more you Playboys will understand of the rest of this. To get back to where I was before I was so rudely interrupted. We laughed again when old Ed said that Tom's nine sons were enough to field a baseball team, and although we all knew he had nine sons and it seemed that there was something missing in each one, none of us saw before old Ed mentioned it that nine sons *does* make a baseball team (yes, I know what makes a golf course, Wiseass).

That was pretty deep all right but not deep the way you wise guys think, scraping your feet and shoveling air with your arms the way you are. Too bad you don't work that hard when there's something to do around here. We considered that for a few years, all the time keeping our eyes on those nine boys to test the truth of what old Ed said, and it seemed he was pretty close to right about the first eight except for Andrew, the fifth born. There was something missing in each one, something not all there. None of them made it to high school. They got to the eighth grade and then kind of piled up and set there two or three at a time for a couple years, drooling and grinning at the girls becoming women, until they were old enough according to the law to go to work. And the daughters weren't any better, all kind of shy, and sad and ugly and dumb. So after a time we all agreed that old Tom seemed to have spread himself thin, not that he had very much to start with, and that only two of the boys might be an exception–the youngest named Tom and Andrew who was about in the middle of the pack.

Old Ed's theory was the only one that seemed to account for all the facts. We gradually accepted it because there wasn't any other explanation. You must remember that it wasn't so much that it was the truth as it was that we *believed* it was the truth. And besides we laughed as we told it over the years to others for entertainment until old Ed's theory kind of seeped into us and became gradually an accepted truth though it was really no more than a speculation and a joke.

I can see you don't understand, but there is nothing I can do about that. You smart cowboys got all the answers anyhow, so there isn't much a body can do to further your education, no matter how hard he tries. But you said you wanted the whole story about young Tom Cassidy so you're going to hear me out, whether you like it or not, unless, of course, you big shots would rather go out there in the alleys and pens and be shovel jockeys and manure pilots for an hour or two or until some trucks or rail shipments come in.

Good. Now that I can see the fear of work has sobered you a bit and I can observe the false masks of constrained seriousness on your pimply faces, suppressing your clever mockery, I shall, perhaps continue without interruption.

We believed old Ed's speculation generally down here in the yards and over in the packing plants. As the years went by, most of what old Ed said seemed true. One of the Cassidy's boys was sent away to the state home for the feeble minded. The oldest boy got six months for sodomy over on the cattle side but he got his job back when he got out of jail without losing any seniority because there isn't anything in the union contract about crimes against nature and so it went for the rest of them, one thing or another, except young Tom and Andrew who both seemed exceptions.

Andrew became important because if he was a good Cassidy, too, like young Tom was certainly growing to be, then there was a flaw in old Ed's theory and maybe we needed a new theory to account for everything. We watched Andrew closely then looking for a flaw so that we wouldn't have to throw out twenty years of considered speculation. Andrew went right through grade school and high school without flunking once, and although he wasn't very smart, compared to the rest of the Cassidy's he was a regular genius. He started setting pins down in the bowling alley when he was old enough to lift the pins and he started bowling when he was big enough to lift a ball. Before he was twenty years old he was the city bowling champion and had the high average in the Classic League.

It goes without saying that we were all impressed by Andrew. Someone said that there was only one way to account for Andrew consistent with old Ed's speculation and that was there was someone in the woodpile, but nobody would believe that because old Tom's Mrs. was a religious woman. Then old Ed himself suggested that maybe Andrew was a kind of mutation, which Ed explained happened to pop up one out of every hundred Cassidy's or so, or in a ratio of about one to every ten idiots.

That seemed reasonable enough, but we took that with a grain of salt because it seemed old Ed was trying to patch up his theory pretty desperate. Besides, he was getting old and senile and was just about ready for his stroke.

Then Andrew got married, which was about the first normal thing that any Cassidy had done in years, except young Tom who was now in high school up there near the top of his class. But Andrew didn't marry just any old bitch who came down the pike like you big heroes will do. Nosiree. Andrew married Miss Betty Kropik who was just about the best looking young woman in town. Even a couple of horny, snot-nosed punks from the country club gang wanted a shot at her. And following his older brother's sodomy it was kind of like a vindication of the Cassidy genes.

Well, love is blind or so the saying goes. She was bowling for Sweet Pickle in the packing plant league that winter and when she saw Andrew throw that ball it was enough for her. They teamed together during, or which was, their courtship, and won the city mixed doubles championship. When it was over, they got married right there in the bowling alley by Preacher Dade from the Storefront Gospel Church down on South Concord street. They stood, holding hands one on each side of the ball return rack between the eighth and ninth alleys with trophies all around and a big wedding cake in the shape of a bowling ball with crossed pins on top and three smaller holes on one side of the cake for her and two larger holes on the other side for him.

Then after they were married three years and still didn't have any children we thought of it for the first time, the something that was missing in Andrew—his flaw, but he fooled us all by having five kids in a row, pop, pop, pop one after the other before his wife had a day's rest, and when he kept on having children, one after the other, we finally decided what was wrong with him: he was the copy of his father and we realized then that, except for the bowling, he had never been different. Somebody said that old Tom should have called Andrew after himself, but then somebody else said the old man probably looked the kid over real close and saw a flaw or himself, which old Ed insisted was worse than having a flaw.

Then we turned our attention to young Tom, believing he was the only good Cassidy and expecting him to turn out special, but we began looking for hidden things too, because of what we suspected when Andrew didn't have any children those first few years.

Tom went to high school and could have gone to college but he decided he wanted to come down here to the yards and be a regular Joe and not a snot-nose college prick. He went into the Navy during the war and saw a lot of action and came back after it was over to his job on the night shift.

Then he made two mistakes: he bid on the ticket writer's job, and he married Peggy Mosher, the waitress in Allen's cafe.

The first mistake he couldn't help. He had to bid on the job or relinquish his seniority privilege for any new positions that might come along. He liked being up there on the catwalk, writing tickets and sliding them down to us. He liked talking to the farmers and truckers and their women on the other side. He wasn't ambitious, but somehow being above us up there where it was clean and separate made him different. Some claimed he got the big head and that he took the job so he could be set off from the rest of us down here in the manure..

The marriage lasted only one night, but we didn't bother to find out that young Tom and the waitress both laughed at the mistake. We didn't bother to find out they were celebrating his birthday on his night off and that they had one too many and that they got married because he joked with her every night when he came in for supper and because she served a good meal with a friendly smile. They laughed about their marriage, even joked about it, and forgot about it as we laughed at him and made a joke of what we believed to be true because he was clean and dry and separate and could now be ridiculed although he didn't know that at first—that it was ridicule. We believed we had discovered his flaw—that there was something wrong with him as there had been with all of his brothers and that old Ed's speculation was somehow both true and false.

It was a French word that he didn't know. He thought at first it was a nickname that we, down in the alleys, had given him. It may even have been a sign of acceptance to him, or reaffirmation of his oneness with the crew. He smiled and acknowledged the words with a wave of his hand as he walked back and forth up there.

There were only smiles at first but the words spread so that even the new men called up to him from the fences in the alleys as he walked from chute to chute writing tickets. Laughter and words followed him across the catwalk above the chutes. " . . .un petit, un petit," and Tom waved back.

Then he guessed or reasoned or maybe somebody told him, for he no longer smiled or waved to us. We began to laugh loudly and gesture with our thumb and finger held closely together and up to the eye. Then we began to squint and strain, trying to see what was between our fingers. We held them up so Tom could see the measurements while the words went from man to man along the alleys down below. The men bent and howled in laughter and slapped their thighs and hit each other on the arms.

Then he stood there for everyone to see after Little Bob stood on the fence and cried up to Tom "un petit, petit, petit, PETIT," and then gestured with his fingers up to his eye (oh, so small) and laughed and fell off the fence to the bricks and lay there unable to get up until the tears came because of the laughing. And Tom stayed there with his pants down around his knees even after we warned him that Mr. Wentworth, the foreman, was coming. And that's how he got in trouble—by staying up there after Mr. Wentworth told him to pull up his pants and come to his office—and not the indecent exposure because like sodomy there's nothing against it in the union contract. Then he was fired the next day after the negotiations between the Grievance Committee and the company broke down. The basis of dismissal was insubordination, but Tom wouldn't have come back had they let him.

There was general speculation about his flaw. Some said that he couldn't take a joke, he was short tempered and pig headed, but others said that wasn't true—that he had never been rash or stubborn in the past, but others came right back and said he had never been tested.

Now that I have come to the end of this story, I can see by the blank expressions on your smartass faces that none of you appreciate what it means to be fired, to lose ten years of seniority, which in an age that has banished God from history is equivalent to immortality, so I guess I'll save my breath to cool my porridge. You can go back to playing pocket pool and reading your magazines about Nazi's whipping naked women, virile young Americans to the rescue, and happy connubial fulfillment.

THE LOGIC OF FLESH

If you were to look with the woman holding the curtains aside and stretched anxiously over the sink to peer out the window, now at this angle toward the gravel driveway, now at that angle toward the barn, you would know it was late November on a flat and treeless land. You might guess it was Minnesota or South Dakota but you would not know for sure; it might be Iowa or Nebraska. The predominant corn fields would tell you that this land was neither too far north nor too far west for corn and that wheat or cattle would be a poor use of this soil and growing season. You would know, too, that there was no sun, and in the light of dusk the land seemed to wear a grim hangover. It was cloaked with a sickly gray as if it had burned itself out, glutted itself in a debauchery of fruitfulness and then lay back chilled and moribund waiting the covering snow.

If you went back across the room with her to the coffee and burning cigarette, you might come to know the kitchen through your eyes as she knew it through her body's touch and labor. Below the sink the slick enameled pattern of white and yellow flowers in the linoleum was worn bare from shuffling feet. An oil heater extended from an inside wall to the center of the room and through the clouded glass of its window a low flame flickered unevenly. There was power operated running water—the groaning, winding electrical pump noise under the living room that fed the chrome plated flattened low slung spigots of the sink. On the other side of the kitchen over the gas stove, with the tubes leading to the metal soldier-bottles at stiff attention outside the window, the bright yellow duck shape of a removed potholder reminded her of the fall cleaning yet to be done.

Everywhere was the faint smell of some permeating essence of oil. Was it a kerosene smell imbedded in the walls and ceiling, wood and plaster from thirty years of use, or was it the paint odor of the glossy walls still clinging to or fading with the yellow brightness?

She thought: Now where has he gone? She pressed her cigarette out and went to the door for the second time. She opened the kitchen door and unlatched the storm door. The wind whined and sucked the door out strongly. She grabbed the knife-edge with her other hand and felt the padded insulation. They had stuffed rags into the cracks in her childhood home. She called out sharply, "Karl," and her voice was blown away by the wind. The wind, unlike the sun or the snow, was a burden of all seasons. You stood up in the wind by leaning into it and always you could hear it moving across the land. It bent the corn in summer and fall, flapping and rustling the blade leaves hotly until they were dry and crackling. Highways were built above the plain level because you could depend upon the wind to sweep the road clean and to drift the snow in leeward ditches. She tried to look around the corner but the weight of the wind on the door forced her back into the house entry.

She returned to her coffee now. As she sat, her dress revealed a bulge below the waist—a slacking weight of weariness rather than complacency or comfort. Her face was fuller than it had been before her marriage ten years ago. Her fingers too had thickened over the years. She could no longer remove her wedding ring without soap. Her padded body not emaciation was proof of her mortality: her decay could be measured by the burden of a slowly growing opulence of flesh that she masked with clothes that fluffed and fluttered and swirled in illusions of chiffon softness.

She thought: What was he doing? Probably talking to them all the way down the driveway with one foot on the running board and them trying to get going. Maybe Karl had come up with another great idea of how to make a living without working. Maybe he had discovered a new hybrid corn that planted, cultivated, and picked itself. Maybe he had discovered an easier way? Put the wife to work—ha,ha—two shifts a day candling eggs at the Cooperative. Karl was a great joker.

She was peaking herself. She had tolerated too much, she had been too easy. Everyone said so. She had watched him drift from one job to another until now he was a rent farmer on a land that would not tolerate delay. The impulse of the seasons was a tyrant he could not deny. Oh, she had been sympathetic at first; he had disarmed her so easily and made her his ally. When he came out of the service right after they were married, he had gone to work at the elevator, but he quit in anger. He told her he wouldn't take crap from anybody, not even Joe Christiansen and he didn't give a damn if Joe owned half of the county. She felt pity. He had such an independent spirit. She still worshiped then, almost mystically, the masculine principle embedded in his knot-hardened flesh that too would decay in time—but unbloated, shriveled rather, gradually to a sinewy mass on the bone-lever frame.

But then there had been other jobs, for Nels in the hardware store, and then selling cars and tractors on commission until he owed so much money to everybody (the child was born then) that he had to get a straight salary job to pay the bills; and then he got fired by the government agent, who said he would not take guff from any loud-mouthed chronic bitcher who talked more than he worked. Karl had his excuses, his justifications. He had a pride but he had been humiliated, and she had been ashamed for the first time when he lost the government weighing job. It was then she began to understand because, beyond a doubt, Mr. Campbell was fair, and besides the body was cooling, cooling ever so gradually. She began to see as if she stood at a distance the grotesque angles of prostration and humiliation that she had mistaken for love. Now she sat waiting impatiently for him to return, rehearsing in her mind all the petty grievances of their married life that seemed to culminate and were symbolized by what Karl had done or not done in a single Sunday afternoon.

Did Karl have to talk so much? Couldn't he listen just once

for her sake? Did he have to know everything? Couldn't Karl hear Donna's man? My God, he lived in California all his life. He told Karl seven times if he told him once that Pomona was at least four hundred miles from Palo Alto. But no, Karl had taken a streetcar from one to the other. Busses now, he supposed.

She got up to check the child, little Jimmy, her little man. She went through the dining room and opened the living room door softly. He was sitting on the sofa with a pillow squeezed in his lap between his knees. He watched television with saucer-wide tired eyes and his thumb had found its way into his mouth. He had tried to put the hogs back through the hole in the fence by himself that morning while his father slept late. He had run this way and that with the big stick until he was almost in tears as the hogs sprinted in squealing grunts out of the corner he had tried to trap them into. The screen was fuzzy snow and the action only vague shadows, but she could tell that there were six or seven costumed girls slowly dancing and carefully cartwheeling across the screen while twirling batons.

She returned to the kitchen and sat wearily again. She dropped her high-heeled shoes to the floor and kicked them under the table. She sipped her coffee dully and rubbed her foot across a hardened gum spot on the linoleum. She felt the light tingling b-rrr sound of the nylon. Outside the sound of the November wind rose and fell, and she could hear above the wind the whine of the taut wire fence that separated the yard from the south pasture.

She heard Karl's footsteps scrape on the drive. The sound stopped for a moment. Then she heard him move across the hardened ground toward the barn. The wind rose, and the sound of the wire fence covered his retreat. She felt as if her twisting insides had opened a healing sore. Karl's disgusting habits tumbled into her mind: the smell of his breath after drinking, the slopping of food as he chewed with his mouth open, the image of him as he picked his nose or scratched his behind sometimes even in public.

She sat for a while listening only to the sound of the wind, still peaking herself for the showdown. Then she heard the Chevy start and the shifting of gears as it drove off slowly. She ran to the door, fumbled the latch, and then opened the doors leading outside. The wind caught the storm door and snatched it from her hands and slammed it sharply against the side of the house. She stood enraged and bitter, with a burning nausea in her throat and in her chest, as she watched the car fade slowly from sight, its tail bumper bouncing jauntily, jeeringly in dip-rock motion.

II

She awoke later to the high taut whine of the second gear of cars coming up the long driveway from the Preston road. She sat up half asleep as the cars backed around to park, their headlights flashing on the ceiling. She fumbled in the darkness for her cigarettes and some matches. Then she lighted a cigarette and listened indifferently, almost numbly to the lurching sounds of the cars coming to rest.

One of the drivers raced his engine before shutting it off, and then she heard the loud roar of laughter and the banging of the car doors. The kitchen door opened and voices entered the kitchen below. Someone sang to the tune of "Red Wing."

> There once was an Indian maid
> Who said she wasn't afraid
> To lay on her back in a western shack

They laughed again. One of the men tripped over a chair.
"Somebody turn on the light before I bust my ass."
"Where's Karl?"
"Where are ya, Karl? You want me to bust your kitchen up? Where's the light switch?"

"Hey! Somebody get the light."
"Here I am. Hold your horses and don't lose your shirts."

> Hooray for Karl,
> Hooray, at last.
> Hooray for Karl,
> He's a horse's ass.

"Attaboy. Attaboy. Three cheers for Karl, the lightturneroner." The men moved about settling themselves in the kitchen. The refrigerator door slammed twice. Somebody asked for a can opener. She heard a voice,
"Did you see the look on that phony bastard's face when I told him I was with the 221st in Germany in '45 and I don't remember a thing happening like what he said."
Then somebody said, "Hey, Karl, get the kid before it all melts."
She heard Karl's unsteady, stumbling footsteps on the stairs and the voices of encouragement. His footsteps sounded up the stairs and then down the hall to the boy's room. She heard him whisper, "Ice cream—chocolate." There was a rustle of movement and the boy's sleepy voice answering his father.
Karl returned downstairs with the boy. Soon the sounds of laughter and scraping spoons came up the stairwell, then the jig stepping of boots stamping on the floor, someone singing, and the boy's laughter. One of the voices grew louder, and she realized someone was calling her.
"Hey, Glad. You awake? How about a beer?"
She heard someone mention what a great gal Karl had for a wife. Karl was a lucky sonovagun.
"C'mon, Glad. Don't be a sorehead."
Karl's voice at the bottom of the stairwell seemed to boom up to her.

"Be a sport, Glad, be a sport." Then a pause as he listened for her answer.

"Guess she's asleep." And he walked away back in to the kitchen.

The boy's laughter continued. He shrieked "Don't... don't" and then peals of delirious laughter as the men tickled him with hooked fingers thrust into his ribs or threw him into the air.

She heard Karl tell the joke she had thought was so funny a week ago.

"Once there was this good looking babe who lived in the forests of Germany when there were many gods, Woden and Thor and all that gang. Well, her name was Griselda or something like that and she had a lisp. She always said th instead of s sounds, like thucker instead of sucker. Anyhow, she met this big guy what must of been seven feet tall at least on a path in the middle of the forest this night..."

She listened to Karl elaborate the story. He added details that she had not heard before and he led his listeners down paths of teasing erotic facts and suggestions and then finally to the punch line. Karl could really tell a story, there was no denying that. One of the men said,

"C'mon, Karl, you're killin' me. Get to the main part.'

Karl continued.

"Well, the next day she met this big guy again and he said to her, 'Do you remember me? I'm Thor.' She says, 'You're thore? I'm tho thore I can hardly pith.'"

Again, she heard the harsh laughter. One of the men could not stop laughing. He kept repeating the last line over and over again, and each time he laughed again the same whining breathless laughter and he choked on the words he tried to utter between his spasms.

In a little while she heard them settle down to a game of pinochle. The voices mellowed into a murmur barely audible. She fell asleep for a while and awakened again as the men prepared to leave. The voices rose and fell as they moved outside.

She heard "G'nite, Karl. G'nite." She heard Karl promise to see them again.

She heard a car start and drive off. Karl slammed and locked the doors when he came back in. She heard dishes clinking in the sink and Karl's footsteps shuffling on the linoleum floor. Karl picked up the boy from the dining room couch and began to climb the stairs. At the head of the stairs he hesitated for a moment and then carried the boy into her bedroom. He laid the child in the middle of the bed pressing his body, sleep weight, against her.

He talked. Was she still awake? He could tell she was. Guess what happened? After Ed's left he went to town for some cigarettes and he happened to drop by the Legion Hall, and Charlie Pederson—she remembered him, used to live between Preston and Milbank on old Route 22—he manages the place now and he wanted to know where the hell he had been. Would she believe it? Charlie wanted to know where the hell he had been. Well, where the hell did Charlie expect he was? There was a dinner out home all afternoon for his sister-in-law who was home with this guy she married in California. So what! Didn't he remember? Remember what? Why he had promised Charlie he would bartend for the barbecue shindig of a National Guard outfit that was having a rally at the Armory. Most of the guys were from the eastern part of the state. Some of them had driven a hundred miles. Could she believe it? He had forgotten completely. He had promised at least two weeks ago. He had to pitch right in because it was getting pretty busy already.

He said more. You wouldn't believe the amount of beer and whiskey they consumed. Nosiree. It was unbelievable. They must of opened eight ponies. He saw Pinky and Al there later. He made ten bucks and they had promised before he left to help Tuesday or Wednesday to get the corn picked. Would she believe it? He had met an old Army buddy from Milbank who had been in Germany with him at the end of the war. Why, he lived only twenty miles away. He didn't even know the guy lived there.

Could she believe it? They hadn't met in ten years and only twenty miles away.

Karl finished undressing and climbed in bed. He threw his arm over the boy and around her back. She felt the boy's warm face and taut-soft arm against her arm and shoulder. He was sleeping quietly. She knew. Flesh of her flesh. Flesh of Karl's flesh. Karl tightened his grip around her back and asked if everything was O.K. Sure. Sure. He knew. Everything was O.K. Did she understand? Sure. He knew. She understood. She listened to the rhythm of Karl's breathing slowly relax and deepen as he fell asleep holding the three of them together, and because she could feel his loosening grip upon her flank and the child's soft flesh against her arm, she knew that just as there is a compulsion of the blood, steady and pulse-strong, in the body eager and warm, there is also a logic of the flesh that rules the heart grown bitter and cold.

CAREER MAN

Toward the end of his senior year of high school, Peterson came home drunk one Saturday night and got into an angry argument with his father about his drinking. His father, a usually mild mannered person, threw him out of the house where he crawled under an evergreen tree on the front lawn and slept fitfully that night. He threw up once on the pine needles and once on his jacket and woke up with a terrible headache the next morning. His mother let him in the house through the back door and he went to his bedroom, locked the door and slept the rest of the morning. For several days his father remained angry; his mother tried to reconcile the two, but neither would speak to the other beyond perfunctory exchanges for the remainder of his days in school.

He graduated from high school with a flat record, and his teachers felt, as teachers usually feel, a vague sense of guilt that they had failed to tap that shadowy inner reality called potential. Some of the test scores indicated real ability, and one teacher felt that Peterson had genuine sensitivity if it could only be developed. But he seemed to defy the individual approach—not in any overt way, of course, the kind that can be documented with examples in a faculty meeting, but in a devious, mocking sort of way.

He didn't want to follow his father into the packing plant, and he didn't want to go to college, and he didn't have anything he particularly wanted to do, except hang around with his buddies who had cars, drink beer and cruise around looking for girls who were looking for boys with cars and beer. When he turned eighteen the summer after graduation, he decided it was time to move along. He checked out the Air Force and the Marines but finally decided on the Navy. He enlisted in August and left unceremoniously for boot camp except for a brief parting farewell to his mother and a younger brother on his way out of the house with a change of clothes stuffed in an overnight bag.. Until then he had told no-one he was leaving.

He went through boot camp without too much anguish. He learned his knots, marched daily on the grinder, went through the motions of orientation. When the overture was made, he duly subscribed to a substantial cash gift for his company commander, a first class bosun mate who was completely sober only twice during Peterson's twelve weeks of training, and on the evening before the final testing, the examination with answers was delivered to the barracks, as was the custom, a reward for generosity.

Toward the end of boot training he was summoned for an interview with a lieutenant who told him that he had scored well in the classification tests and would probably be sent directly to school in Bainbridge, Maryland. The lieutenant read off a list of specialty schools for which Peterson was qualified and asked him which would be his first three choices in order of preference. Peterson did not know and really didn't much care and asked the lieutenant to put down any three. The lieutenant became angry and gave Peterson a lecture about what an opportunity he was getting and how there were thousands, literally thousands, who were clamoring for a chance to go to school. But Peterson just shrugged and said he really didn't care one way or the other. The lieutenant looked over his record again closely and then said that because his score on one of the psychological tests was ambiguous, he wanted Peterson to discuss his problems with the psychiatrist.

Peterson went and talked to the psychiatrist. The psychiatrist asked him several questions and he responded mechanically. Then the psychiatrist explained that the reason Peterson was in to see him was that on a certain test he had failed to prefer, in a healthy fashion, driving a high powered car over raising flowers, for example. Actually Peterson had not read the questions in that section of testing. He had filled in the answer sheet randomly.

Did Peterson understand? No, but he really didn't think it was very important one way or the other. And the psychiatrist said *that* was it—he hadn't committed himself to anything. The psychiatrist proceeded to deliver a lecture, but Peterson's attention wavered out the window and the psychiatrist became irritated and dismissed him. Apparently nothing came of the interview, though, because when boot training was completed, he was transferred to electronics school.

He went home for a ten-day leave, got drunk every night carousing with some old buddies. He had some vague sexual explorations with a chubby and not especially attractive or popular girl still in high school. She was awed by his uniform and claimed to her friends after he left that they were engaged, but he never answered any of the letters she wrote later. It wasn't much of an affair but when he was going east on the train, he remembered his pleasure and her aggressiveness and there welled up in him time and time again a gnawing restlessness.

He arrived at the electronics school a week before his first classes were to begin and was assigned till then to a general clean-up detail with port and starboard liberty privileges. On his third liberty he got a cab and asked the driver for a woman. The cabby took him to a point of exchange and then transferred him to another cab. The second cabby drove about three blocks, parked, and made a phone call from an outdoor phone booth near a new shopping center. Then they drove about a mile to another corner and picked up a thin, dark, oily-skinned girl of about twenty-five who in stooping to get in the cab put her hand on his knee for balance and squeezed him. Peterson was overwhelmed with desire.

When they arrived at the motel, he didn't understand her bargaining pitch at all, didn't know what she meant by the word trick, and agreed to her price just as long as there would be enough time to gratify what seemed an inexhaustible force of lust that seemed to haunt him all the time. During their night together he told her he loved her, and in the morning he asked for her address and telephone number, both of which later turned out to be false.

After two weeks of school, Peterson decided it wasn't worth the effort. He failed several examinations purposely. He was called in to the commanding officer and was abused violently by a short, explosive, mustang Lt. Commander. He was reminded of his responsibilities, of his high potential, and of all the thousands of young men who were dying to get to a school. Peterson could not understand why the commander was so incensed about something he didn't care about. His indifference only made the little man more furious. The commander shouted several questions at Peterson which he couldn't answer without damning himself so he said nothing. Finally, he was dismissed with one more chance, which, or course, Peterson didn't want. A week later, after missing several classes and failing every test (upon which he drew cryptic sexual parodies of his instructors and the commanding officer), he was dropped from the school and transferred to the kitchen staff to complete the remaining five months of his tour.

He liked the kitchen work. It was mechanical and there was much more liberty. He went to Washington, Baltimore, and Philadelphia on weekends, drank a good deal, spent several nights with call girls, had a mild affair with a girl he met at a serviceman's center who took him home and to social gatherings at her church youth club. But nothing materialized and so he tried to ease out of the relationship although once she waited at the gate with her parents in the car, and he had to spend one more weekend at his "home away from home." He went to New York one weekend and missed the train back so he was four hours AWOL. After the mast he was restricted to the base for the remainder of his tour of duty.

He was then transferred to the Eleventh Naval District in San Diego and from there was assigned to a Destroyer Escort preparing for a six months tour of the Far East. He adjusted quickly to the ways of the ship and soon found a modest but secure place for himself in the deck gang. When the ship went to sea for maneuvers and drills prior to leaving for overseas, Peterson became violently seasick in a storm and vomited for twelve hours until all he could get up was bitter green bile, but he was never seasick again and seemed to like the long quiet days at sea and the rhythm of routine.

On the way to Japan, Peterson was promoted to Seaman First Class and celebrated with a bottle of wine he had smuggled aboard and hid in his locker. He shared the bottle with the coxswain of the deck crew who got drunk and mean and decided he was going to kill a "chicken shit" ensign who had been riding him lately. But with the help of others, Peterson subdued him and earned the gratitude of the coxswain who when promoted to Second Class made Peterson his leading seaman.

The ship went into dry dock in Yokusuka for repairs. On his first night of liberty, Peterson had a few drinks and then bargained wildly in black market alley for decorated smoking jackets, fly rods, binoculars, and dainty silken pajamas. He went to a tailor shop and ordered a tailor-made uniform with dragons under the cuffs. While the busy tailor was taking his measurements, he posed for an artist who sketched a near likeness of him in charcoal. Then he went to a night club, had a steak dinner, and hired one of the girls until midnight.

On the second night in Japan he bought a tax free pint of rye whiskey and drank it in the toilet of the enlisted men's club. Unused to so much alcohol consumed in such a short period of time, he became blind drunk and staggered violently through the streets of Yokosuka until helpful shipmates discovered him in a stupor at a street side Shinto funeral ceremony.

On his third liberty, he met a girl who was a dental technician on the naval base, married her in a mock Shinto ceremony before a decaying old priest, and then took his new find to the enlisted men's club and introduced her to everyone he knew from the ship as his "wife." He spent the rest of his liberties with her in a rented room playing husband and wife.

While at sea a few weeks later, Peterson came down with gonorrhea and went to the medic for penicillin. But this bulldog variety had developed a resistance to penicillin and his cure was slow and tedious. He was a cooperative patient, though, and took the good natured ribbing from his shipmates with philosophic equanimity.

When his ship returned to the States, Peterson was promoted to Third Class and the ship was transferred to a flotilla in Long Beach. With the money he had saved overseas he bought civilian clothes, an old Chevy, and rented a locker near the Pike. He took a thirty day leave, traveled around California for a week, lived for two weeks with the wife of a Gunner's Mate on the *Wisconsin* (which was overseas at the time) and then returned, bored, to his ship a week before his leave was up.

Peterson gained a reputation as a fighter when one evening he was challenged in a bar by one of the firemen from the black gang. The fight was over a woman Peterson had apparently stolen one evening in the Moose Club in Long Beach. Peterson was attacked in the hallway at the top of the stairs. The fireman rushed at him and drove his head into Peterson's stomach. With his back against the wall, Peterson reached down and grabbed the back of his attacker's blouse, and as they broke apart he pulled the middy blouse up over the fireman's head and shoulders, binding his arms and cutting off his vision. Then Peterson beat his bound opponent in the stomach and the groin until he sniveled in pain and throttled impotence.

Toward the end of his third year of enlistment, Peterson was promoted to Second Class, but a month later, after getting drunk in several Long Beach bars, he crawled into what he thought was his car and went to sleep. He was confronted in the morning by the angry owner and a policeman, was arrested, bailed out by several shipmates, and subsequently fined one hundred dollars. After the mast in which the captain voiced fatherly concern and amazement, Peterson was reduced to Third Class and restricted to the ship for fifteen days.

In the last year of his enlistment he went overseas again for a six month tour. He was careful this time and avoided any form of venereal disease although he did pick up the crabs through the ship's laundry. He started to gamble heavily on the way back to the States, and when he arrived in Long Beach he tried to make up his losses by playing low ball at the Airport Club, but he lost two hundred dollars the first night.

Then toward the end of his enlistment he had an affair with a divorcee who was four years older than Peterson. Her ex-husband kept bothering her. Once when he met Peterson in a bar with her, he threatened to kill them both. After Peterson moved in with her, the ex-husband called them at all hours of the night and when they wouldn't answer, he let the phone ring to irritate them. But the husband gave up about the time Peterson decided he wanted to get married.

About this time his shipmates began to notice that a sense of responsibility had been settling imperceptibly over Peterson's personality and character in recent months. He seemed to take his job more seriously. He even began to dispense practical wisdom and steady common sense to troubled and insecure newcomers. He even cut back on his drinking. He grew an exquisitely tended and handsome moustache.

A month before his enlistment was up, he told the executive officer that he wished to re-enlist. In due course he was given his rate back and transferred to the San Diego naval training station to report after a sixty-day leave. With his MOP and accrued leave pay, he made a down payment on a small bungalow in La Mesa and was married to the divorcee by a Justice of the Peace in Compton.

Before re-enlisting he was given a complete physical examination, and as a part of a service-wide program of re-evaluation he was given a battery of psychological and intelligence tests. He was in good physical condition, although the dentist did specify that Peterson had a slight periodontal involvement. All of the aptitude tests indicated a high mechanical ability, and his General Classification Test (which was relatively high when he first enlisted) was down twelve points into a safe range, plus or minus five points standard deviation. The Deck Chief and the Operations Officer concurred that he had outstanding practical ability, was a good leader of men, and reasonably reliable. And on the psychological examination he consistently chose driving a high powered automobile over raising flowers. That earlier ambiguous score that occasioned the talk with the psychiatrist in boot camp was deleted and the new score considerably lower and perfectly normal was inserted in its place.

NOVAK ON FEEGAN

Feegan first told that joke right here during the war. He comes into Bonner's Back Room with a straight face and says,

"Well, our illustrious Republican governor, the Honorable Harold E. Stassen, ain't gonna get into the Navy and be a big war hero like he planned. Nosiree."

Then he slaps a folded newspaper on the bar in front of Big George and says,

"It's in all the papers. After them Navy doctors looked him over real close," (if ya watch his shifty eyes, ya can tell he's raggin' us), "they decided that big shot politician or not, they ain't gonna let no guy serve in our armed forces what had only one ball and one thigh."

And we was all laughin' already when he explains the joke anyhow.

"You get it? Senator Ball and Lt. Governor Thye," he says, and then he runs around stickin' his nose in our faces sayin',

"Do ya get? Do ya get it?"

Well, I guess we get it all right. Zenny Kowalski is laughin' so hard he almost chokes on a Kielbasa and we had ta turn him over right there on a card table and pound him on the back and he is still laughin' when he starts breathin' again.

Feegan is like that. Not just explainin' everything when he don't hafta but about politics and that he don't like Republicans too much and thinks Roosevelt is the greatest person who ever lived next to Jesus. He can talk for hours about the New Deal and the NRA and the WPA and Social Security and them goddamn' old men in the Supreme Court what tried to get in the way of progress and the common man. Sometimes he gets sorta weepy when he tells us about the day FDR died. He remembered the time exact. It was 2:33 in the afternoon and he was just goin' to work on the swing shift and thought he'd turn on the radio for the weather, and the news that he died of a stroke come over all of a sudden just like that.

That wasn't his favorite story though. He only told that after he was boozed up on mooched drinks and feelin' sorry for himself and the good ol' days. His favorite story was about the time Roosevelt went to talk to the DAR.

"Now picture this" he says. He always says, "Now picture this."

"Now picture this. All these fancy broads what think their shit don't stink 'cause its two hundred years old and are real proud of rock farmin' and inbreedin' back East and think the Irish and the Poles and the Frogs ain't Americans since they wasn't the low scum of London what had to leave on the Nina and Pinta and the Santa Maria in 1492. Well, they invite FDR to talk to them like they was givin' him some kind of privilege or somethin', and FDR goes there and has dinner with them. Then when the dinner is over he gets ready to speak, and everybody shuts up quiet and they're sittin' there prissy-ass like expecting to be told how great they are, and he leans to the microphone and says in an Irish brogue,

'Fellow Immigrants. Fellow Immigrants', he says, Oh, God, in an Irish brogue. 'Fellow immigrants.'"

Feegan is such a regular in Bonner's Back Room that we all think of him as part of the place like the bar and the card tables and the spittoons. He always wears the same old suit coat about three times too big, and a dirty, colored shirt with an old tie with a couple of weeks of meal drippin's on it. But his face is really pink and clean and he's sixty-five years old and don't look a day over fifty, and he's always talkin' or else moochin' a pipeful or a drink. He's retired now but his life didn't change much after he got his pension and Social Security except he's down here at Bonner's all the time instead of just before and after work. We figure he can talk all he wants. Then he won't kibitz at the games.

Big George Bonner even gives him credit. He says Feegan is a regular floor show almost as good as ten bareass snatch jumpin' all over the place like in them big shot dirty bars in Minneapolis.

There is another thing about Feegan that makes us all kind of let him do what he wants like talk all the time. In the strike of '48 he was the assistant strike captain. When they got that injunction against picketing, he wouldn't let anybody leave the line, and he told that sheriff to go home and mind the peoples' business and not the business of the rich. Then when they got the National Guard out, he stood right there at the entrance and made them young smart punks with the guns push him down to get through with all the scabs behind them. He says that was his finest moment. He walked up and down the picket line tellin' everybody there was nothin' to fear but fear itself, and some of the younger union members, who didn't know Roosevelt said it before Feegan in his first inaugural address, figured that Feegan invented it.

One time we get kinda tired of Feegan. We're all union men and Democrats and besides the union meeting hall, United Packinghouse Workers of America, Local 162 is upstairs over Bonner's and we get enough politics up there. We figure Feegan ain't gettin' enough political opposition. I'm a Truman man myself and though I voted for Roosevelt twice, I figure he's a rich Eastern snob like all the rest and that there's a real difference between bein' the champion of the common man and *bein'* a common man what old Harry was. When he called that music cricket an S.O.B. and did that imitation of H. V. Kaltenborn, I just about busted up. But you can see, I'm not gonna' be no political opponent.

We figured Feegan needed someone to give him some crap for the laughs. Fritz Gottlieb says that his brother-in-law works with this crackpot what hangs around the Legion Hall and wears an overseas cap all the time waitin' for the Memorial Day parade and the Fourth of July. Fritz says this guy was only in the army for a couple of years after the Korean War, but he is one super patriot. Maybe he was awarded the Purple Heart by mistake when he was in sick bay with German measles or the clap. This guy Overseas Cap really hates "King Franklin the First" and "The Jackass Party" and he lets everybody know it, so Fritz's brother-in-law invites him over after work to play pinochle and have a beer and see what happens when Feegan gets goin' on FDR.

This guy shows up with Fritz' brother-in-law. I can tell he don't like things right away when he looks around and don't see no members of the Rotarians or the Junior Chamber of Commerce. Maybe he figures he's at a Communist cell meetin' or somethin'. He don't look too friendly but he sits down to a game of pinochle with Fritz and his brother-in-law and some guy what is related to Big George. Feegan is playin' two-handed sixty-six with Big George at the bar and I am playin' euchre with Highpockets, the Union Steward, and Goosey Jorgenson what will stick his hand in a cup of hot coffee if ya tell him to real fast and sudden like. "Putyourfingerinthecoffee" and over it goes quick as a cat and he always burns his hand and calls us sonzabitches.

Big George begins workin' Feegan up to a spiel on Roosevelt when he promised the mothers of America that their sons would not go overseas while he was secretly making deals with the British to sucker the Germans and Japs into a war against us. It was in a fireside chat or some other political bull like that what nobody believes but what is a good way to rag Feegan.

Feegan sails right in defendin' his hero and before you know it we are gettin' a big sermon on how great FDR is and how he saved the nation and the world and the immigrant and the widow and the orphan and the common man in general.

Overseas Cap begins to get nervous and his feet are twitchin' back and forth under the table. Big George comes around the bar with a bottle and pours both of them each a couple of shots to get things goin' faster. Then right in the middle of one of Feegan's big points Overseas Cap turns halfway around from his cards and spits out between his teeth,

"He wasn't bad for a Jew bastard."

Feegan stops but he figures this guy can't be talkin' about Roosevelt so he goes right along like nothin' happened. Maybe he figures this guy is talkin' about the king of spades. But this guy comes back again,

"Roosevelt. Spelled R-o-s-e-n-f-e-l-t. An American version of an old Jewish name."

Big George gives Overseas Cap another shot. He drinks it down and you can see he is feeling his load already.

"Rosenfelt. Jew bastard," he says again.

And he leans over from the table and looks at Feegan to make sure Feegan knows who he is lookin' at.

"Wasn't a bad president for a communist son of a bitch," he says. And Feegan is really killed. We are chokin' to try and stop from laughin', and Feegan don't say a thing then but stands there blinkin' his eyes which tells me he is gettin' pissed real good.

"Why didn't they lay him out at the funeral? How come nobody seen him? Can you answer that?" Overseas says. He's got this look on his face like he knows God personally and gets his dope from divine revelation, or somethin' like that.

"How the Hell should I know," Feegan shouts at him. "I wasn't the undertaker."

Then Overseas Cap says that he has good evidence, documented proof that Roosevelt is nothin' but a different spelling of Rosenfelt and that there was good reason to believe that he was nothin' but a Jew bastard. Wasn't he always supportin' the communists? Wasn't Stalin himself married to a Jew? Wasn't half the Jews in America from Russia? Wasn't it true that all the Jews what wasn't millionaires was communists what was exposed?

Now I am gettin' nervous. I am not expectin' this kind of stuff. I am expectin' the old rights pitch, ya know, the workers rights to starve and the businessman's rights to be a prick in business, and the rights of widows and orphans and cripples and the blind to earn their own keep in the free marketplace, and that there shouldn't be no big government, and all that self-reliance business what I suppose was pretty good about a hundred years before there was wars and depressions. I am worryin' that maybe this guy's got somethin'. It's true that almost every Jew I know, both of them, is either a millionaire or well on his way, and I guess them Rosenbergers what got the chair are Jews.

"What you hintin' at?" Feegan says. "Who are you? The Secret Service or the FBI. What big shot are you that the government lets you in on its secrets. What's your special pipeline?"

They are both standin' up walkin' around nervous.

"How are you goin' to explain all of them facts. What I know is the truth that's been kept from the public. The dark truth that could destroy. . ." and he presses his fist against his forehead and bangs his hand against the wall by the side door.

"Bull," Feegan says standin' in the middle of the floor and leaning toward forward. "You don't know nothin'. You're just a stupid clod. A small town jerk. You don't know your ass from a hole and you pretend you got government secrets."

"What about all the spies they caught that turned out to be nothin' but Heebs?" Overseas says.

Feegan is gettin' really pissed now. Next to Roosevelt he thinks Bernard Baruch is all the brains behind the New Deal.

"So what, a mole hill don't make no mountain," Feegan says.

"What about Mrs. Roosevelt dancin' with niggers on the newsreel?" Overseas Cap says.

"What you anglin' at?" Feegan says, and Big George is really laughin' but I'm kind of worried.

"How you goin' to explain those facts? I want to know why they didn't open his casket. I want to know why there was nobody allowed to see him."

"So what," says Feegan. "There was too many people what would want to see him, might as well not let any. Besides that's the way rich Easterners do it. They don't let all the hoy poloi in like it was a side show or somethin' with everybody takin' a peek."

Now they are both real hot, standin' up to each other and even Big George and Fritz are gettin' a little worried.

"The paid Jewish press answer," this guy says with a know-it-all smile on his face. "Well, I happen to know a little bit more about this than the public."

"Don't give me that FBI-Secret Service bit agin," Feegan says.

Then Overseas booms out like the voice of doom. "There was *no body* in that casket. Roosevelt didn't die. There was no body in that casket," he says again.

So help me, he says that, and I am gettin' nervous and so's everybody else now. We all look over to Feegan to see what's happenin' and Feegan says,

"So where is he if he ain't in Washington or Hot Springs or Hyde Park and nobody's seen him for about ten years."

"I got documented proof that Roosevelt didn't die. He left this country when he saw the war was about over and flew to his home in Russia."

So help me, he actually says that, and we can't believe this but he has us really worried. We never heard this before.

Then he starts prancin' around the room with his eyes buggin' and shoutin' about some guy named Samuel Untemeyer and how Roosevelt planned Pearl Harbor so's to give his Jewish munitions manufacturing pals business, and all about a pumpkin, and foreign influences, and Yalta, and the big giveaway, and before you know it, we're half believin' him and he offers to bring documented proof which really gets us nervous. 'Documented and footnoted proof by a professor,' he says. Then he starts talkin' about the Bible and the sin of race mixing and how half of Roosevelt's advisors were communists or fags and how any town what don't have an unknown soldier in its cemetery ain't worth its salt. And then he really begins to get me when he talks about all them soldiers what died in vain and Gold Star mothers, and this really gets me. How you gonna argue against that? Even those smart union leaders from Chicago got a warm spot for them, and I'm beginnin' to think that Feegan is a son of a bitch 'cause this guy could really talk. He finishes by sayin' that we're losin' all our freedoms to the communist octopus with suckin' tentacles and Roosevelt was the cause of it all.

When he gets done there ain't a noise in Bonner's Back Room and everybody's sittin' staring at Feegan like he done it all hisself and Roosevelt only helped. Feegan just stood there watchin' this guy and lookin' around at us. It's like a tomb. And then Feegan says, real quiet like,
"Turd balls."
And this guy wags his nose in Feegan's face and says, "What did you say?"
And Feegan says loud now. "Little *round, brown, rabbit* turd balls."

Well, we all see, *just like that*, that this guy is really screwy, and we all start laughin' and he sees we're laughin' at him and not at Feegan, and he knocks Feegan a couple of good ones before anybody can help, and then he stomps out of the bar callin' us a bunch of communist.

We are feelin' pretty guilty when it is all over with Feegan bleedin' from the mouth and still sittin' on the floor so we get him up and give him a couple of shots. We got back to the cards and the next day we are still feelin' guilty so some of us go over to the Legion Club and buy Overseas Cap a few drinks and tell him we're sorry and say that maybe he's right. You know you can't always tell maybe he was wounded in the head durin' basic training or got shellshocked in war games. And when Feegan comes in to Bonner's Back Room the next day we are all kind of polite to him and buy him drinks and let him talk our ears off for about a week.

THE TOLL OF SPRING

No one expected him to live through the winter. Dolan was eighty-four years old and he had almost gone in December from uremia poisoning. But he had surprised everyone. In the middle of February he had felt so well that he had walked several blocks to a meeting at the Lodge one evening in below freezing temperature. The Brothers had been concerned but pleased by his daring, given his age and the rumors of his recent illness.

But in early spring he slipped on a step and fell down the basement stairs and hurt his back. During the first week of convalescence his kidneys began to bother him again, his legs ached from an old automobile injury, and then the symptoms of pneumonia when he seemed to be getting better. In the next few days he grew listless and weak. The doctor, after checking him over, just shook his head and shrugged as he left through the front door. There was no chance for recovery this time. He had a month, he said, two at the most.

Dolan lay in the large brass bed in the room that had been his for forty years. He lost weight rapidly, and when he had his alcohol baths one could see his pale skin, here taut and scaly white, there loosely wrinkled and yellowish grey. His flesh seemed to be melting away, and the knotty joints of his arms and legs, the cage of his chest, and his skull bulged like bas relief beneath his shrinking flesh.

Yet in those last days he struggled manfully for his life, rallying when he seemed to be gone. When he was bad, each breath was labored and there was a suspended pause at the depths of each exhalation and then the sudden rush of air being sucked into the rasping lungs. Then he would rally incredibly and sit up in bed and talk of business, his Brothers, and the years that had slipped away so suddenly, or he would ask to be carried on a chair to the window of his room to look out at the early signs of spring. His moods shifted: exhilaration, gloom, nostalgia, even humor. There were states of confusion as he recalled incidents of the spring of '94 involving grown men and women yet to be born. Grandchildren became children of another year, and once he called for his dog that had died twenty years before. "Here, Pup, here, old girl. Here, Pup, here, girl." He continued listlessly and mechanically to repeat the call.

There were moments of remarkable lucidity, though, when his mind was sharp and his mood, at least at the beginning, enthusiastic. He would sit up propped by pillows and call for his deer rifle.

"Catherine, my rifle, if you please, Catherine." And his wife would have the gun hauled out of the hall closet, and taken out of its case and laid across his lap. He ran his fingers from the butt of the stock to the end sights. He cleaned and oiled the barrel and the stock. Then he recalled in detail the finest buck he had ever taken. He came upon the deer in the pine stubble of a swamp on the edge of one of those perfect lakes in the north woods. The sun was setting and the big buck stood in the marsh silhouetted against the "magnificent glory," his very words, "magnificent glory," of the Minnesota woods. He dropped that buck with a single shot and it dressed out at 257 pounds. And then he seemed to go off into a reverie and his eyes grew dim. He turned and looked desperately at his wife and reached for her hand and began to rub and massage her fingers almost desperately, even sensually until he fell off again into sleep. He called often for that rifle in those last days.

"Catherine, my rifle, if you please, Catherine."

The last time he sat by the window it was late in the afternoon on one of those early spring days that promised so much. Outside a yellow sunlight slanted down, heaved painfully over the rooftops and dispersed itself in the wintered arms of the trees that lined the street like tattered but disciplined troops at perpetual attention. The snow had disappeared except in the shadowed grooves between the houses, and the wind was absorbing the surface moisture from the ground. Rotted leaves strewed the lawns, and water rushed along curbs, cleansing and carrying the refuse of winter in the breech of its force. It was the kind of day the old man loved especially after his retirement.

He would break his winter's confinement on just such a day and stroll, usually with one of his grandsons, along the streets of older homes, homes that he had in his youth and prime helped to build. He wore a black overcoat and his bowler hat and he carried a cane. His grandson would pick up a stick in imitation of the old man and the two of them would set out. When they came to a house the he had built, the boy took his stick and scraped the melting layer of ice off the corner of the last square of concrete in the sidewalk and then after reading closely he called excitedly to Dolan.

"Grandpa, here's one." Dolan would hurry to the boy, bend over his shoulder and read with pride

J. D. Dolan
General Contractor

Then the two would inspect the full length of the sidewalk looking for cracks or breakage, and when it appeared to be wearing well he would beam and shout to the boy,

"And now let's find Silanovich," and the boy would jump and run ahead of his grandfather to the front of one of the largest of the old homes. The boy scraped mud from the square with his stick in preparation. When Dolan arrived and looked at the printing embedded in the cement, he read aloud the letters S.V.K.C.K. and M. and then J.D.D., G.C. and C.O.

The letters recalled the memory of Nicholas Silanovich, immigrant Serb, and he often told the story of his favorite employee. He had hired Silanovich and a whole crew of Serbian immigrants after the First World War when he had received a deluge of contracts for homes. Silanovich and the Serbs were hard workers, so the old man, because of the load of work he had, entrusted jobs to his crew of Serbs and didn't show up until the job was done. It was always done well. He finished the house contract by laying the sidewalk and then imprinting it with his name and title. After one of the jobs in which he had been almost entirely an absentee employer, Silanovich, the spokesman for the crew, came to him in his office with his hat in his hand but a look of indignation on his face. When Dolan finally understood Silanovich through the broken English, he discovered that the men of the crew objected to Dolan's putting his name on the sidewalk after they had done all the work. Dolan explained that he did work: he purchased tools, supplies, materials, handled the payroll, invested capital, sublet contracts. But Silanovich, with all due respect to his employer, insisted that the crew built the sidewalk with their hands, not Dolan, and thus each member of the crew should get his name imprinted for all eternity. Dolan thundered with laughter as he retold the story. "That goddamn Serb was a Marxist through and through," he used to claim, but he also always admitted that Silanovich had a legitimate moral if not sound economic position. He tried to explain to Silanovich in practical terms.

He said, "I don't build a sidewalk big enough to put the likes of Silanovich, Kropolnicki, and Voynovich on it." But Silanovich was not satisfied and Dolan felt uneasy, perhaps even slightly guilty after the incident.

It was soon after this that he was awarded the contract for the largest house he had ever built. It was to be his finest achievement. He put his crew of Serbs into the breech of his creative struggle. His pride of achievement grew as the house slowly assumed form and then substance. It was the largest structure in town, besides the packing plants and schools which he had also helped to build, and when it was finished and his crew had laid out the forms for the sidewalk, he held a ceremony on the morning of the pouring of the concrete. He assembled his men, thanked them briefly for their cooperation, (he disliked any display of public emotion except perhaps irony or bawdy laughter), and handed Silanovich the new cast-iron branding plate he had made for the occasion and read the letters: SVKCK and M followed by JDD GC CO. After Silanovich had impressed the brand into the end corner squares, Dolan stepped over to the imprint and spoke in his best ceremonial voice,

"This home was constructed through the creative and noble efforts of Silanovich, Voynovich, Kropolnicki, Cnobryna, Kropick, and McCarthy under the auspices of J.D. Dolan, General Contractor and Casual Observer." Silanovich solemnly volunteered to stand watch all day to make sure that no boys would deface the concrete while it was setting.

As Dolan sat looking out that window at the signs of new life, he was taken with such a longing that the family removed him from the torture of the vision and refused to allow him to return. There would be no more walks in the early spring warmth and there was no reason the old man should suffer by continual reminders of what would be no more.

Because the old man had not been to church in over thirty years and then only to the wedding of his youngest daughter, they were reluctant to talk to him about a priest. He had never had a violent break with the church. He did not leave the church to join the Masons in a single grand decision of rebellion. He simply drifted away slowly as he followed the course of his duties and inclinations. His leaving the church was part of his maturity. Faith and the practice of religion seemed one of those delicate, personal intimacies understood only by women. Its spiritual benefits were foreign to the masculine soul.

But these were superficial reasons and he knew it. His real reason for leaving the church was that what the church taught was alien to and remote from the facts of experience. Had he been tempted by the devil himself it would have been better, for then he would have fought, probably failed, but at least hated his adversary. But his temptations had been the world and the flesh; he did not hate his opponent. How could one hate the spring, warm rains, green shoots, and promise, or the summer and the leafy fullness of trees, cool lakes, the still evenings of August, or the colors of fall, or the glistening, tingling white of winter. And there was love and fellowship. How could these be transient, unsubstantial. They were all he knew, and they renewed and repeated themselves—their passing was transient, their rhythm and cycle were substantial.

But he knew he was dying and at the nearness of death the church seemed reluctantly relevant. The priest who came was old and tired, and the Dolan seemed to recognize a brotherhood of spirit in the priest's wrinkled skin and grey hairs. After he had confessed and received communion, he chatted quietly with the priest and seemed at peace for the rest of the day, but then that night he was restless and afraid because he felt his strength seeping gradually away. His struggle was slowly becoming passive, beyond his conscious control, and it would soon come to depend solely upon his residual spirit.

When he could no longer control his bowels and bladder, the family, which had been helping in shifts, finally decided to get professional help. They hired a practical nurse, a Mrs. Helseth, and she was a marvel of efficiency and emotional detachment. When she arrived, she brought two suitcases with her and three large bundles of magazines tied with clothesline ropes: there were detective, western, secret love, and even a woman's magazine or two, probably to be read in her more feminine moments which were rare to say the least. After arranging her things in her bedroom down the hall, she appeared in her stiffly starched uniform, looked in on Dolan, and when she came out asked his wife abruptly where the sheets were kept. Catherine reluctantly showed the nurse the linen closet from which the nurse took several sheets and began ripping them into neat squares. The wife objected but she was so confused that her tone was mixed, and her demand seemed almost a pathetic appeal.

"What are you doing? Why are you ripping those sheets?"

Mrs. Helseth only smiled condescendingly as if to a child and said in her most pleasant tone of command,

"Well, mam, we're going to use these to save us a little work. We don't want him urinating all over the bed, do we?"

And then the wife, in horror, guessed at their use. Mrs. Helseth continued,

"Now you be a good girl and send someone out for some large diaper pins, and since I understand your husband has not been doing too well with solid foods, you had better get some strained baby food. You know I can't do everything myself." And then she added as almost an afterthought, "Oh, yes, you do have a rubber sheet, don't you?" and she continued ripping the sheets with professional vigor. Once she adjusted to her new circumstances, which didn't take very long, she did almost everything herself.

The wife went to her children and appealed. The image of her husband as a helpless infant being taken over by that monstrous midwife of death was too much and she demanded that "that woman" be discharged immediately. But the family supported Mrs. Helseth whose practical innovations were soon to produce order and efficiency, at least as much order as could be reasonably expected in death. She was able to handle him by herself and Dolan, who was too weak to get up, followed her about with his eyes, at first full of hate and fear, and later with a glint of ironic admiration. She talked to him in a kind of baby talk as she fed, changed, and rubbed him, or changed his bed. She completed his isolation, his final preparation for death, by setting up visiting hours.

Dolan had spoken to her once and she had been pleased to discover how much he had come to appreciate her efficiency. He had said, "Mrs. Vulture, or is it only Miss?" and she had patted him and pinched his cheek, but it was the only display of affection in the week she attended him.

Once she had even acted compassionately. His wife wanted to see him out of visiting hours. She knocked gently on his door and when Mrs. Helseth answered, "What do you want, Dearie?" the wife answered that she wanted to see her husband. Mrs. Helseth said, "What for? He's asleep," and she answered, "Because he is my husband." And Mrs. Helseth, temporarily put off her guard by the logic of her answer, let her in.

Although everyone was a bit disconcerted by her professional detachment, she soon came to be respected for the role she played in those last days. She sat with the old man hour after hour, taking care of him and reading her way through the stack of pulps she had brought.

The Brothers appeared, but late as if an afterthought. Dolan, of course, was old and life did move on, but they hadn't forgotten him, and so three representatives called the day before he died. When they were told that he had returned to the church, they seemed disappointed and deeply hurt. The wife felt sorry for them. She told them that they couldn't see him anyway because of his serious condition. They stood on the threshold of the door, embarrassed, until she finally invited them in.

She led them to the dining room, set the table hastily, and then served them coffee. They talked among themselves about Dolan, his fellowship, leadership and example, his initiative. He was one of the old pioneers. The world was good for them today because of him. He was kind of a creator who had fashioned out of the wilderness of this upper Mississippi River basin some semblance of order, security and comfort, the substructure of their flourishing bourgeois culture. They spoke in hushed whispers as if Dolan were already dead, and when they unconsciously nodded upward referring to Dolan in his sick bed, it might have been misconstrued as a reference to Dolan's soul already in heaven. When they left, they extended to his wife what was in effect their condolences, for they never appeared at the wake, not with the priest and the rosary, though a delegation did attend the funeral. They shook hands mournfully, looked up to their dying brother with regret, and then left conveying their apologies for having interrupted in such a time of crisis.

Dolan's world, the periphery of his consciousness, began to recede like a dying candle, sucking into itself the remote edges of its vitality. The yellow bars of light that shot through the window beyond the foot of his bed seemed to blur amid the shadows that began to descend and blanket the far reaches of his vision. Soon there was no wall, only a sea of fuzziness, of light and shadows, in which eyes of pity behind masks of affected optimism seemed to float, speak in murmurs, and fade again.

His mind drifted beyond the memory of most people alive. But he could only recall faces, gestures, attitudes, each vision singularly static, isolated without connection to any other image and without any consequences of action. His vision and hearing dimmed until he soon was aware of the world primarily through his touch. As his consciousness seemed to collapse upon him like a shroud, he became aware only of the touch of the bed and the firm, often rough but purposeful strength of the practical nurse doing her duties without compassion, systematically and efficiently.

At about noon on a Wednesday in early April, when it appeared to Mrs. Helseth that there wasn't much time left, the priest, the doctor, and the family were called. Members of the family began arriving soon. They all asked whether he had gone yet, as if presence at the moment of death had some mystical aura about it. There was some discussion and debate as to how the priest was to be greeted. In which hand was the napkin, in which the spoon, or was it a fork, in which the candle in event he was carrying the sacrament, although the oldest daughter who had called the priest told him the viaticum was not necessary, was really impossible because her father was in a coma. When the priest came, the family gathered quickly and quietly in his room around the bed and knelt in prayer during the Extreme Unction. The priest then led the rosary.

The doctor came and left. There was nothing he could do. Although there was no death rattle yet, the sound of the old man's breathing filled the room. He lay on the bed with his head bent sharply back; a pillow had been folded in half and propped under his shoulders and neck. His moustache, gray but yellowed around the edges, stuck absurdly into the air and seemed a kind of filter to the air that passed into the hollow of his lungs. The old man's body seemed an appendage to his breathing apparatus.

Occasionally the wind rattled the glass panes through which a yellow bar of sunlight entered under the half drawn shade and spattered against the wall over the bed. On the table beside the bed was a melange of instruments and bottles which had become the implements and elixirs of life. But Dolan continued to breathe, continued to grasp and struggle for life. After two hours of dutiful waiting and prayer the family began to break up, one by one, until by four o'clock only Mrs. Helseth, over in the corner reading a magazine, was left on the death watch.

Then he died with Mrs. Helseth as his only witness. She had been reading when she suddenly felt the room quiet—except, of course, for the force of the wind on the panes. She did not know how long it had been before she became aware of the silence. As she looked up, she caught with her eyes a piece of lint dropping through the bar of yellow light and she followed it with her eyes through the light until it disappeared in a gently settling, side slipping motion past the moustache between the open lips of the old man.

That was all she told the family of the moment. She shrugged when asked for more detail. That was all she could remember. There wasn't much more. She told them that most of the time it was quiet like that. It probably wasn't much more than what she had said it was, effortless as if the toggles that bound the flesh and soul had been gently loosened.

MY HERITAGE

"A Plague a both your houses."
Mercutio
ROMEO AND JULIET

To begin with, it was usually Grandmother who started it and my father who got in the last word, although it should be stated in fairness to Grandmother that he probably provoked her.

"He is not perfect. He has his little imperfections," Grandmother said. "But there are the good things about Patrick that more than compensate for the few weaknesses and indiscretions that we are all subject to in this vale of tears."

And she nodded toward my father when she inflected the *all*. She intended the word to be comprehensive, to include my father and whatever foibles of conduct he might have. My father smiled and answered in mock Irish,

"'Tis true, 'tis true, Mother dear, begorra—to a degree, to a degree." And Grandmother knew that my father, who was of German descent, implied a great deal more.

What my father implied was simple enough. Uncle Patrick, Grandmother's youngest brother, had two serious faults, (or "indiscretions" as Grandmother put it): he had developed through the years a disposition toward whiskey and an aversion to work. He had become, despite Grandmother's tears and entreaties and later her euphemisms and excuses, a drunken bum and my father used him, symbolically of course (as some kind of generic Irish prototype) in his struggle against what he called "Irish arrogance and smugness," embodied in Grandmother's claim that there are two kinds of people,—the Irish and those who wished they were Irish. And then he added with rhetorical grandeur, half in earnest, half in jest,

"Patrick alone is sufficient proof, I tell you, sufficient proof that five thousand years of inbreeding on that godforsaken island (that even the snakes had left) has resulted in serious racial deficiencies."

And my father shook his head darkly and suggested that it seemed to him a significant comment on the Irish mentality that the snakes emigrated fifteen hundred years before the Irish.

And there were also the Sunday afternoon dinners at Grandmother's when my father, waiting for dinner to be served, had one too many drinks. He would wander into the kitchen and tease Grandmother and before long he would have the knife in the Irish back and would twist it for good measure, and Grandmother, who at seventy years of age should have known better, couldn't resist recriminating.

Once, I remember, after five minutes of specious argumentation on both sides, Grandmother resorted to the ultimate argument.

"Well, if you hate the Irish so much," she said conclusively, "why did you marry one?"

He stood there stunned for a moment and it looked as though he would be certainly and finally defeated.

But with a smile of triumph already beginning to spread from the corners of his mouth he answered,

"Begorra, for humanitarian purposes, of course. Sure and it was the Lord's own work that called me."

And Grandmother, puzzled, tried to dismiss the whole discussion by turning her back and remarking with a touch of bitterness,

"More buffoonery. I have no time for your nonsense."

And my father, following her, pleaded. "No, no, Mother. You don't understand. Hear me out."

Grandmother gave him a last chance.

"You see," and he seemed serious enough, "the Irish national defects," he continued as if reading a papal encyclical from the altar, "like most recessive genetic mutations in nature ought to be reduced in frequency of occurrence. I have humanely chosen," he added grandly, "as my vocation in life to enhance the inbred Irish genetic pool."

It was a set speech memorized in part from a book my father only half understood, and it was followed by a proud gesture of the arm which introduced my brothers and sisters and me as evidence of his great humanitarian achievement.

II

Now, all of that happened a long time ago, but it did not pass without leaving its mark on me. I was actually a very sensitive child, and my Irish relatives were genuine, pre-Civil War, Midwest, American, Irish. (No Johnny-come-lately Boston or immigrant Irish in my family.) In those early years, before I had reached the age of critical intelligence, I was all Irish in my aspirations. I was, to be frank, ashamed of my German name as though it were some kind of hereditary disease or a congenital defect. Most of my friends had wonderful melodious names like McNally, and Cosgrove, and O'Toole. Ireland was the home of Leprechauns and Shillelaghs, and Father O'Callahan and County Cork and Killarney.

Ah, how I cursed the fate of patrilineal descent—especially being German. I could have tolerated being French or Norwegian or even Polish or almost anything but German, the hated enemy of movies and newsreels and newspapers, goose stepping Nazi troops, screaming dive bombers, extermination camps, mass rallies, violence and brutality. I used to dream that my German name was all a hideous mistake, that I had been secretly adopted and that some day the dark cloud of my German ancestry would be dissipated, revealing me in a sudden blaze of glory as a one hundred percent, true son of Ireland.

Once, during one of my summer tours of duty as an altar boy at early morning mass, I confided my difficulties to Father O'Callahan and he comforted me with the thought that being just a little bit Irish was enough because that meant you were a whole lot better than everybody else. Well, I wasn't just a little bit Irish; I was a full fifty percent which I figured made me a giant among men. Unfortunately, whatever sympathy and support Father O'Callahan lent me was only temporary, for although I may have been a giant among men taken from the population as a whole, I was still a half-breed midget among my relatives and friends who one hundred per cent Irish.

But later rather than sooner, even I matured. By the time I reached adulthood, what little Irish heritage I had acquired had faded. It had been a heritage, when viewed objectively, with little significant accomplishment and certainly no direct influence on me. All I learned about Ireland when I was young came from movies like "Going My Way." It was a priest-ridden land of tenors, sentimentality, blarney, and hot headed brawlers. Later I learned that there were no philosophers, no scientists—only a handful of artists who unanimously concluded that Ireland was a sow that devoured her own brood. And what had been the Irish contribution to America? Alcoholism and crooked politics. But back in the days of my childhood I suffered all the agonies of ethnic ambivalence and somehow most of what I suffered was in one way or another connected to Uncle Patrick. He was the central figure of my father's attack, the obvious weak link, the chink in the Irish armor. Grandmother knew he needed defending more than anyone else and my father sensed her vulnerability.

Uncle Patrick, himself, was short and stocky, of indeterminate age and uncertain stability. I was always uneasy in his presence as if my existence along might unbalance what seemed a precarious emotional equilibrium. But his temperament was usually calm, though he spoke in elliptical fragments, his words exploding like sharpened barbs. His eyes were an empty blue, always watering, except when he spoke and then they narrowed into pugnacious intensity. His nose was red and irrigated with random purple and scarlet veins, his cheeks were like road maps—the red veins representing main highways and the thin purple lines representing secondary and provincial back roads.

For Uncle Patrick, Grandmother's house was home, and through the years they had formed a pact of sorts—tacit but alluded to often enough to become an understanding. He could wander as he chose, but he must promise to do his Easter duty and to report once a year for at least two weeks of physical and spiritual restoration. She in turn promised Patrick a respectable funeral and burial, "a last anchorage" as she put it in the hackneyed metaphor and sales idiom of Grandfather's undertaker, "secure, stationary, peaceful..."

Uncle Patrick wandered east and west, hitch-hiking, on the rods or in boxcars, occasionally working for a meal or money for whiskey. He had in the prime of his life and for no apparent reason renounced the society of civilized men and all its works and pomp. Patrick often visited Grandmother's distant relatives and vague childhood connections as far away as Boston and New York. Each year, sometime around Christmas, we reconstructed his itinerary of the year from the hurriedly jotted notes on the back of cards from those whom Patrick had visited.

It as usually after some Sunday dinner in early January. Grandmother moved us, the grandchildren available, into the living room that was used only for special occasions. It was clogged with the remnants of death and the past and although I came to dislike the yearly ritual, I always felt obliged to indulge Grandmother in her whims because my father used to tell me, confidentially of course, that she was getting a little senile and although I didn't know what the word meant, it sounded bad enough to merit my compassionate cooperation.

Grandfather's Morris chair was still arranged in his favorite position near the front window and his cuspidor was sentimentally ensconced at the foot of the chair. An embossed plaque of the poem "Trees" was attached to the wall above his chair. On one of the tables, curiously arranged almost like a religious shrine, were pictures of two nuns and a priest, cousins whom I had never seen and felt had also died, until one of the nuns shockingly appeared at a family outing and played softball with us. On one wall hung the most agonizing wooden crucifix I have ever seen, carved by a remotely related craftsman from Ireland, and which later became after Grandmother's death a prize which led to some bitter words and a temporary rift in the family.

The ritual was simple. We spread a large national road map out on Grandmother's living room rug. She sat in state in a grotesquely Victorian, winged chair, her throne. As she read cards and letters and dictated to us, we marked with big X's in red crayon the places Uncle Patrick had been and the date. Then we marked out in black crayon with rulers, the way the crow flies she insisted, the probable route and with arrowheads indicated the direction. Once when we had finished, my father commented that he thought Patrick would visit relatives for years without visiting anyone twice. He added that the Irish were like the Poles and Swedes (and Grandmother clicked her upper plate in violent repression when Father made the comparison) thick to the fifth degree.

Whenever Uncle Patrick returned, which was usually once a year according to the agreement, he was indulged as if he were a helpless child or the soft-headed victim of some violent tragic incident. When my mother and Grandmother spoke of Uncle Patrick, they often did so in hushed, reverential whispers. Grandmother hinted that he was one of the victims of the Great Depression, a defeated child of his times.

"Poor, poor Pat," she would whisper to herself after he had left again. "What he might have been but for '29."

She was always evasive about details and her confusions when not challenged soon became facts in her mind. My father allowed her tragic and somewhat romantic version to stand uncontested, but he often said to my mother, when he became riled at the imaginary verisimilitude which Grandmother invented to support her fictions,

"The truth is things got bad for Patrick with Prohibition and *she* didn't get around to noticing until October of 1929."

And then he would repeat himself over and over again and pace the floor in angry demonstration and reaction. But Grandmother was not alone in her euphemism and convenient self-deception. Uncle Patrick came to be considered by the family, to my father's despair, as a kind of lay mendicant, a begging, unordained friar, and although his life at first seemed a waste, his wanderings soon assumed in the imagination of the family the aura of a religious pilgrimage.

III

But, *alas* and *alack* too, as in literature so in life, we plunge headlong toward our prosaic destinies. Hour becomes day, day becomes week. Week becomes month, etc. In short, time flies.

One spring Uncle Patrick returned to Grandmother's never to wander again. The signs of time and decay were already upon him. He lasted little more than a year, for he never mastered the whiskey that led to pneumonia and death.

And the time that flies also had its effect upon my father. The greatest change, the most fundamental erosion, that took place over the years was in my father's attitude toward Uncle Patrick. He came to regret that he had ever mentioned Uncle Patrick in his arguments with Grandmother.

In that last year Uncle Patrick often came to our house in the evenings (to escape Grandmother's surveillance) for supper and to drink with my father into the night. And they talked and talked. I understood little of what they said except for the politics. I remember the pirate-booty metaphor was central to their political discussions and reflected the fundamental assumption that the world was populated by two kinds of people—thieves and fools. Along with such traditional stalwart "pirates" as John D. Rockefeller, Jim Hill, and J. P. Morgan were such recent figures as John L. Lewis and Winston Churchill. The greatest pirate of all was Franklin Delano Roosevelt, the prince of thieves. Wall Street, Hollywood, and England had the greatest concentration of pirates and their victims were distributed rather evenly throughout the rest of the world.

Occasionally, as in the case of President Roosevelt, there was a certain admiration in the use of the word, but whenever "pirate" was used with approbation it was automatically implied that the victims were such fools that they deserved to be cheated out of their share of the loot.

I once thought that there might be compassion or justice at the root of their political attitudes but such was not the case. Most of the booty had already been distributed rather unevenly in favor of someone else. They simply regretted that it had not been doled specifically to them. They never entertained any sympathy for a theoretical socialism which would require an equitable distribution of the wealth. They accepted their unequal fate heroically and gained some satisfaction from the position that *anyone* who had been successful was *ipso facto* morally suspect.

There was a kind of structure to their discussions. They would begin, after cigars had been lighted and my father offered Uncle Patrick a small one for the road (he didn't leave for at least three more hours), in a political argument and Uncle Patrick would modify my father's outlandish and wildly exaggerated charges with his explosive barbs and then my father would retrench, qualify his statements, and then they would find some common ground and proceed to discuss things in general on a level of abstraction I could not follow. Before I was sent to bed, I could sense that both of them (there were many more short ones for the road) had reached a level so marvelously detached and Olympian (and alcoholic) that they seemed to be discussing Man as if they were not members of the human race, as if they were foreign observers of human folly.

It is difficult to explain my father's attitude after a year of philosophic discussion and drinking with Uncle Patrick, a year which ended in Patrick's death. It wasn't just that he was a victim of a certain time in American history—a time of deliberate ethnic, racial, and national segregation in city neighborhoods or in rural communities, a time of religious bigotry and racial and ethnic hostility. My father had a mind, how shall I say, not satisfied with sufficient causes—a mind concerned with ultimates, with absolutes. He was a bona fide second-rate philosopher, a curious sort of rationalist who demanded order or predictable consistency in the world about him even if no order existed in fact. As he grew close to Uncle Patrick, he became faced with a living paradox. Uncle Patrick was like Prometheus or Lucifer, somehow grand even in the blackness of damnation; he was *great* even though Irish.

IV

At the wake Father was the only one to mourn. Everyone else seemed to think that Uncle Patrick's death was a blessing. Father took two days off work; he was the first to appear at the wake in the afternoon. He told Mother and Grandmother, before all the arrangements had been made, that he thought there ought to be some restraint, some "class" to Uncle Patrick's funeral. He didn't see any reason the wake had to be an opportunity for a convocation of the Gallagher and McDermott clans. He said to my mother, "Now, let's not make a goddamn three-ring Irish circus out of this."

I must admit, though, what with all the hot dishes and jello desserts that were sent over by kind neighbors or brought by the relatives; and what with the hot rolls from Mrs. Lundeen who lived across from the school grounds; and the Norwegian casserole from Mrs. Olson up the street; and the Swedish meatballs from Mrs. Anderson; that although it never became a "goddamn three-ring Irish circus" the wake took on the tone if not the substance of a smorgasbord style family picnic.

Uncle Patrick was laid out in a mahogany casket with silver handles right smack up against the south wall of Grandmother's living room between Grandfather's Morris chair and the wood-carved crucifix. He wore one of Grandfather's dark blue suits and one of my father's best striped ties. All afternoon flowers were delivered until the casket was banked to the ceiling with remembrances. Even Grandfather's chair had to be moved to make room.

During the afternoon of the wake my father moped. He hovered on the far edges of the living room and occasionally walked over to the casket to view Uncle Patrick and shake his head gloomily. We went home about five o'clock for supper, but he wouldn't eat. He had several drinks and began to mutter to himself. We all returned to the wake about six-thirty.

When we walked into Grandmother's living room again, we discovered that a marvelous transformation had taken place in our absence. The casket had been slanted askew of its original flush position and the left rear corner had been tilted upward obliquely. The flowers had been rearranged on tables of varying levels in tiers to the side and behind the casket, and the lights of the living room had been redirected or extinguished to heighten the effectiveness of the floral arrangement and Uncle Patrick. Everyone was talking quietly and nodding their approval.

We soon learned that this remarkable artistic accomplishment was to be credited to the undertaker's assistant, a recent college graduate with a major in mortuary science and a minor in theater arts. He stood inside the archway of the living room smiling benignly, with his hands clasped behind his back and his feet set apart. His upper lip was graced with an incipient moustache and he rocked up and down from his heels to his toes, surveying his handiwork with obvious satisfaction.

I could feel an atmosphere of gay festivity. The street for a block in two directions was packed with cars. Mourners were arriving every minute. They came smiling through the front door, sobered when they saw Uncle Patrick laid out so fine, said a prayer or two on the kneeler next to the coffin, and then moved slowly into the dining room and kitchen, picking up something to eat on the way. The food was spread on two large tables one in the dining room and the other in the kitchen. Then they filed out the back or side door onto the lawn and into the cool September air where they took up again the conversations they had begun before briefly praying for Patrick. Everyone behaved so rationally—everyone except my father, of course—who was seething with anger at the "sideshow" which had replaced the circus he had feared.

The spirit was contagious. I hadn't been there ten minutes when I went to the back yard with my cousin, Mickey, and some other boys to play "Red Rover." We played in whispers out of respect for Uncle Patrick, but as we raced back and forth and tackled and grabbed, we became too noisy and were solemnly rebuked by Mickey's father, Uncle Michael who was already drinking a highball—somewhat hypocritically we all agreed considering his pompous and self-righteous criticism of our good spirits and fair and sportsmanlike play.

When I went back inside, Grandmother got hold of me and grabbed my hand and held it for about fifteen minutes while she talked to the friends and relatives who conveyed their condolences. She didn't say a word to me. She just held my hand and squeezed it every so often. When she took me over to the casket, I was suddenly afraid that she was going to make me kiss Uncle Patrick on the forehead as she had had me kiss Grandfather five years before, but she only took my hand and patted it on Uncle Patrick's brow and murmured, "Poor, poor Pat" a few times. Then we went back to the other side of the room and she let my hand go and picked up the hand of one of my cousins.

About nine o'clock Father O'Callahan came to say the Rosary. Everyone knelt down (except the Protestants who stood uncomfortably against a back wall or went outside). When the Rosary was over the wake seemed to diffuse, to decentralize. The women went to the kitchen and began to wash the dishes and the men wandered into the far corners of the unlighted back yard and began to talk. In time, I drifted out there and found my father, whom I had not seen since early evening, on the edge of the circle of men exchanging stories of the good old days.

Someone passed my father the bottle that had been circulating. He took two long swallows, tipping his head way back, and then passed the bottle on. While one of the men was talking quietly, he suddenly raised his head, his voice boomed and broke the quiet murmur of conversation. He had been working his thoughts out in a deep concentration. He had apparently reached a moment of truth: he had resolved in his mind (we were soon to discover) the paradox of Patrick's life. He delivered with a deep passion and a rough eloquence an elegy on Uncle Patrick, and I might add that as drunk and impassioned as he was, his parallelism and antithesis never faltered.

Father began by reviewing the facts of Patrick's life. It was difficult, he said, to comprehend the odd mixture of virtues and vices in Patrick. He personally had considered all the evidence carefully through the long years of his close association with the deceased. He had come to admire Patrick; he felt that the good far outweighed the bad, and, indeed, Patrick was to be admired for having labored under certain handicaps in life. He personally had come to the conclusion that Patrick was, indeed, an exceptional man. But How, he asked, How? How was this possible?

Patrick displayed the deficiencies of the Irish on a grand scale, to be sure, but he was more than a typical Irishman. In order to account for the paradox, for the contradictions that Patrick embodied; in order to understand how Patrick, the typical pugnacious, drunken, lazy Irishman, had managed to systematically bilk the Irish for thirty years by playing to their shabby emotions; in order to comprehend how Patrick was able to live and drink for three decades off phony Irish patronage to the fifth degree of kindred and to trade for a profit in sham sentiments and self-deceptions and yet manage to mature beyond the superstitions, vulgar pretenses, and petty stupidities of the Irish race; in order to account for how he had managed to make capital, as it were, of the very defects he exhibited to a greater or lesser degree in his own character; in order to account, in short, for Patrick's ability to transcend the limitations of his racial background it was necessary for my father to assume—and without any reflections on the virtue of his wife's grandmother or his mother-in-law's grandmother or that long line of respectable Irish women or Irish Motherhood in general—it was imperative for him to assume that somewhere, somehow, sometime there must have been a German in the Irish woodpile.

V

Now, I do not want all of this to seem flippant or irreverent. After all, Uncle Patrick, Grandmother, and Father are all dead now and that isn't any joke. Besides, few things in my family have ever been taken without some awareness of the tragic potential of the human condition. Life is after all a serious business. Father's drunken elegy out there in the back yard was not considered lightly by anyone, especially Mother.

A few days after the funeral, Grandmother got me alone and after a long and tedious monologue she drew a moral for me so that I might benefit through negative example from my father's disgraceful performance. (I was thirteen years old at the time, and everyone agreed badly in need of moral training). I do not wish to belabor her lecture too much, the substance of which was simply this: my father's speech illustrated one of the most important principles of human behavior—people who live in glass houses shouldn't throw stones.

When she was done, I asked her if that wasn't the same idea as people who live in tin cans like Prince Albert shouldn't throw can openers, and she said,

"What?"

I repeated myself and she said (even though Irish she had a soft spot in her heart for good old Prince Albert),

"What is Prince Albert doing in a can?"

And I said,

"It's a joke. Prince Albert is a smoking tobacco and you call the drug store and ask them if they have Prince Albert in a can and when they say 'Yes' you tell them 'to let him out.'"

"Oh. Is that what the younger generation thinks is funny nowadays?"

I noticed that her glasses were slipping down toward the end of her nose.

"I don't know about the younger generation but we really got old man Gerike mad when we called him."

Grandmother seemed to have lost the train of thought so I asked her,

"Is that the same idea?" and she said,

"What idea?" and I said,

"About people living in tin houses." And she said,

"Who lives in tin houses?"

And I said "Who lives in glass houses?'

" I was using glass houses only as an illustration," she said.

"Yeah, Grandma, I know. I was using tin houses as an illustration, but is that the same, tin houses and glass houses?"

She thought for a moment and answered slowly, nodding her head,

"I guess so. Your joke is not very clever but it is an apt analogy. Yes. I suppose it is the same."

Having finished instructing me, she turned away and proceeded to the more important duties of consoling my mother and forgiving my father, who had already made a gesture of reconciliation by promising to begin attending AA meetings.

THE GOOD BOWLER

a short novel

For his teeth seem for laughing around an apple.
There lurk no claws behind his fingers supple;
And god will grow no talons at his heels,
Nor antlers through the thickness of his curls.

"Arms and the Boy"
Wilfred Owen

PLACE
A River City in the Upper Midwest

TIME
Early November 1966

CHAPTER ONE

His clay grew tall according the will of the flesh, but the statistical data are unimpressive. He is slightly under the national average in each measurement, perhaps five feet, eight inches tall and one hundred and forty-five pounds soaking wet. Neither does he come at you boldly with flashing eyes and squared shoulders to take command. Rather, he recedes toward the edge of things.

He lives on the fringe, the shoreline of the main stream, and participates vaguely and passively, if at all, in the cherished cultural accomplishments of Western Civilization. He is twenty-one years old and his christened name is Frederick Eugene Gerbracht. He lives out there somewhere in the hinterlands—in a trading and meatpacking center along a great river. He belongs to a vast inarticulate subculture which is bounded on the east, philosophically, by the editorial offices of the Reader's Digest and on the west, artistically, by the Lawrence Welk Music Makers.

You must not judge him too harshly; regardless of appearances he is neither barbaric nor corrupt. He simply wears man's smudge and shares man's smell. He participates eagerly in the fruits of original sin: he refuels three times a day like the fallen machine he is and he must work by the sweat of his brow. He, too, must face the common lot of ignorance and death. He is for all his affectations of masculinity quite innocent of the knowledge of good and evil.

Since he has completed only twelve perfunctory years of school, he may safely be classified as uneducated, but like all true-blue Americans he believes in freedom or the illusion of freedom though he cannot articulate this faith. It is not any grand concept; in its highest form it is little more than the opportunity to be a stranger, the power not to belong. It isn't even rebellion. More often it is only the freedom of motion, the meager command over nature that he can feel in the controlled arch of the perfectly delivered bowling ball. Sometimes his freedom is little more than the illusion of alcoholic euphoria which temporarily seems to reconcile all differences and alleviate all pain.

But he is willing to pay a price to perpetuate this illusion of freedom. He is consciously willing, even eager, to trade one form of entrapment for a larger, more comprehensive form of entrapment because in the exchange he will feel the release of escape, the breaking of the bondage of the past, and for a brief moment he will think he is free.

He is going now. The final decision, determined by the United States government through the courtesy of the local Selective Service Board, has made his flight easier, less personally responsible. He would have gone anyway—enlisted—but there would have been an argument at home, accusations of ingratitude. Besides, he would have been scorned and ridiculed by his friends and fellow employees. One is supposed to hate the army and love one's home.

He has already passed his physical, received his notice of induction. Now he must only restrain his eagerness, pretend he has been wrenched from his life's desire, affect to scorn the army and the government and this shallow pretense of a war. But in his heart he is eager and in twenty-four hours he will be delivered. He is preparing now to leave.

He is already imagining a future time, another place, but he makes a conscious effort. He says to himself: "This is the last time I will do this or that, see this or that." Tokens of the present and the past are strange and useless to him, impediments. He feels guilty, knows he ought to feel some sense of loss or debt of gratitude, but he cannot feel the obligation.

Although his father accepts his departure as an ordinary event in the normal order of things, his mother has hovered about him for over a week. Her solicitude is smothering. She has said little so far, but her eyes have been growing in sadness and concern. He can't do anything for himself, she has been right there wanting to help in any little way she can, silent, long-suffering, waiting on him.

Detached and passive he has been witnessing the ritual of his own demise. He remembers his grandmother's funeral. There was the opening of the casket, the arrival of the first mourners at the visiting hours, the closing of the casket, the church, the grave, each a new peaking of grief but each followed by a gradual lessening of the load of pain and loss.

For five days now, each dawn has brought a new plateau of significance. There has been his fifth to last breakfast, and his third to last lunch; his favorite foods have appeared with uncommon frequency. She has hovered, hovered, hovered—silently watching. And now he is into his last day, and she is down to each last meal and to each and every simple habit.

He is afraid that if he picks his nose she will sigh, after she has admonished him, of course, and in her quiet, sad exhalation he will be able to read: this is the last time my son will pick his nose here at home. But he is not yet free. He reads the signs of her expectation. She has not said very much, but, alas, that does not mean she has nothing to say.

CHAPTER TWO

"Hey, Ma."

Gerbracht speaks over the top of the morning paper. He is slumped in an easy chair and his feet paw an ottoman as he reads.

"Hey, Ma-a-a-a," he tries louder but without looking up. No answer again.

He is dressed casually in faded suntan pants, the cuffs of which have been rolled up so that his white sweat socks will show. His sport shirt is open at the collar so that the white of his T-shirt will also show. His hair has been groomed neatly and it glistens from the hair oil in which it has been drenched. The heady aroma of an alcoholic after-shaving lotion wafts after him when he moves, and if you look closely, you can see the thin layer of finely textured powder that covers the skin of his face, smoothing and enveloping the incipient pimples and filling the cratered peaks of those that have been squeezed.

He crushes the paper flat into his lap and persists in calling her now not because of anything important he has to say but because she has not answered his call. Besides she has the irritating habit of slinking off and sneaking in, of being ubiquitously present and absent.

"Hey, Ma, where are you?"

As he stands up, he notices across the room and above the sofa that his mother's favorite banner hangs crookedly to the right from its golden rope. It is white silk with gold tassels and fringes and is embroidered in gold thread. It is inscribed with a religious sentiment.

Jesus saves, if you can find
In your heart to be kind.

He straightens it and steps back, surveys its new balance, and satisfied with his work walks across the room toward the kitchen door. In the hallway he hears the weight of steps on the floor upstairs. He stops, reverses his direction toward the stairway. At the foot of the stairs he leans on the banister and cupping his hands into a megaphone shouts,

"Ma-a-a. You up there? Hey, Ma-a-a-a."

"You calling me, Freddy?" a voice muffled by distance answers.

"No, Ma. I was yelling to myself."

"I didn't hear you." The voice is clear now as she appears in the opening at the head of the stairs.

"You were downstairs a minute ago," he says. "I wouldn't yell except you're always sneaking off."

She is about to answer him but checks herself and asks,

"I thought you were reading. Did you want something?"

"I don't know. A couple a minutes ago I thought I wanted something. Now I can't remember." He stalls for a few moments, reconsiders the conditions which prompted his first call, and then, upon remembering, is disappointed by the banality of his question.

"I remember now. I just wanted to know when you want me back this afternoon."

"I suppose five or six," she says. "Uncle Fritz will be coming early; he said he had some business after."

She comes down the stairs and follows him back into the living room where he sits once again to read.

"Is that all you wanted?" she asks and is immediately apprehensive he might take her question the wrong way. She peers with concern and sadness at him, and he stirs and fidgets under her stare.

"Naw, I got a few other questions. If you don't sneak off again, I'll ask them when I finish this article. Just let me finish this and I'll be right with you."

He doesn't seem angry. She walks around the room setting things in order. She gathers the magazines scattered on the coffee table and on the other ottoman and returns them to the magazine rack. She looks at the banner, cocks her head, and leans across the sofa to adjust its balance.

"I just straightened it," he says without looking up.

Her arm freezes in mid-air and then jolts back as if she has received an electric shock. She steps back, turns, sits on the sofa, and muses as she waits for him to finish. This is her only child. The depression and war delayed her marriage to Henry who spent four years in the army, two miscarriages, and a legacy of varicose veins have restricted the size of her family. She does not want to lose him, yet it is not just the fear of military action that bothers her. She is as anxious about his moral well being as she is for his physical survival. There is corruption everywhere, of course, especially in the large cities. In the daily newspaper and in weekly magazines she reads of violence and degeneration in Chicago, New York, Los Angeles, Detroit.

But it is not just the corruption of the City. Her fear is deeper, more fundamental—of the weaknesses of human nature itself. The environment that nourishes is simply a poor prop to our fallen nature, not the cause of our downfall.

It is her pride that she has been a firm support to her son though now that he is leaving, she is frightened by the certain truth that her moral influence over him will be inversely proportional to his distance from her. She wonders: Will he be strong enough? Will he be a credit to my care?

In time he looks up from his paper and decides to have it all out and done. He hesitates, watches her as she sits primly, her head tilted to one side and her hands clasped in her lap.

"I just wish you hadn't done it, Ma," he finally says. "You should of just let me go quietly. You shouldn't of invited everyone to say goodbye. I'm gonna feel like a real stupe."

"I didn't do it all for you," she answers rising instantly to this opportunity and walking forward. "Some people would like to say goodbye to you even if you don't want to say goodbye to them."

"I could of gone around and said goodbye casual-like tonight and tomorrow morning. It would have been easier that way."

"Yes, and you would have forgotten somebody and then I would hear about it. Oh, did Freddy leave?" she mimics."He didn't even stop and say goodbye. And then I would have to make excuses for you. No. This way everyone has been told, and if somebody doesn't show up, well, it's their fault, not mine."

"You mean they're all invited! I haven't seen Uncle Fritz for two years. I don't see I owe him any goodbye. Besides, he'll get into another argument with Pa and you won't be able to hear yourself think with them two going at it."

"They won't argue. Fritz won't be here that long. You will just have to put up with them for one night. He is your godfather, after all. Since you'll be giving your time to the army for the next few years, you can spend at least one night with your family. Who knows what might happen. There is fighting, you know."

"Aw, c'mon, Ma. I'm not gonna do any fighting. It may be over any time now. It's not like World War II. It's not even like Korea. Besides the casualty rate is much lower."

"What if it escalates?" she says.

"It's more likely they'll get going at the negotiating table."

"Well, what difference will that make?"

"Well, it'll make a lot of difference. If it's like Korea, they'll just sit around out there every night throwing flares up to make sure nobody cheats. I worked with this guy who spent a year right in the middle of it all in Korea and he said that for the last two months all they did was dig a foxhole all day and sleep in it all night, after the movies, that is. They put up this great big screen with loudspeakers and the guys just laid in their foxholes and took turns watching the movies. Even the Gooks watched.

"And we got a guy down at the plant who was just discharged. He spent two tours of duty near Saigon as a lifeguard at a Rest and Recreation center."

"What about Eddie Kardin? Was he catching a movie or

swimming when he was killed?" Her mother's heart always bleeds for other mothers.

"Aw, Ma. He's been the only serviceman from town to get killed so far. I read the facts, the statistics about this one. Only ten percent of servicemen see action anyhow. I got as good a chance as anybody else to go to school and get a specialty training, learn to be a mechanic or an electronic technician, something I can use when I get out."

She feels dissatisfied with the course of this discussion. She hasn't managed to get to the heart of the matter. She is wandering timidly on the periphery of her concern. She has had this difficulty before. Everything specific that she wants to articulate somehow comes out in harmless generalities. Even now with a catalogue of concrete anxieties, she complains to him vaguely.

"Oh, I don't know. I don't know." She shakes her head. "There's so much corruption in the world today. It's like in the time of our Lord. That was a time of decay. People were pagans. Worshiped false gods, sought pleasure. I don't know."

She turns her head away, but looks at him out of the corner of her eye to see if she has had an effect. The image which has been haunting her all week returns. It is a grey, stone bas relief of a Roman vomitorium. She does not remember whether she ever saw a picture of it in a magazine or whether she read a description of it and has recreated it in her imagination.

A young man is sprawled lengthwise, luxuriantly, on soft pillows along a trough with flowing water, his toga is draped about him. He is forcing two fingers down his throat, stone-frozen forever in this posture of satiety and self-indulgence. Behind him is a low table upon which are piled quantities of food—fruits, meats, wines. Reaching for a slice of meat which has been drenched in rich gravy is a young, voluptuous, stark naked courtesan who, laughingly, waits to serve the young man as soon as he has relieved himself of prior indulgence—the digestive tract being too slow a process for the seekers of life in Roman times.

The image revolts her, but she has been unable to purge it

from her mind for over a week. She doesn't know why. It appears to her also as a photograph of a painting. The parallels to the present are terrifyingly relevant.

She thinks that ours too, is an age of license and self-indulgence, of topless bathing suits and naked waitresses. All the old values are gone, gone, forgotten. How can she communicate her fears? How can she warn him, for example, of the sex gatherings she has read about where men and women parade naked and change partners six or seven times a night? These stories must be true; she has read about them in a responsible religious magazine. It is impossible for her to even mention the subject of sex to her son; and her husband refuses to do his duty, insists his son probably knows more about it than they do. But she means attitudes, not facts; he has been indifferent to her plea.

Atheism, homosexuality, LSD, marijuana, free love, juvenile delinquents, beatniks, hippies—all, all, all publicly accepted, drunken parties, summer riots, pornography, destruction of law and order, inter-racial marriages; and communists everywhere, at the universities, in government, hiding their identities, corrupting our youth, betraying our country.

Oh where, where will it all end?

"If you're worrying about me going to an orgy or something like that, forget it. I ain't good looking enough," he says trying to help her get everything out into the open so it can be exorcized and forgotten.

She blushes. Has he been reading her mind? She has read that two individuals, for example, who are close somehow know what each other are thinking without the exchange of words. Why did he say that just then? But it's not his mention of sex that disturbs her.

"There's nothing wrong with your looks. You're an attractive young man and don't go tearing yourself down all the time. Self-respect is the basis of all right moral action."

She would like to add that neatly ironed clothes, shined shoes, brushed teeth, clean shaves, and short hair cuts are the bases of self-respect. She believes firmly in the domino theory of moral degeneration. If one habit or one virtue goes, the rest will follow. It's an automatic and irrevocable progression from the first uncorrected sloppy habit—from long hair, for example—through loose women to the opium den and complete physical and moral ruin.

"Aw, Ma. Don't worry about me. I'll be O.K."

She wonders: Is he trying to end the topic of conversation before I bring it up?

She says with sudden anger: "I can't help but worry. I'm your mother, you know."

"I know, I know," he says. "I call you `Ma' all the time."

She disregards this.

"I worry about a lot of things. Not just the fighting. I worry about the wild boys you might get in with and the bad girls."

She blushes again. "You'll get out to California and forget all about home and never come back. You know this could be the last night at home for the rest of your life."

"I get a leave in a couple months and thirty days a year."

"I mean permanently, as a member of the family."

"I suppose you got me married off to some dame already and living in Los Angeles or Pasadena, coming home once every ten years, or not at all like Uncle Orville."

"Yes. I mean exactly that. Orville never came home from the service." Her jealousy flares. "He married your fancy aunt in San Diego and nobody has seen hide nor hair of him since, except for our visit to see him four summers ago, and then he lorded over everybody with his swimming pool pretending he was just trying to be a good host."

Memories of their vacation to San Diego four years before emerge. He sees again the brown and golden girls clad in bikinis as they walk in rhythmic sensuality along the beach. And there as they pass, the ripples of whitened flesh along the thin lines of cloth and thigh flickering with each step promises of sunless delight.

"Uncle Orville is all right, Ma. He wasn't putting on the dog. That's the way everybody lives in California. You can afford to build a swimming pool and nice house for cheaper there than here because you don't have ten foot of snow all winter."

She doesn't answer him and sits quietly then stands up and begins to walk into the kitchen.

He thinks her silence is final. It wasn't as bad as he thought it was going to be. He turns again to the newspaper, lights a cigarette, and settles back in the chair. She stops and turns toward him.

"I wish you wouldn't smoke so early in the morning, Freddy," she says.

He is startled, jerks forward.

"What difference does it make if you smoke in the morning or at night or in the afternoon?" Now what? He thought she was all done.

"I don't know. I just heard it isn't good for you to smoke so early in the day. I think I read it in *The Reader's Digest.*" She argues earnestly. "That's a wonderful magazine, you know. I hope when you're gone you'll read it."

"I heard down at the plant from those college guys who work in the summer that that's the phoniest magazine out. They said that it's all full of lies so that they can sell the magazine by telling everybody about cures to diseases and that everything is great." He sucks on his cigarette.

"College boys," she says and an image emerges of bearded protestors with glasses and long, dirty, disheveled hair carrying signs against mothers. "Smart alecks would be more like it. Well, you listen to your mother for a change. I have found a great deal of satisfaction reading it. I have found many things to be true in it from my own experience. Why, just last month was an article by a famous corporation president who went to New York City and after five years left and went home to a little town in Ohio. Well, the upshot of it all was that he said that New York was no place to live and bring up children and that there was no place like home."

"Aw, Ma. They put articles like that in on purpose so people will think that being nobody in some jerkwater town is great."

"And what is wrong with being satisfied? What is wrong with accepting your place and doing a good job? What's wrong with being average?"

"Nothing, Ma, nothing. I don't want to argue now." He squeezes the cigarette out in an ash tray.

"I didn't mean for you to put it out. I just wanted to warn you against too much smoking."

A pause. She sees his matches on the end table, walks over and picks them up.

"You shouldn't strike a match without closing the cover. See it says, `Close cover before striking.'"

"Jeez, Ma. I know you're supposed to close the cover before striking. I can read."

He moans to himself. What next? What next? He thought she was all done but he guesses now she has only started. She closes the match book cover and turns away from him. In the middle of the room she whirls about and asks,

"What are you going to do today?" She says this sing-song with studied, cheerful indifference but he receives it as suspicion.

"Nothing. Nothing at all. I'm going to the plant to pick up my check and put half of it into traveler's checks like you said I should. I suppose I'll meet Ernie, go to Bud's and hang around there a while. There's nothing else to do. But that's O.K. That's what's fun. Doing nothing just for one day."

"What about tonight?" she says without any attempt to mask her suspicion.

"Ernie's trying to get me a blind date for later. After nine o'clock."

"Ernie? What kind of date would Ernie get you?"

"He hasn't got one for me yet. He's got his date, this girl he's been going with. She's trying to get a girl friend."

He says this as if nobody wants him, as if five girls have

already declined and she responds as he anticipated. She bleeds for his shy, simple purity.

"Well, you'll probably be better off if he doesn't get you a date. I can just imagine what kind of girl Ernie Hanson goes with." She has a vision of a most voluptuous peroxide blond with a coarse, foul, sensual mouth.

"She's a nurse, a student nurse at the hospital. He's trying to get her roommate for me. We thought we'd go to church first for a few hours and sing hymns and then come home and listen to your Lawrence Welk records."

She doesn't hear him. A nurse. Visions of social mobility. They make good wives and mothers. But a shadow appears to darken her happy speculations. The hospital is Catholic. Is she? Is she?

"Is she Catholic?" she asks.

"Who? Ernie's girl? I don't know."

"No. Not Ernie's girl. Your date."

"I don't have one yet. I don't know which girl it will be until they find out who is off tonight."

"She may not be Catholic. They have girls from all faiths training at St. Joseph's. Besides, it's only one date." An afterthought looms. "You have to watch the Catholics. They're thick and narrow. They take all the children, too."

"Aw, Ma. I ain't gonna marry her. It's just a blind date, if everything works out."

"Blind date or not," she instructs, "Every girl you go out with should be considered a possible wife. And you should treat her with the same respect you would accord your mother or your wife."

He doesn't respond to this. How can he? She's so far out of it, so far out of it. Beyond either instruction or repair. But, suddenly and unexpectedly, she lets off her probing. She knows he will leave for the day; she doesn't want him to go away angry. She goes upstairs, pretends to be busy for a short while and then comes down with the family photograph album. Gerbracht, who is still sitting in the living room lazily weighing the pros and cons of leaving, chides himself, when he sees her coming, for not moving faster. She pretends she ran into it accidently while looking for a hat in her bureau.

"Why, look what I found," she says.

He knows it was not an accident. He knows she intends to bind him with remembered obligation. He cannot escape; it is the price he must pay. He must recall these memories—more hers than his—and admit his bondage. He wonders whether he really remembers or only reaffirms her prodding and reminders. But he has done his duty for today. The worst is over. He can put up with this for five more minutes.

The book begins with his baby pictures. He wonders if his parents' existence began with him. There are no other pictures of them before he was born. It strikes him as strange. He blurts in a kind of exasperated demand that startles her.

"What did you and Pa do before I was born."

She recovers in a moment and casually mentions the job she had to help support her family at home after Grandpa died. And then there was the war, of course, an answer he gets to almost every question he asks, or the Depression. No, he didn't mean then. He meant after she was married to Pa.

She points to a picture in the book. There he is when he was not quite a year old. "You were such a good baby," she says congratulating him but in a tone of absent reverie that suggests she is talking about some child that died in infancy. His father holds him and he stands in front of the lilac tree. It has been cut down since then to make room in the yard for the patio that his father built. She comments about something very funny that happened then but he cannot remember what she is talking about. It doesn't seem very funny to him but she laughs and he grins.

"Oh, oh, oh. There you are on the black and white pony." He is two years old and smiles proudly. He wears a cowboy outfit complete with boots, miniature ten-gallon hat, bandana, and vest all furnished with the pony. The badge on the vest shows he is on the side of the law—one of the good guys.

His grandmother paid to have the picture taken by the man who carried the camera over his shoulder and led the pony up and down the streets. His mother said the man was Italian, ruefully she said this as if he should have carried an organ grinder and led a monkey rather than a camera and pony. His grandmother died of cancer quickly, it was a blessing. His mother says: Grandma sure loved little Freddy.

They continue the tour through his childhood—birthdays, summer vacations, camp, Boy Scouts, confirmation, graduation. . As she turns the pages he looks with a growing depression at the images of this stranger, these shadows of his mother's memory. She sees the child and the grown young man as one—two stages of a process of being with a single essence. He sees each stage a different essence, a different identity, as though each day is a sloughing of the old garb, of the old identity. He knows that for him there will be no growth without forgetting. The photographs have recorded his oneness in time. As he watches and listens he remembers that all of this will be over in a day, and that soon he will be free to be nothing to anybody.

This stream of images which connects him to the helpless child and to the mother who fed and fondled him is her illusion, and so he does not rebel. He has had it out with her; his day will be easier. He even tries to "remember when" and sometimes he adds something she has forgotten and she is surprised and touched and feels a joy and believes that her grip upon his destiny has been re-affirmed.

CHAPTER THREE

Now he sets forth on this final morning walk. If you will follow him from a distance you will come to know this city through eyes unshackled of his past. From your detachment you may even come to know a measure of the uneven terms of his birthright—of the fullness and poverty of his heritage, for this walk is a return to origins.

And even if you were to see only through his eyes, your vision would not be altogether distorted, for he sees now with the eyes of a stranger. These streets no longer define the limits of his experience, the terms of his entrapment, and because he sees without emotion, it seems he beholds his world transformed.

High above the industrial and rail center which sprawls along the river bottom, the residential area has developed on the slightly rolling land which flows westward from the ridge of the bluffs. The streets have been arranged on a north-south axis according to the unalterable canons of the Land Ordinance of 1785 which presumptuously disregarded all natural boundaries—all rivers, lakes, and mountains—to assert once again the illusion that human logic is superior to divine caprice.

There is a particularly necessary application of logic to order community life in this city, for it was originally a river town and then a rail center out of which developed a meat packing industry. The residential area is protected from social pollution and commercial vulgarization by ironclad zoning ordinances, as if everyone 'on the hill' is ashamed of the packing plants and stockyards, the bars and truckers' hotels down below which are the life blood of the community. But however they have insulated themselves by law from the source of their well being, the east wind too often bathes the homes and schools and churches, the quiet, orderly neighbor-

hoods in the stench of the packing plants and stockyards. Sometimes on a summer night the wind will waft into still bedrooms the cries of anguish, the bellowing moan and terror of cattle being yarded to pens to await the morning market and eventual slaughter.

This city has been divided into two sections: the north end is better than the south end. There is, however, a consolation prize for you who believe in progress: there are clear signs of decay in the north end; the younger generation of the older, established families are moving to the newer, more fashionable districts developing near the golf course west of town.

It is all a feverish attempt to get beyond the sound and ubiquitous smell of the commercial center. But, alas, the east wind finds them out. The stench persists, though weakly, in the remotest perimeters, reminding us as it drifts with the wind that there are limits to social engineering.

Here the terms of our history have been temporarily reversed: the outlying districts, the most recent western frontiers of this expanding city, breed snobbery not democracy. It is the pervasive smell of the past, of origins, which is the common experience, the leveling influence here. All are bathed in an obnoxious equity.

And contrary to general opinion this is good. With democracy on the decline in America, it is good to take an occasional whiff of the stockyards or, to get to the heart of the matter, an open sewer pipe or septic tank to remind us of the common humanity we try so desperately to escape, to remind us less fundamentally but no less profoundly that pure democracy probably does not exist short of a society of practicing plumbers.

But there is loveliness here, too. The clear air, no east wind today, is refreshing and Gerbracht steps with strong strides to the corner and then crosses to the left. The trees are bare; the dead leaves have been blown into banks and drifts on the sidewalks. He goes out of his way to kick through them. In the cold, yellow sunlight the grass is still green and in the gutters the wet matted leaves glisten a mottled gold and dark brown.

And there is a loveliness of order. The houses, trees, streets are *pleasantly, rationally arranged. An occasional, but regularly spaced, church steeple aspires above the mundane accommodations which seem to have brought happiness and satisfaction to the vast majority of the city's residents. It is only below the cliffs along the river bottom where you can find ugliness and violence; nevertheless, all roads lead there regardless of social pretensions and all feet hasten there in order to pay for the good life of the higher plateau.*

This city is still ordered by the industrial whistles and sirens. Like Gerbracht many of the employees of the packing plants still walk to work and home again in response to the imperative urging of the steam whistles. When Gerbracht reaches First Avenue, he can see below him the expanse of the plants, yards, and railbeds that stretch from left to right more than two miles. Of the ten thousand residents, perhaps a third are employed directly in the packing plants.

He can remember coming here with his father to this First Avenue vantage point to witness one of the great stockyards fires. He remembers flames shooting hundreds of feet into the air and the embers that glowed in the night for a week after the fire was officially declared under control; he remembers that in the daytime the smoke rising from smoldering wooden rails and planks lasted for three days.

In the distance two enormous, black smoke stacks dominate the disorderly, sprawling pile of grey bricks which is the main packing plant. And to the right the stockyards sprawl for a mile in two directions. Across the top of the pens, the catwalks, designed for convenience in yarding livestock, stretch from one end of the yards to the other. And beyond them are the covered blocks of pens for the hogs and sheep.

As Gerbracht descends the street that will bring him to the commercial center of town and then to the entrance of the packing plant the buildings thicken in frequency and substance. The main thoroughfare which leads to the heart of the city is called Grand Avenue and in its day it was considered a wide street. Today, though, the buildings along each side impinge upon its breadth. The side-

walk descends from the top of the bluff at such a steep angle that he must hold himself back lest he plunge headlong down the incline.

Near the bottom of the hill Grand is crossed by several streets which run parallel to the bottom of the bluffs and are therefore narrow and crooked. The buildings are older, and they grow older and larger as he proceeds toward the packing plant and the original structures still standing, unseen, buried far beneath the additions and expansion wings added over the years.

Grand Avenue is level. Gerbracht approaches Broad Street, the main north-south thoroughfare and the last commercial street before the railroad tracks which separate the business district from the industrial area. Here, it is like any other city, barely distinguishable from any trading center: stores and shops, banks and bars, and restaurants.

Two buildings, however, are distinctive. The one, the Stockyards Exchange Building, was built over fifty years ago and is an excellent example of architectural totemism. It is modeled after a middle eastern mosque with towering red brick minarets as if the first fathers of the market wished to inspire each succeeding generation of traders with all of the subtle, shrewd, crafty techniques of the Turk, the Arab, the Armenian rug dealers, the modern descendants of the ancient Persian merchants.

The other structure located across the street was modeled after a Grecian temple complete with Ionic columns. The Farmers and Merchants Bank is housed here. It was originally intended by the city fathers to be a counter force to the Exchange building. The design suggests the conservative "golden mean" as a fiscal policy although it is unfortunately true that this bank was one of the first to collapse in the depression.

The packing plant itself, the outer walls of which begin just across the railroad tracks, is an architectural wonder. It is the result of the successful blending of late medieval English gothic, turn of the century state penitentiary, and public high school auditorium circa 1925 styles. Gerbracht enters the main gate and approaches the security office where he has dutifully punched his time card five days a week since he finished high school.

CHAPTER FOUR

"B-R-A-A-A-K."

"Who said that?"

"Said what, Fats?"

"Made that noise. You know what I mean, goddamnit."

"B-R-A-A-A-K." From the other side of the room the sound grows in intensity and pitch. It has all the feeling of a personal insult and it is delivered from behind one of several hands covering feigned coughs or yawns.

"Now, goddamnit, cut it out." The guard is flushed with anger. The men stand around the edges of the room. Some sit on the benches against the wall. All wear masks of innocence.

"What the hell you talkin' about, Fats? I don't hear nothing."

"You know damn well what I mean. If I hear it once more, I'm going to clear this place out. You can all wait outside for your checks."

One of the men steps forward and with a great display of indignation demands: "You're not going to throw me out. You're not going to make the innocent suffer because you can't find the guilty. You'll carry me out first."

"B-R-A-A-A-K," from the other side of the room and suppressed laughter from everywhere.

"Screw you. Screw all of you. Screw the night crew, screw the union, and screw the Democratic Party."

"While you're at it why don't you call the paymaster and tell him to get screwed too?"

"He ain't got the guts."

"C'mon, Fats. Call him up and then we'll all get out of your hair."

Roars of laughter now. Frank Burton, alias Fascist Fats, has a drab olive uniform and a Sam Brown belt but he doesn't have any hair.

"Daddy," a voice squeals in falsetto imitation of a child. "Daddy, why do some men wear those Sam Brown belts?"

"Well, Son," same voice, deep base, "it's so they can hold their fat guts in so's they can see their pecker when they piss."

"Thanks, Daddy." Falsetto again.

Gerbracht walks into the middle of this, steps to the counter, and asks the guard for his check.

"There ain't any checks here yet. Look around you. You think these fools would be here if their checks were in. They'd be up on Broad Street drinking their money up."

"B-R-A-A-A-K."

"Goddamnit. Shut up." The guard glares past Gerbracht. For an instant, he thought Fats was shouting at him.

Frank "Fascist Fats" Burton is the corporeal embodiment of the unseen order. For two years now Gerbracht has punched into work under the surveillance of Fascist Fats who sits each morning like an angry Buddha on a stool in the window over the time clock. Gerbracht has often punched his card with a certain quiver of guilt, a vague apprehension that he was doing something wrong. He has long been intimidated by Frank Burton's shifting, suspicious eyes. He doesn't know that the guard's only responsibility is to make certain no one punches more than one time card.

Gerbracht turns away from the counter and confronts smiling, taunting faces from all directions. That sinking feeling that they are laughing at him catches at his throat and he turns around, a reflex action, as though there might be a rip in his pants or as though someone may have surreptitiously attached an obscene sign to his back.

He moves quickly across the room to a bench. Eyes do not follow him. Heads do not turn. He is safely beyond them. He sits on the bench, stretches his legs, and leans against the wall. He can wait for his check; there's no hurry. When the others line up to get theirs, he'll mosey up behind them. A voice above the drone of conversation is directed to him. "Hey, how's the old bowling arm?"

Gerbracht looks up. Now standing before him is the union steward of the night gang.

"Hey, Clem," he says rising to greet him. It has been over a year since Clem Yanich, Gerbracht's straw boss when he was in the box factory, transferred to the night shift to get the hourly bonus and to recruit new union members.

"What department you in now, Fred?"

"I'm not working any more, Clem. I'm all through. I'm picking up my terminal check." Gerbracht smiles, a flicker of victory on his lips.

"Got a new job? Going back to school? I always said you should go back to school."

"Not exactly," Gerbracht says.

"Well, what you going to do?" Clem asks. Gerbracht hesitates.

"Well, I'm going into the army. I mean, I've been drafted. I didn't have any choice."

"The army!" Clem shouts as though he has been betrayed. "The goddam army! You poor bastard!" Clem laughs.

Gerbracht winces but argues back weakly. "What do you mean? I can't see the army's going to be any worse than working in this friggin' hole the rest of my life. Punching the time clock every day and hounded to work all the time; shifted from one department to another—one day I'm cleaning guts—the next day freezing my ass off at ten below zero in a freezer and then the next week I'm sweating in the smoke house."

"You're lucky they never sent you to the hide cellar."

"I even spent two days there," Gerbracht says with a smile. "I was a hose and brush man."

"But there are a few differences between this hole and the army you haven't thought of," Clem says.

"Yah, I've thought of them but I can't see they're that important."

"Well, let me list them for you. First, is the money. You don't have any union getting you a higher salary. The saddest part is they don't pay you the price of a good piece of ass. Second, you can't quit any time you want to and get a new job and if they decide you're going to Alaska and freeze your tail good, you're going to Alaska and you got no say one way or the other."

"It's only for two years," Gerbracht says gloomily as Clem catalogues the disadvantages he already knows. Besides, I might get sent to California."

"Yah, and you might get sent to Mississippi. But that isn't the worst part. The biggest difference is you have no rights. You're nothing and if some prick says `shit', you say `what color?'. The army might be tolerable if the enlisted man had a legitimate grievance committee to protect him but you're not gonna have any recourse. It's a one way operation, and you got no say and no grievance committee to bail you out."

A loose circle of Clem's friends has drawn around them. One of Clem's friends sitting nearby interrupts. He leans toward them.

"It ain't so bad as when you and I was in fighting a real war. Now they got a new uniform code of military justice and you can get your own civilian lawyer in the military courts if you want. The sarge can't clobber ya any more. No cruel or inhuman training. You can even pick your own speciality before you go. No. It ain't like when you and I was in, Clem, killing the Germans and Japs so young punks in diapers could grow up and occupy the surplus women at two bucks a throw. It's peace time lend lease now. We lend our old enemies young studs to do the job for all their men we killed."

"Big heroes," Gerbracht says. "Big heroes. Too bad you can't wear your uniforms any more to pin your medals on."

"Hey, the kid's got a little spunk," Clem laughs.

"Yah, but not enough to tell that fat bastard off," someone says. "Did you see him back down?"

"What do you mean back down? I didn't back down."

"You backed down. He bluffed you right out and you ain't even an employee any more."

"What do you mean?" Gerbracht says.

"That's right," Clem says. "He's got no hold on you at all and you take his crap. I saw it. You just turned heel and ran away. Now the company owes you that last check and they have to give it to you. He's got no right to hold it back from you."

"But what can I do?"

"You go back up there and tell him you got terminal pay coming—that you're not on the night shift. You tell him that Mr. Lindstrom told you to tell the fat, stupid guard at the gate that you got terminal pay coming and that if he can't find it in one of his drawers that he is supposed to call up the main office to get it and that if he doesn't call, you're supposed to call Mr. Lindstrom yourself and tell him that the fatass guard won't lift his fat pinky to get your check and you say the word fat as often and loud as you can."

Gerbracht wavers.

"C'mon, Gerbracht. Show your spunk. They're gonna steamroller you in the army if you don't start proving you're no pushover."

As Gerbracht begins to walk to the counter, Clem whispers encouragement.

"Atta boy. Remember tell him Mr. Lindstrom."

"Who is he?" Gerbracht asks trying to stall.

"He's the paymaster," Clem answers. "Now get your ass up there and demand your rights."

Fortunately Gerbracht is rescued by a messenger who enters the security shack and delivers a stack of envelopes to the guard. The men on the benches get up slowly and begin to drift toward the counter forming a line based upon the principle of seniority of arrival. Clem disrupts this orderly arrangement.

"Make way," he yells. "Make way for the soldier on his way to the war."

The men grin. They step aside for Gerbracht. Clem shoves

him to the front of the line. He addresses his fellow employees: "At least *we* can show proper respect for this young man about to lay his life down for his country to make the world safe for democracy. At least we can treat him with kindness and consideration."

"I ain't going to lay my life down for anybody, Clem," Gerbracht protests. "I don't plan to get killed. And I got all day. I can take my turn."

Clem has pushed him to the counter and now has his arm around Gerbracht's shoulder in a fatherly embrace.

"If you had come to the union hall to receive the last payment for services duly earned, you would not have received the scorn and indifferent dismissal recently rendered you by this representative of the fascist order, by this fat slob of a glob of a fascist prick. At least we still have some love of country and respect for our fighting men left."

"I'm not going to answer you today, Clem," the guard says wearily. "I'm not going to sucker for your bait, so's you can show off here for your pals again."

He flips the envelopes with his thumb.

"What's your name, kid? I guess we can find your check first. I'd hate you to think the only genuine patriot in this room didn't do his bit for the boys in the service."

Gerbracht tells him his name and the guard fingers the envelopes, finds his near the bottom and hands it to him.

"So you're going into the army, huh, kid? Too bad. Gonna become a world policeman taking care of the interests of the French and English bankers and the international trade unions. We can't take care of our own business and we got to be taking care of everybody elses," Fats says.

"Fred, my boy," Clem says, "this guy thinks we fought the wrong country when we fought Germany—not that he did any of the fighting, mind you, and that the President of the United States is a conscious agent of communist conspiracy."

"At least the Germans were white men and gentiles and not a

pack of communists and yellow bastards. All white countries should have got together and destroyed Mongolian Russia and China. Now look at the mess we got. China and Russia flouting us. Even our former allies giving us the finger after we reconstructed them and put them back on their feet. And all of them together with the Black countries in the United Nations telling us what to do and sending our soldiers all over the world getting killed for somebody else." Fats draws an asthmatic breath. "And not even fighting the way we can. Tying our hands behind our back, restraint of power and the rest of that bull crap. And do you know why, kid?"

Clem shrieks laughter and the men in chorus laugh with him. Sensing the mockery, the guard suddenly withdraws.

"I'm not talking any more. I have work to do. And if you don't get back in line, I'm not going to give any of these checks out to anybody."

Clem, grinning, withdraws on tiptoe to the end of the line, and Gerbracht feeling guilty for receiving preferential treatment waits just inside the door for Clem to get his check.

Gerbracht follows the older men out of the plant gate and to the right toward the commercial center of town. The sidewalk is narrow, pressed between the fortress walls of the outer perimeter of the plant and the wide brick street which serves to shunt the huge cattle trucks around the yards to the proper unloading chutes.

Gerbract hears the thunder of a tractor and trailer as it approaches from behind him. As the truck passes he hears the nervous, urgent squealing of the hogs which have been crammed into two levels of the trailer. Steam from their urine and perspiration rises through the ventilation slats and trails off behind. Gerbracht's nose and eyes smart from the ammonia vapors which float suspended in the air behind the truck. When they come opposite the cattle chutes, the older men slow down. Clem turns around to Gerbracht. They are afraid he is tagging along.

"We're going to cross here, Fred. We'll see you around. Keep up your bowling. You got a future there," Clem says.

"Yeah, we'll see you," one of the men adds.

"Yeah, yeah," Gerbracht says. They realize Gerbracht is following them out of politeness. He is not really going their way.

"I'm sorry I'm going in the army," he says.

"That's O.K, kid." Clem waves his hand in forgiveness.

"You couldn't help it," one of the men adds.

"I wouldn't of gone if they hadn't drafted me," he lies.

Clem shuffles awkwardly then extends his hand in farewell. When Gerbracht feels Clem's grip, he is surprised. The hand offered is limp, ineffectual.

"Don't get your pecker burned in some L.A. whorehouse," one of the men advises.

"You were a good worker," Clem says. Then he turns on his heels and plunges across the road behind a passing truck.

CHAPTER FIVE

After he cashes his payroll check and purchases traveler's checks, Gerbracht leaves the bank and walks northward. His steps quicken as he passes the clutter of neon signs which overhang the narrow sidewalk; he moves rapidly beyond the boarding houses and tenements which are clustered on the edge of the commercial center to where the buildings thin and Broad Street once again becomes simply a north-south highway.

Six blocks north of the entrance to the packing plant the highway runs along the bottom edge of one of the steepest river bluffs. Two blocks farther on a slight bend on the railroad side of the highway is Bud's White Fire Gas Station—Gerbracht's immediate destination—where his best friend Ernie Hansen works and where he is certain to be entertained after a fashion by the station's popular proprietor—George T. (Bud) Anderson.

There is an eagerness in his step as he arrives at the front door of the station during the pre-noon slack hour. Through the plate glass window he can see Ernie standing just inside the door, his arm resting on the elbow-high bench which holds the cash register and the charge plate press.

Before he enters, they communicate in pantomime. He waves his arms and mouths some words and Ernie answers with a nod of the head. When he enters he asks with a grin,

"What time?"

"One at the latest. I came early and helped him with some grease jobs and oil changes. He gave me a lot of crap but I think he was only kidding. He knows he couldn't run this friggin' place without me."

Gerbracht settles into a dilapidated Morris chair against the inner wall. He knows that without Ernie's assistance he would be a total social failure. Following his father's early death, Ernie was raised by an easy-going, permissive mother whom Gerbracht has idealized as a counter-image to his own mother. Ernie is draft exempt because of a heart murmur resulting from rheumatic fever in childhood.

From one of the side windows Gerbracht can see immediately below him the switchyard and in the distance he has an unobstructed view of the northern-most extension of the packing plant—the old ice house, a graying, warehouse structure which formerly stored the thick blocks of ice cut from nearby lakes. Beyond the warehouse perhaps a half mile farther is an earthen levee and beyond that the river. The front window faces along the highway and commands a full view of the several islands of pumps which have been spread lengthwise for fifty yards to accommodate the diesel tractors with long trailers.

"Hey, where's Bud," Gerbracht asks after he has settled comfortably in his chair. Ernie jerks his finger toward the door to the men's room and before he can say anything, Gerbracht hears a flush of water. The bolt of the door clicks and slides and Bud Anderson emerges buttoning his fly. He appears startled for a moment, but then throws out a hand of welcome. Bud continues to grip Gerbracht's hand as he shakes his head and says, "Well, here's the Soldier Boy. Fred Gerbracht a soldier. Little Fred Gerbracht in the army."

He speaks through teeth clenched tightly on his pipe. Though the pipe is rarely absent from his mouth, it is rarely lighted.

"Goddam, a soldier," Bud says, "and he used to come in here when he wasn't hardly knee high."

Despite his appearance—his pin striped coveralls, his red mackinaw, and his reversible hunting cap—Bud conveys an aura of professional solidity. To those grown beyond his tutelage— such as Ernie who has been overexposed—he is known as the "old bullslinger," but to those like Gerbracht, inexperienced in the ways of the world and relatively underexposed to Bud's wisdom, he is a veritable fountain of truth, a reservoir of deep-researched, easily digested magazine-article facts sufficient to serve a young man in the first days of an uneasy independence. Gerbracht enjoys listening to him; he has often read up on cars or accidents so that he could prime Bud into a discussion. Bud usually tailors his conversations to the interests of the audience of young men who gather about his station in the early evenings to work on their cars in one of his unused hydraulic lift stalls. Bud has become the mediator of maturity for those no longer irresponsible but not quite ready for responsibility, and his station has become a clearinghouse for their attitudes and opportunities. Gerbracht has been one of Bud's favorite listeners.

Gerbracht is about to speak when the service bell rings. He looks up to see a car slowing at the second island.

"I'll get it, Ernie," Bud says and has already opened the door.

The car that has stopped for gas is a new Plymouth. As Ernie closes the door he says to Gerbracht,

"If you really want to hear old Bud go off at the mouth, tell how great you think the new Plymouth is. He's got a thing against them. The other night he must of spent an hour telling Benny Johnson how stupid his old man was for buying one."

Ernie smiles and spins a finger around his ear and points toward Bud. He shakes his head. Gerbracht looks down toward the railroad yard and watches a switch engine slowly make up a train of empty cattle cars.

When Bud returns and takes up his stand at the side of the cash register, Gerbracht says,

"They claim that the new Plymouth is about the hottest thing on the road. They're running away with all the stock car races. One hundred and thirty-two miles an hour average for two hundred laps in the Daytona."

"Plymouth. Plymouth," Bud says through his teeth. "They've been selling that goddamn car to senior citizens for thirty years. Now they put two, three hunert horses under the hood so little old grandmothers can hot rod it to the supermarket. Jesus, what next? Those people in Deetroit are crazy. That Lawrence Welk bunch don't want three, four hunert horses to go get a loaf of bread." He shakes his head sadly. "They come and they go—the hot ones. They come and they go. Since the war ther've been three or four supposed to be real hot. First there was the Merc and then the Eighty-eight, then the Pontiac and the Ford, and now, for Christ's sake, even the friggin' Plymouth." Then he adds, "One thing certain—they suck up the gas. Man, do they suck up the gas. Good for business though, so I can't complain."

Bud removes his pipe and sucks air and saliva through rounded lips and sunken cheeks, the sound of a hoggish fuel pump at seventy-five. "Gramps gets his new Plymouth out on the four lane super-highway and gets his rocks off going seventy-five, eighty. He can't make it fifty miles, the old fart's got to fill the tank. They don't get ten miles a gallon at those speeds."

Bud replaces his pipe and clamps down again firmly on the stem.

"Not ten miles a gallon?" Gerbracht says. "What about those claims of twenty-one miles a gallon?"

"At seventy-five M-P-H? Not ten miles" Bud affirms.

"No shit?"

"No shit," Bud asserts emphatically and sucks upon his pipe.

"Some of them foreign cars can really move out without burning too much gas," Ernie says. Bud hates foreign cars.

"Foreign cars. Foreign cars. What good are they? You got to be either a millionaire or a damn fool. You can't get parts when something goes wrong. They're so friggin' small and light that every time a semi goes by they almost get sucked under. And they ain't so fast. I just read where that wop car, the Ferrari, what's supposed to be so hot, can't even compete with American cars any more in those Big Prick races."

He pauses for breath.

"Besides, they're a drain on the economy. Too many American dollars leaving the country. I read the other day that one of the big steel companies told their employees to buy American cars or get another job. Can't blame 'em. Even the unions backed the company on that. If we don't consume our own cars, then production is cut back, and then people lose their jobs—and all from buying foreign cars."

"What about the Victory-three? One helluva car I hear," Ernie says.

"Can't corner. No stability." Bud grows serious. "You should have been with me the night we scraped that big golfer off the Interstate. He was driving a Vi-3. Big status symbol. Big deal. Country club bullshit," he adds bitterly. "Well, he's dead now. Had to use a blotter to get him all off the pavement and all he tried to do according to witnesses was take a corner at forty M-P-H."

"Only forty miles an hour?" Gerbracht asks.

"Forty M-P-H. Any American car, even Ernie's old '37 Ford with a high center of gravity could do that."

"Any American car? No shit?" Gerbracht says.

"No shit!" Bud asserts emphatically.

The silence that ensues is finally interrupted by Bud himself.

"Soldier boy. Cannon fodder. I sure hate to see you go, Fred. You might not have had to go at all, you know, if things had gone different."

Bud has warmed up sufficiently to turn directly without justification or provocation to one of his favorite subjects—the decline and fall of the German Wehrmacht.

"If Hitler hadn't made so many stupid, friggin' mistakes, he might have beat the Russians in '42. Then we could of whipped him. Then there wouldn't have been any Big Three or Big Four. Just a Big One. Us—the good old U.S.A."

"If your aunt had balls, she'd be your uncle," Ernie says. But Gerbracht, anxious to learn what he can from this old master of fact and opinion, leads Bud on.

"How is that, Bud? How could it all have been different?"

"Well, first of all the big mistake Hitler made was not continuing his attack at Moscow, the center of the heartland. He thought he could focus farther south at Stalingrad and then take Moscow in the spring after he had taken Stalingrad and cut off all the supplies from the Black Sea. Then American guns and tanks couldn't get to the Russians."

"I thought the Germans got whipped at Moscow," Ernie says. "They didn't have any choice about where to concentrate their attack. I saw newsreels and it showed the Germans froze to death all over the place. Too much friggin' snow and too goddamn many Russians."

"There certainly were some tactical disadvantages with the winters," Bud says. "But whatever reason, he failed in his overall strategic plan. He had to get the heartland—Moscow first and the rest would fall automatically."

Bud shakes his head at Hitler's incredible stupidity.

"And he went against the advice of the high brass, the German general staff, and all the theories of the heartland and conquest."

Bud pauses to suck the saliva flooding his lower teeth. He swallows hard while continuing to grip the pipe stem with his teeth.

"The turning point of the war was the battle of Stalingrad. The Germans lost two million troops there alone." This he says matter of factly.

"Two million troops?" Gerbracht gasps!

"Hell, that's nothing. That was just a beginning. All told there were twenty million German and Russian troops killed on the Eastern front alone."

Gerbracht tries to grasp the enormity of this slaughter but all that he can visualize is the cartoon image of the marching Chinese from "Believe It or Not" by Ripley. He cannot recall all the details accurately but he can see again those anonymous coolies with the conical rice paddy hats, 500 million of them, two abreast marching around the girth of the world in endless procession. Trying to comprehend, Gerbracht turns them into troops marching, marching relentlessly and mechanically unto death. Faceless, nameless, plodding myriads of men—the cannon fodder of six short years of war.

"But twenty million is only a beginning," Bud says. "There were twelve million more non-combatants mostly Jews and political and religious opponents of the Nazis put to death in concentration camps." He counts on his fingers trying to recall the totals accurately. He looks toward the river in abstract concentration, hoping, perhaps, that the endless flow of water will help him summarize the staggering totals. He accounts for Japanese losses in the millions: "75,000 troops and non-combatants alone, at a single shot in Hiroshima." He scratches his head trying to recall the specific Allied losses, British, French, Dutch, American, excluding the Russian losses which he had already enumerated. He checks each country off on his fingers and then adds the figures quickly in his head. America was fairly low with only three hundred thirty thousand.

"Fifty-five million, more or less," he says with mathematical finality.

"Fifty-five million!" Gerbracht says. " Fifty-five million!" He tries to visualize one recognizable face among the nameless dead but only the image of those plodding Chinese coolies marching for all eternity comes to mind. He tries to see himself among the masses of the dead but he cannot identify. It is all too remote, too incredibly bizarre.

" Fifty-five million!"

"Fifty-five million," Bud repeats.

" No shit?"

"No shit!" Bud asserts emphatically. "But that was just World War II. If you count World War I and Korea, and a few other minor skirmishes, you get a grand total in the Twentieth Century of one hunnert million."

Bud waits for this figure to sink in, to achieve its maximum effect before he continues.

"It's almost natural, though, with populations getting so big. Man has devised greater means of keeping the totals down. Why in the next war alone, the experts predict each side will lose one hunnert fifty million in the first two or three hours. It's a natural law. The larger the populations, the bigger the bombs. It's an automatic law of history like pestilence and famine in the old days."

Bud is interrupted by another customer. When he returns, Ernie sets him off in a new direction, a direction he has always found more interesting than a catalogue of the dead.

"What about the wounds, George? Tell Fred about all the troops that get wounded without getting killed," Ernie says.

"Well, butt wounds are the biggest percentage," Bud instructs. "There are four or five wounded for every one killed and of these thirty-four per cent are butt wounds. You got to learn to crawl flat, stay low behind fallen trees or in ditches or you get your ass shot off."

Gerbracht visualizes this situation and makes a mental note of Bud's advice.

"Then there's the worst wound of all. Getting your balls or pecker shot off. Happened a lot in the First and Second World Wars. Although you don't hear about it too much, there's been a lot of stories written about it."

"Stories written about it? What would anybody want to write about that for?" Gerbracht asks.

"It's not so much the wound but what happens when the wounded man goes home after the war to his wife or girl friend. Tragic complications and all that."

Bud bites hard on his mouthpiece and looks toward the river.

"That doesn't sound tragic to me. Sounds like it ought to be pretty funny," Ernie says.

"Well, I suppose you could make a funny story about it, but Ernest Hemingway didn't."

"Did he write about that? I thought he just wrote about fishing and bull fighting."

"You might say almost everything he wrote about had to do one way or another either with some guy that had his balls shot off, or was afraid he might have them blown off. Why, his main story was written about this guy that was shot where it really hurts, and after the war he goes back to his fiance who was a high-class English babe. Well, he can't do anything and they're really in love. It almost drives them crazy. She runs all over Europe screwing every Tom, Dick, and Harry in frustration cause her boy friend can't lay her, and he even breaks down crying once and he's a pretty tough cookie. They made a movie about it with Tyrone Power and Ava Gardner"

Bud pauses for emphasis.

"The Lost Generation," he says nostalgically.

"The Lost Their Balls Generation, huh?" Ernie smiles. Then skeptically, "I find that story pretty unbelievable. There are other things he could do to keep her happy or did he get all ten fingers and his tongue shot off too?"

Bud wags his head, takes his pipe out of his mouth and taps his temple with the stem.

"Be too hard on him, getting all heated up and not getting any satisfaction. No. Too hard on him, psychologically." He taps his temple again for emphasis. He points to Gerbracht's belt buckle with the stem of his pipe and says seriously,

"You just take care of the family jewels, Fred boy. I read somewhere that ten percent of all wounds received are castrations."

"Ten percent?" Gerbracht asks.

"Ten percent!" Bud affirms through his teeth.

"Hey, Fred, old buddy," Ernie interrupts, "don't say 'no shit' again, will ya? You're giving me a terrible headache."

"All right, Ernie, old buddy," Gerbracht laughs. I won't say 'no shit' again."

High overhead Bud spies a flock of snow geese migrating southward. Because the river loops to the northeast and then sharply to the west just north of town, the geese cut across country along the edge of the bluffs and rejoin the river to the east of Bud's station. Three or four flocks a day come directly over the station, and Bud, great hunter that he is, cannot resist the desire to dry shoot their pass.

He opens the door, steps into the driveway, and raises an imaginary shotgun to his shoulder. He aims, leading the geese as they pass and then squeezes the trigger three times. After each squeeze his shoulder jerks absorbing the recoil of the gun.

Back in the station he takes up his stand again just inside the door.

"And it was all a terrible waste," he says. "All the dead and wounded. Most of the deaths could have been avoided. Strategic, tactical errors. Stupid generals, incompetent officers, the friggin' high command."

Gerbracht wonders if Bud means that those killed in action were not engaged in heroic individual struggle? Does he mean that most of the dead were victims of error and stupidity? Gerbracht has always conceived of the war as an individual action. A marine storming an island beachhead, the fighter pilot in hot pursuit of the Jap zero, a ranger with blackened face on patrol behind the enemy lines, the paratrooper with a carefree grin plunging into the void shouting "Geronimo," and more recently the Green Berets. He has also conceived of the war almost solely in terms of the Pacific, the romance of tropical islands from the war movies he has seen.

There has always been something impersonal, remote about the invasion of Europe: thousands and thousands of ships and planes and tanks, millions of troops, the long, slow-grinding war of attrition. Occasionally Gerbracht visualizes a dashing tank commander but invariably the tank runs out of gas. Logistics. Supply. Superior numbers. No grace or beauty. Snow and mud, like Korea except with a purpose.

"I have a hard time believing that, Bud," he says. "I suppose there were a few mistakes, but I can't believe most of the troops killed were killed by the errors of their own generals." He shakes his head in disbelief. He is convinced by the mood of his own dissent. "I can't believe that, Bud. I can't believe all those men died in vain."

Bud does not seem disturbed by this challenge. He looks at Gerbracht and sighs. Bud decides that any twenty-one year old kid about to go in the army certainly cannot afford any illusions.

"Ever hear of Tarawa?" Bud says this with a touch of battle-weary sadness in his voice.

"Sure," Gerbracht says. "Everybody's heard of Tarawa."

"Ever hear the true story of Tarawa?"

"What do you mean, the true story of Tarawa?"

"I only use it as an example. Would you agree a pretty heroic chapter in American military history was written there?"

"I guess so."

"How many casualties do you think we received in the first week of that engagement?" Bud asks.

"I don't know. How many?"

"Six thousand. Six thousand on that little beach in the first three days. Six thousand."

"Is that a lot? Gerbracht asks.

"Is that a lot?" Bud thunders. "Is that a lot? Why that's just the highest relative casualty rate for any operation in the whole goddamn war."

Bud taps the dead ashes from his pipe, takes out his pouch, fills the pipe and slowly works the tobacco into the bowl with his forefinger. He replaces the pipe in his mouth and says,

"Do you know why Tarawa had the highest casualty rate of any operation in the war?" His voice is calm—the calm that precedes catastrophe. Gerbracht confesses he has no idea why the casualty rate was so high.

"I figure you know about ocean tides. They come in and they go out?" Bud asks motioning with his hand the movement of the tides.

"Yah. I've been to San Diego once to visit my uncle. We went fishing and he told me about them."

"Well, when the tide is in, the water along the shore is deep and comes up on the beach. Right?"

"Right," Gerbracht says.

"And when the tide is out, the beach is wider and the water along the shore is shallow. Right?"

"Right."

"Now on amphibious landings they drive the landing craft up on the beach. As the front end drops down the marines pile out and run for cover on the beach. Right?"

"I guess so. I saw a movie about it on T.V. once."

"Now, if you were a marine what had to go ashore, when would you want to land, at high tide or low tide?"

"Hey, this is a regular quiz show," Ernie says.

Gerbracht thinks, considers all the possibilities. He can't really decide one way or the other.

"Take your time," Bud says. "Think it out."

Gerbracht thinks it ought to be high tide but he doesn't want to make a fool of himself by guessing wrong.

"Hell, I don't know, Bud."

"Think about it from the marine's point of view."

"I'm trying to, Bud. I'm trying to."

"Oh, tell him, will ya, George. We'll be here all day," Ernie says.

"High tide," Gerbracht guesses.

"Right. Good thinking, Fred. And the reason is the higher the tide the farther the LCI's can come up on the beach. The farther they come up, the less open beach the marines will have to run across in order to get to cover. Right?"

"Right. Right. Right," Ernie says.

"You mean they sent them marines in at low tide?" Gerbracht finally asks.

"You bet they sent them in at low tide. The friggin' high command what's supposed to know about those things made a mistake and instead of calling the whole thing off, they kept pouring the troops into the slaughter. The LCI's ran aground about a hunnert yards from shore and those poor marines had to wade all the way in real slow in the water up to their waists instead of being able to run just a few yards to cover. The Jap snipers had a field day."

Bud raises an imaginary sniper rifle to his shoulder, aims down its imaginary barrel and begins picking off imaginary marines wading in the imaginary water.

"Pow. Pow." He swivels and takes fresh aim out the window. "Pow. Like shooting fish in a barrel."

Gerbracht winces.

"They ought to hang every admiral and general at the end of every war—on both sides. Just on general principles," Ernie says.

"Oh, there were a lot of good officers. Don't get me wrong. The really bad ones got shot by their own men, accidentally, of course. I'm just trying to warn you not to expect too much of the high command. They make stupid mistakes like everybody else. You got to salute their uniform and obey their orders but you don't have to think they're great. There's nothing in the book says you got to love them."

Gerbracht is mildly depressed. He vows to obey their orders, but he swears to himself he will never like any of them. He'll keep his distance from the high command. Not volunteer for anything. Do his job and shut his mouth. Keep his nose clean.

But he can't get those poor marines out of his head. Sitting ducks, clay pigeons, the cannon fodder of folly and ignorance. He wags his head in sympathy and identifies with their plight. Bullets splat in the water all around him. He struggles against the movement and weight of the surf, his rifle high, until one of the snipers finds the mark. Flesh ripped, torn, bludgeoned. An instant of agony and then instant sleep. Is that the way it was?

Bud bites hard on his pipe, stretches the edges of his mouth into a grin, sucks air, and swallows.

"Ho. Ho. Ho. Here comes your old pal, Ernie," Bud says. "J. F. Taylor, coming for his weekly fill."

Ernie jumps up and looks out the window. A smile spreads across his face as he sees a car in the southbound lane about to make a turn into the station.

"Here he comes, Fred. Here he comes. The guy I've been telling you about with the cherry Buick."

A two-tone grey, 1941 Buick is waiting to turn into the station. There is an arm hanging out the window, but Fred cannot see the driver. When the cars from the opposite direction pass, the Buick creeps across the northbound lane. It dips into the gutter and as the front end begins to rise on Bud's entrance ramp, the car stops. Ernie breaks out laughing and slaps his thighs.

"Goddamn. Every time. Every blessed time."

They can hear the roar of the engine. Then the car lurches forward toward the first island of pumps.

"He's gonna hit them for sure this time, Bud. He's gonna hit a pump." Ernie rushes his hands over his eyes and turns away. Fred sees a bob of white, a sudden flurry in the car, as it quickly turns to miss the first pump. Then a sudden jamming of brakes and the car stalls out parallel to the first island. Ernie is looking out toward the river, his back to the impending crash.

"I can't look. I can't look," he cries. There is a long pause. No sound. Bud places a sympathetic hand on Ernie's shoulder.

"It's O.K., Ernie. He made it. It's O.K. He missed the pump. Everything's O.K."

Ernie turns around slowly.

"I've got to sit down for a minute. I can't take it like I used to."

Ernie gropes for a chair. "So help me, Bud. If that old son-of-a-bitch ever hits anything with that car, I'll kill him. I'll ring his scrawny, friggin' neck."

"I thought you were worried about the gas pump," Fred says.

"Gas pump, hell," Bud says. "That's replaceable. Insured. But you have never seen a car like that."

"Is he always that late with the clutch?" Fred asks.

Ernie says with disgust, "Sometimes he tries to shift without it. It's a crime to let him even touch that car."

"Give him some credit," Bud says. "He's the one responsible for the condition it's in."

There is no movement in the car.

"Aren't you going to wait on him?" Fred asks.

"Oh sure. In time. In a few minutes. But he's in no hurry. This is his weekly trip on the town. He won't get out until we get there. He probably won't even get out. Once, when we were real busy and didn't get to him for about fifteen minutes, he just sat there and fell asleep at the wheel."

"How old is he?" Fred asks.

"About a hundred and ten, more or less," Ernie says.

"Eighty-eight," Bud says. "He's been coming in once a week for about ten years now."

"Sit down and take it easy, Bud," Ernie says. "I want to show Fred that car. Let's go take care of the old bastard." Ernie opens the front door.

They approach the car from behind. The windows are rolled up. Ernie raps on the glass beside the old man's head. There is a jerk and then the slow lowering of the window. Fred looks at the car closely now for the first time. He can hardly believe what he sees. He walks around it slowly feeling the finish, examining the chrome. It is flawless—no chips, no dents, it glistens evenly in the sunlight.

"Fill 'er up, Mr. Taylor?" Ernie shouts.

"What? What?" the old man says. "No. No. One dollar's worth. One dollar's worth will be satisfactory."

"Yes, sir," Ernie shouts.

Fred walks to the gas pump. Ernie whispers,

"You pump the gas. Give him a buck's worth slow. I'll clean the windows. When you're done, grab a paper towel and clean the inside of the windshield so you can see the upholstery and the floor mats. Absolute cherry. Then pull the hood release and we'll check the oil and water. The engine is the main thing."

Fred winds the gauge to zero, unscrews the tank cap, and inserts the nozzle. As he presses the release valve, he hears the gas fall into the tank. He leans to inhale the fumes.

"Want to sell this car, Mr. Taylor?" Ernie shouts. "I know someone will pay a good price for it."

The old man doesn't answer. The gallons are tolled. Fred slows the pump and stops at a dollar. He turns the gas cap back on and replaces the nozzle. He rips a paper towel and runs around the car, opens the front door and sits on the seat to clean the inside of the windshield. As he finished reaching across in front of the old man he pulls the hood release. He sees Ernie motioning to him from the front of the car. He jumps out and together they raise the hood.

"Would you look at that?" Fred whispers in awe. "Would you look at that?"

"The entire engine, all the points, wires in the motor well, distributor, air filter, everything has been completely waxed. He does it twice a year. It must take the old bastard half a year to do one coat."

Ernie checks the oil stick and Fred unscrews the radiator cap and replaces it.

"How many miles on it?"

"About nine thousand."

"Does he want to sell it?"

"Naw, but I ask him anyhow. He quit answering me about a year ago. When I first asked him, he said he would sell. His asking price was twenty-five hundred. Twenty-five hundred friggin' dollars. You wouldn't think the old buzzard would know the market like that. He may be old but he ain't looney. In five years if this car is kept in its present condition, it'll be worth more than that. Some restored Model A's are going for two thousand now."

They withdraw their heads from under the hood and Ernie closes it gently.

"All set, Mr. Taylor." He waves to the old man.

Ernie says,

"And George says he never had seat covers on it."

They walk back to the station as J. F. Taylor starts the car.

"Listen to him ride the clutch," Ernie says. He puts his fingers in his ears. The engine roars but this time the car does not lurch. It creeps forward slowly to the ramp with its engine racing, the old man depressing the clutch just enough to apply only a fraction of the engine's power. Then he lets the clutch out quickly and takes his foot off the gas. The car coughs into the north bound lane, almost stalls, and then recovers as the old man shifts into second.

Back in the station Bud has Mr. Taylor's charge book.

"One dollar's worth of regular," he says as he enters the figures in the book. "Always the same. One buck's worth a week. He never uses it up, so the tank gets fuller every time. Then I don't see him for a couple weeks. When he shows up next, his tank is empty. Takes a trip, I guess."

"More likely he forgets to turn the motor off when he gets home," Ernie says.

"I hope so," Bud says with growing emotion. "I hope so. I hope he doesn't drive very far. He's a goddamn menace. Ought to keep everybody over seventy off the road. I mean it. They ought to make them take a test every six months. It's a crime the accidents they cause."

"Well, he'll be off the road for the winter pretty soon. When you going to drain it and put it up on blocks?" Ernie asks.

"His daughter ought to call pretty soon. They take him to Florida right after Thanksgiving," he explains to Fred.

"Let me do it this year, George. Just call me. I'll do it for nothing. Any day, any hour. I just want to have it all to myself for an hour or two. When I think of my stupid car, I get sick. All the work I've put in restoring it and it's nothing—nothing at all—compared to that Buick. The hours I've spent in junkyards."

Bud scans the sky for more geese. Ernie turns a sullen eye toward the switch yard and the river beyond. He cannot erase the memory of the striking contrast between his car and Mr. Taylor's Buick. They sit without speaking.

Now business begins to pick up. Three consecutive cars keep Bud busy. Then a customer pulls in for a grease job and oil change. While Bud is busy at the gas pumps, Ernie opens the stall doors, directs the car forward, and sets the blocks. He raises the car and begins to drain the oil when Bud returns to take over. Back in the office, Ernie asks,

"What time is it, old buddy?"

Fred checks his watch. "Twelve-thirty. Why?"

"I got a phone call to make for you during the noon hour. You would like to know if you got a date tonight, wouldn't you?"

Ernie feels in his pockets.

"Hey, old buddy, you got a dime you'd like to invest in a piece of ass?"

"Here you are, old pal. You can refund it if I don't get anything."

The pay phone is located, shoulder high, next to the toilet entrance. Ernie deposits the dime and dials. He turns his back to Fred to speak in privacy. Fred fidgets in his chair.

"Hello. Could you connect me with Frances Conroy, please, 234... Thanks, sweetheart." He waits several moments. Then he begins to talk quietly and laughs softly into the phone. Fred smiles unconsciously in sympathy with whatever intimacy has been exchanged. Ernie speaks loudly now and turns around to look at Fred.

"You say everything's all set then?" He laughs, nods and winks at Fred.

"She's a knock-out, you say..." He pauses to listen. "What's my buddy like? Well, Fred's no Mr. America, but he's a big spender."

Fred blushes with pleasure at this characterization and pats his wallet confidently. She won't expect anything he can't deliver. Ernie puts his hand over the mouthpiece.

"Hey, Fred, they want to know how big your prick is. She said penis but she's a nurse, you know."

"Tell her fourteen inches. By the time anybody finds out the truth it'll be too late."

"Twenty-one," Ernie says nodding into the phone.

"Twenty-one!" Fred shouts. "Twenty-one. Nobody'll believe that, you dummy. They're nurses. They've seen something."

Ernie laughs so hard he has to apologize into the phone.

"I'm sorry. I'm laughing at this buddy of mine. He's a real

card." He looks at Fred, smiles, listens patiently, nods occasionally, says 'yes' now and then. He draws himself upright in conclusion.

"All set then, Francie baby. Eight o'clock. We'll go bowling and then out some place. Right."

With his finger, Ernie depresses the lever closing off the call, but he pretends to continue the conversation.

"Hey, baby. Wait a minute. Don't go yet. Listen. This buddy of mine is real horny; wants to know what he's going to get tonight. You know, it's his last night home and he don't want no sweet virgin or prick teaser."

"Well, for example, what's her bust line. How big are her tits and can he nibble 'em for a while first . . . What? . . . forty-two inches before the silicone treatments. . . wild. . . I'll have a bite myself."

Fred jumps up and wrestles the phone from a defenseless Ernie who is limp with laughter. Fred listens to the hum of an open line.

"Thanks a lot, old buddy. Thanks a lot." Fred feigns anger as he hangs the receiver up but he is quietly pleased that everything is all set, even though the girls are nurses and probably Catholic.

"Hey, old buddy," Ernie says still laughing. "I'm hungry. Let's cut out of here. You've listened to enough of Bud's bullshit to last you ten years. He unloaded a truckload on you today."

Fred is still uneasy about one point: "She asked how old I was, didn't she? You know, when you said twenty-one?"

"You'll never know, will ya, old buddy. It'll give ya something to think about all day."

As Ernie leaves to get his car which he parked in a narrow alley adjacent to the south end of the station, Fred yells through the doorway to where Bud is working.

"Hey, Bud. We're going to take off now. We'll see you."

"Just a minute, Fred," Bud answers. He enters the office wiping the grease from his hands. When they are sufficiently clean, he ceremoniously extends his hand for a final shake. Fred is mildly embarrassed.

"You take it easy now, Fred. Remember, take care of the family jewels," Bud laughs.

"Don't worry, Bud. I'll buy an armored jock."

"I'm going to miss you around here. You were a good customer," he says in the elegiac mood as though Fred has just been buried.

"The old man will keep coming in."

Ernie pulls into the driveway and guns his engine.

"Well, we'll see you, Bud."

"Don't take any wooden nickels," Bud says as Fred opens the door. Fred steps into the driveway and opens the car door. Bud follows him and shouts after him, "Don't do anything I wouldn't do." He stands framed by the plate glass window and he raises an arm in finals salute.

As Fred slams the car door and looks back at Bud, his arm poised in parting benediction, he is moved by a fleeting sense of nostalgia.

CHAPTER SIX

In the old days, the Stirrup and Spur Bar and Grill was the lobby of what was then the Metropolitan Hotel which, following its first days of glory and responding pragmatically to the real needs of a packing plant and stockyards society, soon degenerated into a brothel. Recently, the hotel section of the building has made a respectable social recovery: the first two floors above the ground level have been remodeled to house a medical clinic and two dentists.

Yielding to progress and the spirit of urban rehabilitation, the prostitutes removed themselves to the new motels on the outskirts of town, and a separate entrance was partitioned to the upper floors so that the patients of the medical facilities need not be embarrassed by sharing the hallway with the drunks who come stumbling and cursing from the Stirrup and Spur all hours of the day and night.

The high ceiling is painted aqua and trimmed with thin slivers of gold. Along one wall, where a toilet in one of the hotel rooms above once gagged and flowed over soaking down the paint, there is a large pale yellow blister. You are not supposed to be able to see this; everything has been done to dim the interior. The large picture window squarely in the middle of the street front has been shaded with Venetian blinds and heavy curtains. A neon beer sign hangs facing the street but only the edges of the red light show inside. There is a large horseshoe bar with padded stools. There are a few booths along one wall and a television set sits on a stand high on the closed, wall end of the bar.

When they enter through the chambered doorway, Gerbracht, struck by the artificial gloom, has difficulty adjusting his eyes. He feels vaguely uneasy, unnatural. He can detect the odor of stale beer modified by faint perfume vapors. Behind the bar a light above the cash register silhouettes the balding head of the bartender, who when he turns to serve them reveals in his smile long, narrow teeth tenuously attached to the bone sockets of receding gums.

They sit on stools and order beers. Gerbracht pours his beer into the glass and drinks. He shivers when he swallows the cold bitterness. He doesn't like beer. He doesn't like whiskey except mixed with ginger ale.

"Want to watch T.V., boys?" the bartender asks.

"Yeah," Ernie says. "Turn on one of those programs where celebrities play word games."

The tube lights, lines dance, and Arthur Godfrey, guest panelist, comes into focus.

"There's a lucky sonovabitch," the bartender says. "Had the Big C and beat it. Nat King Cole wasn't sick three months and poof. What are ya gonna do?" he shrugs.

"Must of been about ten big stars got it in the last few years," Ernie says. "First there was Bogart and then Dick Powell, Gary Cooper, and John Wayne."

"What about Clark Gable?" Gerbracht asks.

"Naw, not the Big C," the bartender says. He taps his breast with one finger. "The ticker. Same with Tyrone Power."

The bartender leaves to wait on other customers. Gerbracht drinks the beer now in larger swallows. The first bitterness is gone. They watch the program without real interest. Ernie grows irritated at one of the contestants who fails to grasp an obvious clue.

"Stupid ass," he says. "Why don't they get somebody on there that knows something. Don't they screen the idiots, give them an I.Q. test first or something."

The bartender returns and pours a shot for himself below the bar level on the glass drain. He looks up at the television and says,

"Cooper had cancer of the intestines. They say you get that from eating too many charcoal broiled steaks, all the carbon from the fire. And Bogie had it of the throat, too much booze."

He drinks half his whiskey.

"What you boys doing here so early in the afternoon? You working nights?"

"No," Ernie says, "I got off at noon and my buddy here is going in the army tomorrow. We just came by to meet some of his buddies as soon as the packing plants let out."

The bartender introduces himself. His name is Willie Maloney. He spent four years in the army himself—chasing poontang all over Europe. He looks around to make certain no one is watching, then he produces two jiggers on the bar and pours each a shot of bourbon. He raises his own glass to eye level.

"Here's to luck in the army."

Gerbracht throws his head back pretending to take a big gulp, but he only sips a small amount. It burns the roof of his mouth and his throat. He washes it down quickly with some beer. His eyes fill with tears. He does this three more times before the glass is empty. They order another round of beers and Gerbracht offers to buy the bartender a drink.

Gerbracht drains his first bottle of beer into the glass, drinks it down, and goes to the toilet. When he returns, there is another shot of whiskey before him, and Ernie and the bartender are talking in hushed conspiratorial whispers and laughing.

Gerbracht listens to Ernie tell a story. It is about a bartender and the electronic engineer. He has heard it before, but it is funny enough to listen to again. As he listens, he begins to feel the first effects of the alcohol: the whiskey bottles on the shelves behind the bar take on an extraordinary beauty, a larger and larger significance. He looks at the labels with increasing delight and interest as he sips the second shot and washes the whiskey down with beer.

He listens to Ernie tell the story and finally arrive at the punch line. "There, I've proven my point. You don't know shit and you want to talk electronics!'"

Despite himself Gerbracht breaks into laughter. The bartender doubles over for a moment and when he straightens up again there are tears in his eyes.

"Oh," he says, "oh, I got to write that one down. I got to remember that one."

He goes over to the cash register and brings back a pad and pencil. He writes notes on the paper, checks Ernie for a few details, then rips the paper from the pad and folds it. He puts the folded paper into his wallet carefully.

"I'm saving this one," he says laughing. "I'll try it out first on my old lady tonight."

"How about a couple more beers? " Gerbracht says and puts a five dollar bill on the bar. He opens two more beers, then empties the ash trays. He rings up the last round of drinks and brings the change as Fred leaves a large tip on the bar. Ernie turns to him with a smile on his face.

"You're a good boozer, Fred baby," he says, "and a big spender but we better make this the last drink if we want to have a few later tonight."

"Ernie, buddy," Gerbracht says, "I know you're right about Bud. I guess I let him bullshit me too much today. I'm sorry about that. It's not that Bud's such a great guy. It's not that at all, but if you had my old man, you'd think different."

"I understand your problem, old buddy. I understand your problem." Ernie shakes his head as Gerbracht recalls a catalogue of grievances.

"It's not only that I have to almost fight him to use the friggin' car once in a while, or the way he complains all the time. It's not just that. It's like he's always looking for an argument. According to him nothing is worth anything. He goes to a movie, for example, and squawks for a week how phony it was. He squawks so much I feel like giving him his ticket money so he won't feel he's been cheated."

Gerbracht pauses reflectively.

"That's it in a nutshell. He feels he's always being cheated. I remember once after a Twins game we went to this Chinese place in downtown Minneapolis. I never had such a good time eating out like that, but when we were done, he claimed we had been cheated on the meat, that there wasn't enough meat in the chow mein. When we went to pay the check, he got into an argument with the Chinaman who owned the place and he was so loud, the Chinaman offered to give us another meal. And the old man walked out saying he wouldn't want to get cheated again, not even for nothing."

Gerbracht lights a cigarette and drinks off his beer.

"I tell you, he's like that all the time. He fought our neighbors for about a year over the grading of the alley. He won't talk to my Uncle Fritz who was in charge of everything when my grandmother died. He claimed my ma didn't get enough money. And whenever anything goes wrong he blames it on the Jews. If Bud is right about what the Germans did, there ain't enough Jews around to blame everything on."

Suddenly, he is done, exorcized and cleansed. He has nothing left to say. A benevolence descends upon his spirit. Gerbracht even looks with a kindly inward eye upon his father. And just as suddenly the bar is filled. The working day at the packing plants is over. The bartender is now busy cashing payroll checks. The men with whom Gerbracht has worked for the past few months find him gazing benignly at the string of smoke curling up from his cigarette.

The men are all older than Gerbracht; they have come to have a drink with him, to pay him a final tribute. They are full of advice. They reach into the reservoirs of their pasts, for his future is their past. Drinks are bought all around. Gerbracht accepts another beer but only sips it slowly. He listens intently to their advice as he drifts down the bar. He loses track of Ernie who has met other friends.

They josh him and he pretends to take them seriously.

"Is that right," he says. "Japanese pussy is horizontal? No kidding?"

"Yeah, yeah," one of the men says, "you got to slip it in side saddle."

"And remember, too," one of them says, "short arm inspection ain't the same as small arms inspection. Nosiree. You take a bath for one of them."

"Right, right," he says happily.

"And don't drink any coffee in basic training. It's full of saltpeter."

"What's that for?" he asks.

"So you can't get a hard-on. Since you won't be seeing women for a couple of months, the high muck-a-mucks, the army brass, figure you'll be better off with only two legs."

His straw boss gives him serious advice: "Don't knock the army," he says. "It isn't so great, but it's an opportunity, a helluva better opportunity than you'll get here. Everything is set here. The only way you can get ahead is by seniority. It ain't like the old days when if you didn't like the way things were going, you could take off, go west, get a piece of land. Not any more. Everything's closed up."

Gerbracht nods seriously. Someone grabs him by the arm, squeezes it.

"Pretty scrawny thing to stop a bullet," a voice says. "The army better fatten you up a bit before the slaughter."

Gerbracht loses his sense of time. After a while he even loses those who came to drink with him. He wanders along the bar talking with strangers. When he accidentally notices a clock, he realizes it is four-thirty. What happened to the time? It seemed to be passing so slowly. He is already sobering up. He only has an hour or so before he must go home. He searches for Ernie and finally finds him.

"Hey, buddy. We got to get going. I got to be completely sober by six o'clock."

" We got to oxidize the booze," Ernie says. "We need to run it off. We'll go to the Y, work out. Have a cold shower."

"Well, let's go then," Gerbracht says. "Let's oxidize right now, buddy, 'cause I've only got a little while before I have to walk a straight line past all my friggin' relatives."

CHAPTER SEVEN

"What did you do all day, Freddy?"

Martha Gerbracht noted a wavering out of focus look in her son's eyes when he came in.

"Oh, nothing much. Went to Bud's. Then had lunch and a beer or two. Then we went to the Y and had a workout."

Except for the "beer or two" she is satisfied her son has had a constructive, moral day. She is especially pleased by the YMCA workout; physical fitness, according to the President's Council on the same subject, has become almost a patriotic duty. She makes a mental note, however, to mention the evils of alcohol to him—that it is a poison, that it contributes directly and indirectly to thousands of deaths each year, and that it is the acid of the soul, the corrosive fluid that can break down our moral fiber—but she refrains from preaching now, her mood is too buoyant.

She has had a busy, busy creative day. She cleaned the house, prepared the food for the evening guests, had her hair done, and bought a new dress. She bought and wrapped two farewell gifts for her son which she is now eager to award him in affectionate farewell.

He notices a warmth and softening. There is a patch of color high on her cheeks. Her tight curls do not become her. They suggest a girlishness incongruous with her flabby, white-lumpish flesh, but Gerbracht senses a renewal of spirit that might finally be translated into a temporary holiday from her moral seriousness. When he has read these signs in the past, she has been unable to repress her joy though not without some sense of guilt.

She calls him to the kitchen where she gives him his presents, neatly wrapped in paper she has saved from past presents. These gifts were generated out of the few moments of anxiety she experienced in this otherwise satisfying day.

Her hair had already been set. Her head was in the dryer and she was reading her favorite magazine when she came across an article entitled, "Death Stalks Camp Behometh," and the equally terrifying sub-title, "The Secret Killer More Deadly Than a Bullet That Fells Our Young Men: Spinal Meningitis." The article began with the story of a young man returning to his barracks after a day of drills. His head ached and he felt warm. He had no appetite for supper that evening and went to bed well before taps, foregoing his letter writing and customary game of cards.

After a comprehensive and detailed summary of the progress of the symptoms, the introduction to the article concluded with the dramatic announcement of the death of the young man, and a compilation of the tragic statistics of this dread disease.

Terror gripped her heart. She wanted to bolt from the salon, but she was trapped with her hair in rollers and her head in a machine. What to do? What to do?

She continued to read. Another case history; but, fortunately, this young man survived. She began to feel a little better. She continued to read eagerly to find out why one man died and the other lived.

The article quoted several authorities. Jargon and mystery. There was no clear-cut answer. Then the author of the article with fiendish indirection took the reader back to his case studies and the individual backgrounds. After pages of circumlocution, the conclusion drawn was that the young man who lived had had a higher resistance to the dread disease because of a balanced diet. The one who died had a vitamin deficiency. The article concluded that the mothers of America need no longer experience the tragic, needless deaths of their sons and daughters if they would judiciously supply them with vitamin pills.

She felt relieved when she had finished the article, but she could hardly wait to get to a drugstore. To take her mind off her anxiety, she began reading the issue of last July only to run into another article of concern: "Why Crime Reigns in Our City Streets." This article also began with a story, this time of a young man new to the city who was robbed and beaten when he tried to help what he thought was a little old lady cross the street. The little old lady turned out to be a sixteen year old juvenile delinquent, the lure for a gang of teenage hoodlums.

Later with the comforting assistance of the druggist, she had little difficulty selecting the right bottle of vitamins, but the money belt in the military style was another matter. She finally located one in a war surplus store after trying three men's clothing stores and one department store.

Now, while she finishes washing a few dishes in the sink, he opens the package which contains the belt first, uncoils it, and exclaims, "Geez, Ma, thanks. I can always use another belt." He doesn't quite know what to do with it.

"It's not just another belt, you know," she says, turning from the sink. "It has a secret compartment for your money, here." She turns the belt around in his hand and unzips the compartment.

"Would you look at that?" he says. "Would you look at that?" He runs the zipper back and forth. Then he takes a bill out of his wallet, folds it, and stuffs it in. He closes the zipper, takes off his belt, and puts this new one on.

"Is this ever great, Ma!" he says. "Is this ever great! I can keep a hundred bucks or so in there and if I ever get knocked over the head, nobody will find it." He pauses as he buckles the belt.

"It has a military style buckle," she says and smiles.

"Yah, I noticed that and it fits just perfect at the third notch. Just perfect."

When he unwraps the bottle of vitamins, he claims they are great, too. Just what he needed. He slips the bottle of vitamins in his pocket as though to say they are so important he won't ever let them out of his possession.

Gerbracht shifts his weight back and forth from one foot to the other uncertain what to do next. Then, he crosses the room and opens the refrigerator. He peers in and sees the plates of sandwiches under waxed paper.

"You're not having everybody for supper, are you?" he asks.

"I've only made sandwiches and coffee. I told them they could stop by any time between six and eight o'clock and it's almost six now. Your father will be home pretty soon and Uncle Fritz said he was coming by early because he has an appointment later and has so far to drive."

"Can I have a sandwich now, Ma? I'm hungry."

CHAPTER EIGHT

"I'll get it," his mother cries when the doorbell rings. Gerbracht hears her open the door and a voice.

"Can you tell me where the Gerbrachts live?"

"Oh, you just be still, Fritz," she says. "Don't try to be funny with me."

Gerbracht looks through the kitchen doorway into the living room and sees his Uncle Fritz enter.

"Where's my namesake godson, the soldier boy going off to war?" Fritz yells into the kitchen. "Hey, where you keeping yourself? I got a new Cadillac convertible out here I'm selling for three hundred bucks to any guy named Fred who is going into the army tomorrow."

"Oh, Fritz, don't be foolish. He can't go in a car, and don't try to make a joke of everything. It isn't pleasant that he's going."

"Well, it ain't a wake, either. I don't ever go to wakes. You can't sell cars there, and I'm not about to let this turn into a wake. I drove twenty miles to say goodbye and to be downright honest with you, I wish I was going and he was staying here to sell cars."

Gerbracht goes into the living room, tucking in his shirt as he goes.

"Hi, Uncle Fritz. Long time, no see," he says extending his hand.

"How ya been, boy?"

"You got a Cadillac you want to sell me so's I can get to basic training in style?"

"You bet, Fred boy. A big coon convertible. Chartreuse with fuchsia upholstery. Only three hundred down and the rest in monthly payments of $147.50 for the rest of your life."

"I'm going into the kitchen to check everything. You men can talk alone," his mother says.

"Say hello to the kitchen chair for me, will you, Sis?"

"Oh, Fritz, be still." She laughs a nervous titter.

Fritz is divorced, the clown of the family and Gerbracht's mother has the annoying habit of laughing at everything he says whether it is funny or not. He has a round, jovial face, sandy thinning hair, and a razor-thin moustache. He is known as a flashy dresser. He is a car dealer in a town about twenty miles away. Gerbracht has been taught by his father to believe that his uncle is a phony blow-hard, but Gerbracht has always been attracted to him.

Fritz clasps his hands behind his back and walks about the room, carefully inspecting the family portraits. Gerbracht sits on an ottoman and waits for his uncle to sit down. Finally, Fritz makes his way to the sofa, settles down in it with a heavy sigh, and says to Gerbracht with sudden seriousness,

"Well, Fred boy, the big day has arrived. You can get the hell out of here for good. You can do anything you want now without everybody talking about it for two or three weeks." He winks. "Just don't get caught and you'll get a Good Conduct medal."

"You liked the service didn't you, Uncle Fritz"

"Liked it? I hated it at the time, hated every minute of it. But I was a damn fool then. If I'd stayed in, I could retire in just a few years from now and have the rest of my life to myself with a good steady income. I wouldn't have to spend my life sucking around everybody to make a buck. Good security, too. Lots of guys I know younger than me retiring already. You take it from me. If you like it at all, stay in, and don't get married."

"You know, I've talked to some guys and they say the same thing. There's a lot of crap you have to take, but if you keep your nose clean and do a halfway decent job and use your head, it can be pretty good."

They are interrupted by Mrs. Gerbracht who serves them a plate of sandwiches and some coffee. She leaves as silently as she came. Fritz waits for her to get beyond earshot and then leans forward and says,

"And there's a lot more advantages that don't have anything to do with the army. There's a lot of women running around in this big old country and if you get to Germany or Japan with the occupation forces, man, you'll have it made." He pauses. "There's only one hazard. Stay away from the queers."

"Did you meet many?"

"Meet many? Only about two or three a day. The first time I was in New York City I was propositioned to go up into three separate apartments overlooking Central Park in less than half an hour. They all got apartments overlooking Central Park."

He begins to laugh and looks guiltily over his shoulder to make certain his sister cannot hear. His voice is considerably lower as he leans toward Gerbracht. "I have to tell you this story about this big black coon we had who went on leave to Harlem when we were at Dix in Jersey. Well, he come back from a weekend and we said to him, `Hey, Adams, you get anything up in Harlem?' And he says, `Yeah, I got me somethin' but you'll never guess what.' And we all said, `Tell us about it.' And he says, `You see dese knuckles?' And he shows us his knuckles all scraped up and says, `Can you figure out how I end up with dese knuckles, man? Well, sho' nuff, I'll tell you. I go to this high-class bar up on Lennox Avenue and I meet me a piece what am a piece. Man, is she beautiful, and she goes for me. She sit down and right away there is a hand goin' up my leg, so I say to her, le's get goin' to some quiet place, so she says she got a room only two blocks away and so we go up there fast.' You ought to hear this big buck tell this story. Oh man, he was mad." Fritz settles back lost in reverie.

"Well, what happened? Don't leave me hanging."

"`Well,' Adams says, `we git up into that room and I am hot to go but all she wants to do is play around with me and finally I go for her panties and man-oh-man-oh-man, up I comes with a hand full of nuts.'"

Fritz breaks out laughing.

"Man, you should of seen the look of disgust on that nigger's face when he told us that."

"You mean it was a man?"

"A man is right, but not much of anything when that big jig got done with him. I've never seen anybody so mad in my whole life."

"You mean this man had dressed up like a woman?"

"Why, sure. They do it all the time. Female impersonators. Sometimes they are in night club acts." Fritz sips his coffee and squints critically through the steam at Gerbracht. "Boy, you got a lot to learn but I suppose the army will teach it to you fast. That ain't no outfit of sweet virgins, I tell you. And stay out of the bars, too. Don't go gettin' mixed up with any B-girls. They're as bad as the queers."

"What are B-girls?"

"Bonus girls. Why, they sit around in the bars gettin' paid to lead you on and spend your money on booze. They get a percentage of what you spend. Oh, you usually get something in the end, but it costs too much. My advice is to go to church."

"Go to church? But you were just telling me about all the women everywhere."

"I suppose you think women don't go to church? Based upon my experience, almost everybody that goes to church is a woman."

"What good is going to church going to do?"

"Well, the plan is to go to church in your uniform. Now these girls that go to church all the time are just like any other woman, they got desires, but they like to think it's love and holy."

Gerbracht takes out a package of cigarettes, offers one to Fritz. They light their cigarettes as Fritz continues.

"When they see you in church a few times they figure you're not just any old horny serviceman. Pretty soon the minister will ask you to the youth club and before you know it you got more women than you know what to do with. The simple truth is,

Freddy boy, the biggest pimps in the world are the clergy and you better take advantage of them while you're young. The only thing they do for you when you get old is bury you. The beauty of it all is that it doesn't cost a dime, you get free meals, and if you play it right and are careful, you can get everything you want. Take it from your old Uncle Fritz, a passionate nice girl is better than an old whore any day of the week."

Uncle Fritz looks toward the kitchen again, afraid his sister might hear. Gerbracht turns around guiltily, then back and says,

"But you can't do that all the time, Uncle Fritz. Somebody will catch on."

"Naw, nobody will catch on. You play three or four churches at once and since nobody knows you, you can get away with murder. You can't do that here. You go with one girl and everybody has you married. There is something to being a stranger. If I had my way, I would wander all over being a stranger in one city after another. As soon as they got me pegged I'd move on, and become a stranger all over again." Fritz's eyes grow misty. "It's exciting and mysterious. There's always a new woman, always new friends, always something you've never done exactly like it before. It's freedom, man, it's freedom. Just think, Fred. The whole goddamn world don't know you and you gotta be stuck in this town where everybody knows everything. Is that justice? Now I ask you, is that justice?"

"Hey, do you make leaving home sound great. I'll be honest. I kind of feel that way myself. There's a lot of things I haven't seen or done. And so many people I've never met. I sometimes feel I can't wait to go. You know something, Uncle Fritz, if that draft board hadn't hurried to get me, I was going to enlist anyway except that you have to sign up for four years but you only get drafted for two."

The two have reached a peak of romantic wistfulness. After some moments, Fritz breaks the silence with a laugh.

"You're a chip off your old Uncle Fritz's block, boy. I'd give you some of my old phone numbers that I picked up in the service, but I guess the gals would be a little old for you now."

"I suppose there's a new crop coming along."

Fritz slugs Gerbracht gently on the arm. They stand up and walk toward the kitchen.

"Yep, a whole new crop just ripe for picking. You keep my advice under that hat of yours and when the time comes, give a thought to your wise old Uncle Fritz."

"Hey, Ma, is there anything for dessert?"

"There's strawberry shortcake. It's all ready in the ice box. There is a can of whipped cream inside the door."

"It ain't an ice box, Ma. It's a refrigerator."

"I'll call it a refrigerator if you stop saying ain't."

As Gerbracht walks into the kitchen his mother and uncle hover in the hallway briefly then walk slowly to the living room.

"Where did you say the whipped cream was?" he yells.

"In the refrigerator door," she answers.

"O.K. I got it. Right here in the ice box door."

"You know, Martha," Gerbracht hears Fritz say, "I honestly wish I was going into the army again. I'd have my whole life ahead of me instead of most of it behind. I'll tell you I wouldn't do the same things again. Nosiree. I'd of stayed east in New York or gone out to California with Orville."

"It's not so bad here. The grass always looks greener somewhere else, but you take your own problems with you," she says.

Gerbracht returns to the living room with a can in his hand. He leans back against the doorway, puts his head back, and squirts some whipped cream into his mouth.

"What are you doing?" his mother cries out.

"Just having me a shot of whipped cream, Ma."

He leans his head back again and squirts some more in his mouth.

"Stop that this instant. It's not clean. It's filthy."

"I'm not touching the end. See! Besides, this is my last day at home and I've always wanted to do it."

She comes toward him and tries to take it away from him. Fritz retreats behind her and signals to Gerbracht.

"How about giving me a shot, boy. I've always wanted to do that myself."

Just as she gets to him, Gerbracht tosses the can to his uncle who leans back and squirts a shot into his mouth. She turns toward Fritz.

"Stop it now," she says half laughing. She runs back to Fritz but just as she gets to him, he tosses the can back to Gerbracht. They continue to play keep-away, until she is laughing, giggling with breathless delight.

"Give it to me!" she cries.

"Come and get it, Ma."

"Come and get it," Fritz says.

"Give it to me."

"Hey, Ma. You want a shave?" Gerbracht squirts her in the face.

"No! No!" she screams. "It's in my hair." She falls onto the sofa laughing. "Get a towel quick," she cries, "before it ruins my hairdo."

By the time Gerbracht returns from the bathroom she has stopped laughing. His uncle looks at his watch.

"Holy Cow, it's six-fifteen. I have to see a farmer on the way home. He wants to trade an old cattle truck and I have to give him an estimate."

"Don't go yet, Fritz," Mrs. Gerbracht says. "Dottie and Frank are coming over in a little while."

"Don't go, Uncle Fritz. We'll get a game of Euchre going after while. Maybe I can win a down payment on that Cadillac."

"At two bits a game?" Fritz laughs. "We'd have to play for three weeks, twenty-four hours a day."

"Pa will play and I got a pal coming over later who will be a good pigeon to clean out."

"I am almost tempted to stay, but I really got to go. I have an appointment at 7:00. No 9:00 to 5:00 in the sales line," he finishes.

"What are you driving, Uncle Fritz?"

"This week I am driving a red Oldsmobile convertible. A demonstrator. Want to drive it around for a few minutes?"

"Do I? Let's go. You can give me some more advice on how to get along in the service."

"Don't go far now," Mrs. Gerbracht cautions.

"Nah," Gerbracht says. "We'll just drive around the block."

The night air is clear and cold. By the porch light Gerbracht runs down the front steps toward Fritz's car, parked directly in front of the house. As he goes around the back of the car, he slides his hand along the cold metallic paint. In his excitement he has forgotten his jacket. He feels the chill.

As he opens the door, the interior light erupts. He slips into the driver's side, a cold leather bucket seat, and waits with the door half open until Fritz makes it to the other side of the car.

He shivers when his uncle opens the door. Fritz slams his door. For a moment they sit in the darkness. Gerbracht hears his uncle wrestle for the keys in his pocket.

He snaps his seat belt and caresses the hardened slickness of the steering wheel and the dashboard. When Fritz hands him the keys, he searches for the ignition, inserts the key, turns it to the right, and listens to the starter and then the quick catch of the engine. As he turns on the lights, he begins to feel the power of the engine spread gradually through his body.

"How's the pick-up, Uncle Fritz?"

"She'll do sixty-five in second in less than a block if you know how to drive her."

"I know how to drive her," he says.

"Well, let's see you move it out then."

Gerbracht slips the stick into low and pulls slowly from the curb. When he has straightened the car into the lane, he depresses the gas pedal thrusting the car forward. At thirty miles an hour he shifts as quickly as he can. From the corner of his eye he can see his uncle sitting impassively watching the road ahead. He slows for an intersection. The car dips into the cross street, rises over the hump, and dips once more as he passes the street lamp post.

He thrusts the pedal down again and the car still in second gear surges forward.

"Jesus, why don't you drive this goddamn car if you're going to. You won't get to no sixty-five in a block at this rate," Fritz says.

Gerbracht peers down the tunnel of light, and sees the bare arms of the trees silhouetted in the distance. He feels his uncle's foot on top of his and the stubborn pressure of the floorboard underneath.

CHAPTER NINE

Henry Gerbracht is dissatisfied. He sits waiting for his son to return. Unhappily, what he rehearsed in his mind all day now seems insignificant. Perhaps, the rehearsals lessened the passion and seriousness with which he planned to deliver this first and final valedictory to his son.

He thought all day of this last speech. By four o'clock he had settled the major points and their order in his mind. After work he dropped by the Legion Club and delivered an impromptu version of it to the bartender. He left for home satisfied that everything was set. But somehow he has lost his enthusiasm.

He would like to redirect the course of his emotion. He tries to rile himself by resurrecting forgotten insults, old injuries. He sits pretending to read the paper.

"Please don't be angry tonight and embarrass us all," Mrs. Gerbracht says to him from the kitchen. "Try to be civil. It's his last night."

"Maybe I should go out so you won't have me bothering you."

"Now, don't start pitying yourself. I'm having a hard enough time the way it is trying to be cheerful so he'll remember us with smiles on our faces."

"I want to talk to him alone before he goes. I want to tell him what it's really like so he won't leave here expecting the army is going to be a bed of roses."

"I'm going up to change now. Don't disillusion him too much. He's got to want to go a little bit or he'll be miserable," she says.

He talks out loud as if to his wife though he knows she has gone: "I'm going to tell him the truth as I see it." He gets up and paces the room. "I bet Fritz is telling him how to get along. I hope he tells him how to be careful with women so he won't get the clap like his Uncle Fritz did from some barfly in New York. All that time everybody was worried about him in the hospital all he had was the drips."

Outside there is the roar of an engine and in a few minutes Fred comes back in.

"Hi, Pa," he says. "Wowee! That is some automobile, I'll tell you. Fritz says it will do sixty-five in second in less than a block."

"Fred," Mr. Gerbracht says firmly. "I want to talk to you before you go and before everyone else comes. Come in here and sit down."

Gerbracht sits reluctantly on the sofa as his father stands above him and then begins to pace.

"I suppose Fritz has been telling you a lot about the army and what to do?" Mr. Gerbracht asks.

"He told me a little bit. He said it wasn't so bad and that there were a lot of new things a guy could do."

"Well, I'm gonna tell you different. Did he tell you the crap you have to take from some chicken-shit second lieutenant? Did he tell you that it ain't no picnic to march all day and do drills and shoot that stupid rifle and have some big horse's ass eat your ass out for not looking right? Did he tell you about the loneliness that gets you when you're on a short overnight pass and walk the streets of some godforsaken town just wishing you knew somebody to talk to? New York City is a great big honky-tonk with everybody trying to screw you good for four bits."

"I know about that. I heard the worst." Gerbracht squeezes his hands together, looks at the floor.

"Well, the worst is that you never leave yourself behind. The world don't change because the names of the streets are different or the land has a different lay. You probably figure it's going to be one good time after another. Well, it ain't true. Life ain't like that. You're going to meet the same kind of people you know here, except worse. You're going to do the same things, have the same kind of friends, and make the same mistakes all over again. Nothing is going to be changed just because the scenery changes."

Suddenly he feels spent. He wonders: Is that all I had to say?

"I'm not expecting miracles. I'll be getting out in two years, three at the most. It ain't the end. You talk like I was going off forever and that I wanted to go and not come back. It ain't so bad here, but everybody likes to see something different for once in their life before they settle down. That's all I want, a chance to see something different and learn a trade. Maybe learn how to be a mechanic or electronic technician."

"O.K. I just didn't want you to go without somebody telling you what it was really like." He feels a vague satisfaction that his duty is done. He goes across to his chair and retrieves his newspaper from the floor.

"Thanks, Pa. I'll keep my eyes open and stay out of trouble. Don't worry about me."

Mr. Gerbracht settles into the stuffed chair with the paper. "I don't plan to worry about you. I just don't want to pick up the pieces of another Fritz who came out of the army a bum and hasn't settled down yet. That's what your Uncle Fritz is, you know. An army bum who never grew up past twenty-two. He'd have been better off to stay in."

"Yah, I know. He said so himself."

"If you ever need any money or anything, don't forget where you're from."

"No, I won't. Thanks, Pa. Speaking of money," Gerbracht says beginning to smile, "Ma made me put half my money in traveler's checks in case I get robbed or something. She even bought me a belt with a secret compartment." He shows his father the belt. Mr. Gerbracht glances at it perfunctorily and returns to his paper.

"Yeah, sure. Your ma got her purse snatched in Chicago once," he says. He pauses and adds an afterthought: "You all set for tomorrow?"

"Yeah, Pa. We take a bus to the junction first, then the train."

"Don't be too late tonight. You got a long, hard day tomorrow."

The doorbell rings. Gerbracht crosses to the stairway hall and shouts, "Hey, Ma. They're here."

"Well, answer the door. I'll be down in a minute."

As he walks across the room Gerbracht turns to his father. " What advice do you think Aunt Dot will give me?"

Mr. Gerbracht says as matter of fact: "She will tell you what to eat and how much."

Gerbracht laughs: "Boy, I guess you got her pegged." Mistaking his father's factual statement as irony he adds: "You're pretty funny sometimes, Pa."

"Funny? Who's being funny? What the hell you talking about?"

As he walks to the door Gerbracht halts and turns around. "Aw, forget it, Pa. Forget it. I thought you made a joke on purpose."

CHAPTER TEN

After the cards, the kibitzing, and the crocodile tears after the cribbage and rattle, and rap rummy he plays with his aunts and uncles and cousins because it is their wordless and therefore a relatively painless gesture of farewell, Gerbracht is released to his own pursuits. As Ernie drives across town and before they pick up their dates at the student nurses' residence hall, they stop at a liquor store for a pint of whiskey and a six-pack of ginger ale. Gerbracht pours off two or three ounces of ginger ale and fills the bottle with whiskey. He puts his thumb over the end and shakes it. He gives the bottle to Ernie and they pass it back and forth.

He does not expect much, but his date turns out much better than he had hoped. "What a pair of headlights," Ernie says behind his hand on the way to the car. Fred avoids looking at her. Her name is Joyce Toomey. She graduated from high school the same year Gerbracht did, worked a year to save money and is now in her second year of nurses' training.

He says little. She probes, questions, waits patiently through the long silences which punctuate her questions and anticipate his answers. Since he graduated from high school, he has been working in the packing plant. Too bad he is going in the army, she commiserates. He agrees and wishes he were already on his way.

She is Catholic, very, very Catholic, and he is Protestant and very little of that. Lutheran or Methodist; he goes to either, when he goes. His father is one, his mother the other.

After they have settled in the car, the girls resume their conversation. It is about a certain doctor. Gerbracht misses his name.

Apparently there is little correlation between his competence as a physician and his personal warmth and understanding. They also mention something about O.B. and pediatrics, tours of duty, and a D&C, a procedure in which somebody gets scraped out.

"I hear you're a pretty good bowler. We're all looking for lessons tonight," Joyce says.

He is momentarily startled. It is his idea to go bowling. What if he can't pick up the spares? He has had nights when he can't hit anything.

"Oh, I'm not that good. Ernie's been exaggerating."

"He told Francie you had a 236 one night."

"Yah, but did he tell her I had a 121 in the game right after? You wouldn't believe it. A 236 followed by a 121, a hundred and fifteen pin difference, and I tried just as hard in the second game."

"Maybe that's why you did so poorly. You tried too hard."

"I suppose so. I was trying for a 600 series. That's the way you can tell a really good bowler—if he averages over 600 for a three game series. I don't come near that; my best season average was 176 two years ago."

"That's good enough for me. I've only been over a hundred once." She laughs.

When they arrive at the bowling alley, the girls excuse themselves. The leagues are still in progress. Ernie is dazzled. He has never been here before. He digs his toe into the thick wine carpet.

"Geez, a friggin' palace. Look at this place. Last time I was bowling was at old man Johnson's on Broad Street. Upstairs above the old Green Lantern." Ernie reminisces. "Used to take your life in your own hands going there at night. Once I went there with this buddy of mine, Dick Lesker. He was a pinsetter and they had this room in back where the pinsetters played cards and things when they weren't setting pins."

They walk forward and stand behind the spectator seats. Two shallow levels below them are the crowded benches and in the approaches, waiting for balls to return, are the gaudily attired league bowlers. The hollow sound of tumbling pins, the whine of the ball on wood, shouts of triumph, despair, encouragement. Topper's Bar. The Keyhole Inn. Happy Jack's. Robert's Meats. Ellerton's Drugs. Hank's Bar and Grill. Truckers' Inn. The commercial league. Flashes of glorious yellow, red, and blue satin and above the approach on a narrow gable of the ceiling, the scores of each match projected by the telescore in black and white boxes of shadows, and hurried hands marking the figures and symbols and vanishing quickly into nowhere.

Squeals from the left draw Ernie's head toward the first ten lanes. Women bowlers from the Packing Plant League. Sweet Pickle. Administration 1. Sausage. Fancy Meats. Administration 3. Smoke drifts upward from crowded ash trays.

"Hey, look at that down there." Ernie points toward the women.

"Yeah, a ladies' league." Gerbracht is preoccupied.

"Where's the pinsetters?"

"All automatic now."

"How do the balls come back?"

"Under the alleys."

Progress. No question about it, Ernie decides. Progress. Just getting rid of the crummy pinsetters is progress. He returns in memory to the pinsetters' room in Johnson's Bowling Alley and finishes his story.

"I went to Johnson's this Saturday with this old buddy of mine and there wasn't much doing so we played blackjack until I lost the quarter my ma gave me. At a penny a game that was hard to do. Then these older pinsetters wanted to play this game of chicken. We all took our pants down and sat in a circle on the benches. Each of us had a book of matches and we took turns burning hair off from around our pecker and balls. After we lit the match, we had until it went out. The one who burned the most off was the winner. I was about thirteen or fourteen. Didn't have much hair to start with so I really burned my old dinger trying to get close enough to win. My ma made me smear butter all over that night."

Gerbracht hasn't been listening. Without laughing, without even acknowledging that he has heard Ernie, he starts off to the Pro-Shop, a glass cage to the right of the entrance. Ernie wanders along the carpeted runway discovering as he walks new and wonderful evidence of the progress that bowling has made in ten short years: a soda fountain, a cocktail lounge, and Good Lord Almighty, a friggin' nursery where mothers can leave their brats while they bowl up a sweat with the girls.

In the Pro-Shop under the brightly beaming Don Carter clock, Gerbracht runs his hands over the new balls on display. He inspects the shoes, and feels the grip on the ball valises. One ball in particular catches his eye; it is translucent red. Light penetrates two or three inches but is diffused and dissipated in the density of the center, but light directed at an angle along the surface glows, illuminates the frozen swirls of molten glass. It is like a gigantic agate glass marble. Class. Real class. He caresses the slick-hard surface. He bets it would cost plenty, maybe fifty or sixty bucks even.

The plate glass near his head rumbles, flutters from a knock. He looks up to see the girls beckoning him from the other side. They carry their coats and motion to him to hang them up. He meets them in the runway and takes their coats to the racks. He hangs his own jacket up also. When he returns to the girls, Ernie has joined them.

He looks at his date closely now for the first time. Her forehead is hidden by long, square bangs. Her straight black hair is shoulder length, but the ends curl under ever so slightly. Her face is broad, her cheekbones wide and high. She is no striking beauty, but she is put together well. She wears a white blouse, an olive green plaid wool skirt, and red knee length stockings. She carries her sweater first, then decides to put it on. Because she fastens only the top button, the folds of the open front fall away at an angle draping her breast. Like blinders they partially hide and yet accentuate a well developed breast.

Francie, Ernie's girl, is dressed in tight lavender slacks and a lavender turtle-neck sweater with horizontal white stripes. Her honey-blond hair is piled carelessly on top of her head. An occasional curl comes undone and falls loosely across her forehead.

The league bowlers are beginning to finish; carrying balls, sweaters, shoes, and purses, they begin to file up from the approach areas and congregate at the tables behind the spectator benches awaiting friends yet to complete matches. Scores in the men's league over 200 and in the ladies' league over 170 are announced over the loudspeaker. Ripples of applause greet each name and score.

At the counter Gerbracht gets shoes for everyone and a scoresheet. They have been assigned Alley 23. He leads Ernie and the girls to the benches, and they sit to change shoes. Gerbracht appears composed, but when he puts his bowling shoes on, his leg trembles, jerks when he lifts his foot off the floor. He wishes he could plunge right into the bowling, perhaps warm up with three or four frames as he does before the leagues.

He escorts the girls to the ball rack, helps them find a properly fitted light-weight ball, then walks toward the racks where the sixteen pound balls are stored. Ernie passes him with his ball and joins the girls who have already placed their balls on the return rack and are sitting on the benches behind the approach area.

When he arrives at the rack where his ball is usually stored, he is mildly flustered to discover the space opposite ball number 241 is empty. He looks around expecting someone to return the ball now that the leagues are over, but when he looks toward the alleys, he realizes that most of the bowlers have left. With growing dismay he realizes that whoever used ball number 241 for the league matches is either not going to return it or is still using it.

He is comforted when he remembers that either 239 or 240 is an adequate substitute, but the ball he removes from space 240 is ball 74 with a thumb hole so wide he can insert three of his thumbs without achieving a firm traction. Ball space 239 is also empty.

Now in growing desperation he begins a hurried investigation of the storage racks and the ball return racks. Why couldn't the sonovabitch who used it last have the decency to put it back? Why does this have to happen on his last night at home? He goes hurriedly from return rack to return rack, spinning balls, checking the finger grips, scrutinizing each probable-looking ball for the magic number.

But after checking most of the storage racks and half of the return racks, he returns angry and petulant to the others.

"I can't find my ball," he says. "It makes me so damn mad. Why can't people return the balls to the racks like they're supposed to? Now I've got to look all over the stupid alley."

"Aw, forget your ball," Ernie says. "Just find one you can lift and with holes that aren't too small. I took the first one I could get my fingers into."

"Listen," Gerbracht says. "You three go ahead and start. I'll catch up when I come back."

"We'll wait for you," Ernie says. "We're in no hurry. Just come back before the alley closes."

"Why don't you order a round of drinks?" Gerbracht suggests. "I'll find a ball in a few minutes."

"Good idea," Ernie says. "Don't hurry."

He leaves them again and continues his inspection tour of the return racks. He feels a mounting anger toward Ernie whose comments smacked of mockery. After ten minutes he has made it to the first alley. There has been no sign of his ball or either of its acceptable substitutes. He can't delay any longer. In the storage racks he finds ball 301. Although the thumb hole is too big, it has the right spacing. He used it a few times before, but had difficulty picking up spares.

The girls are drinking Tom Collins and Ernie has ordered a whiskey and ginger ale for him. Gerbracht stands and drinks rapidly, finishing his drink in two gulps. He assumes a seat at the scoring lectern and fills out the names, putting his own name last.

"Ready to bowl?" he asks. Ernie finishes off his drink, and places his empty glass in the holder.

"All set to go," Ernie says. "Who's first?"

"Francie, then you, then Joyce," Gerbracht says. "I'll score and go last."

There is an awkward sensuality in Francie's delivery. She has no form and delivers the ball on the wrong foot. It drops heavily to the alley and begins to roll slowly with a throbbing groan. It catches the trough of the worn path of the hook bowlers and follows a gentle curve to the 1-3 pocket. The pins tumble as if in slow motion. The 4 and 7 pins remain standing. She squeals and jumps up and down. Her face is flushed with excitement when she returns to the approach area.

"Nice ball," Gerbracht says. "If you just had a little more speed or mix that would have been a beauty."

"What do I do now?" Francie asks.

"When your ball returns, you can throw once more at the 4-7 combination. If you carry them, you get a spare and a pin bonus in your next frame."

Her ball bobs up onto the rack. Her second throw is more emphatic than her first. As the ball bounces on the wood and sputters weakly into the gutter, she puts her hand over her mouth and sneaks back to her seat on the bench. The others laugh.

"Well, you can't get them all," Ernie says.

Ernie has little form. Although he is right handed, he approaches the foul line from the left hand side. He throws the ball as hard as he can and makes no attempt to hook it, but the angle and force of his delivery result in a "back-up." His ball crashes into the 1-2 pocket and carries all the pins with explosive force. Ernie falls down over the foul line following his delivery. He crawls back on his hands and knees with a satisfied grin on his face.

"Nice form," Gerbracht laughs.

Joyce's delivery is another matter. He realizes that she has a natural form, something that could be developed. She holds the ball above her chest, rocks forward on her toes and with a ramrod back moves with stately grace toward the point of delivery. At the last moment, without bending her back, she kneels in a kind of sliding genuflection, and releases the ball. It rolls with moderate speed on a slight angle toward the 1-3 pocket.

"Nice ball," he shouts. "I think you're going to hit the pocket."

Her ball is light on the king pin and she leaves the 7 pin standing. With her second ball she takes careful aim and clears the pin with a solid hit. She jumps with restrained joy.

It is now his turn. His legs are jumpy and his hands are sweating. He extends his hand over the warm air vent to dry the perspiration, then he steps up to the approach area. He picks up his ball and rests it on his hip holding it with one hand while the automatic pinsetter resets the pins. His approach run is relatively short, a four step delivery with the first two steps almost half steps. He sets himself for delivery by turning his body at a slight angle and then carefully inserts his fingers into the sockets. He holds the ball in front of him waist high, concentrates on the pins before him and then moves forward, slowly down the right side of the approach. His final step is a long glide on his left foot. His action is explosive as he delivers the ball with a twist of the hand. The ball starts down the alley almost in the right gutter. As it gains distance on the wood, his hook begins to take. Two thirds of the way down the alley, it begins to hook sharply, too sharply it seems. He watches the shot from his follow-through position, his arms suspended like bird wings. It's going to hit the head pin high. It will probably be a split he decides, but the ball hooks more than he expected. It crosses to the left of center, barely touching the head pin, sending it spinning flatly. The head pin levels the pins on the right side. His ball drives through on the left. Gerbracht has made a cross-over strike, but he knows it didn't feel right, that it was really a lucky shot. There is something not quite right about the feel of the ball.

By the fifth frame the pattern of his failure has been established. He cannot control his hook. In the second frame the ball broke high leaving a baby split which he failed to convert. In the third frame he tried to take something off the hook and his thumb slipped. The ball didn't hook at all and managed to carry only the 6-9 and 10 pins. Then in his attempt to pick up the spare, the ball crossed over leaving the 1 and 3 pins. He retraces the steps of his delivery, trying to discover some flaw in the rhythm of his approach.

After completion of the fifth frame, his score is 57. Ernie is well ahead of him with 83. Between the fifth and sixth frames, he again searches for an adequate ball. He is once more unsuccessful. When he returns, he complains,

"The thumb hole is just too big." He shakes his head. "I can't control my hook."

"Why don't you throw a straight ball," Ernie suggests.

"I can't," Gerbracht shrugs. "Besides, you have to keep going with your strongest game. You can't panic out and start changing your delivery or you won't be able to hit anything."

But even though he stays with his strongest game, he fails to score but in the seventh he spares and says,

"I think it's coming back."

But it doesn't come back. He finishes the first game with a 127. In reviewing the game he counts three splits and two cherries. He shakes his head. Joyce, who has managed to bowl a 92, encourages him.

"It'll come back. Don't worry, Fred."

Ernie tries to cheer him up: "Look on the happy side. It's probably the only time I'll ever beat you."

"That's happy for you," Gerbracht smiles weakly.

"Look at me," Francie says. "I only had a 42."

"But you haven't been bowling twice a week for five years."

The second game is all gloom. Gerbracht simply can't pick up a spare. Ernie's game gets stronger illustrating by contrast his failure. Although he manages three strikes in the second game, one a solid hit which everyone applauds, he finishes the game at 132. His rhythm, his timing, his control—everything is off; he struggles to smile, to laugh it off, to appear casual in the face of defeat. He is angry at himself, at fate, at the bowling ball, but mostly he curses and damns to hell the anonymous bowler who failed to return ball 241 to the storage rack.

The girls and Ernie decline to bowl the third game. Francie has a blister on her finger. But they all encourage him to bowl another. We're in no hurry, they say. Work it out, they encourage him.

"I'll score for you," Ernie says.

"You sure you don't mind," Gerbracht says. "I thought if I bowled faster, if I didn't wait between shots, I might get my timing back."

He orders another round of drinks and goes to the line to bowl the final game alone. He decides to make one adjustment in his delivery. He holds the ball a fraction of a second longer, thus lofting his ball ever so slightly upon release. Because the ball does not hook so sharply, he gains greater control.

The tempo of his bowling increases. There are no long pauses between frames. He settles into a rhythm. By the fourth frame he has broken into a sweat. He can feel the perspiration between his legs. Between deliveries, he nervously shifts from one foot to the other.

"It's coming back," he says. "I think I'm in the old groove again."

He turkies the eighth frame. He can blow out and still have a substantial score, but he spares the ninth and tenth and strikes out for a 218.

"If I hadn't had that split in the third," he says retracing his score frame by frame with his finger, "I could have gone over 220 easy."

For a while as he changes his shoes and returns his ball to the rack, he is elated, but by the time he pays for the games and catches up to the others who have preceded him to the car, he is depressed. Whatever the score of the final game, he admits to himself, the simple truth is that when the pressure was on, he couldn't deliver; when he wanted to produce, he choked.

CHAPTER ELEVEN

Things usually get worse before they get better. That is, unhappily, in the nature of things. So it is an adverse turn of the wheel that has brought Gerbracht and party across town to the Capitol Highway and thence to the Buckaroo, a restaurant and bar located four miles north of the city.

The wagon-wheel chandeliers with incandescent candles, the knotty pine wall paneling, the two by four murals portraying the various natural scenes from the land of sky blue waters, and the evenly spaced tables with red and white checked cloths create an atmosphere of democratic elegance. There are even touches of rustic authenticity, an old spinning wheel, for example, to suggest a frontier heritage.

Fred and Ernie order steaks and the girls order shrimp. An argument ensues when Ernie says that not eating meat on Friday is stupid. Francie argues, "What's so stupid about it?" Ernie answers that the only reason she doesn't eat meat is because some Pope was in the fish business a long time ago. She retorts with the analogy about the long distance runner who must train his body with practice and self-denial if he is to win the race. Not eating meat is an exercise in spiritual self-discipline to help us in the race of life, she says. Ernie shrugs.

"What if you love fish and shrimp or lobster?" he says. "How are you building spiritual muscles by eating something you like better than meat?"

Francie doesn't answer and a tense quiet settles on them. Now what is a poor situation becomes even worse, for striding across the room to join them, smoothly sidestepping tables and waitresses and chairs, his hands thrust in his back pockets comes

Floyd Carlton III, son of Floyd Carlton II, local car dealer and sportsman.

Floyd Carlton is the all around young man of social advantage and athletic prowess. He is now a junior at the university. Fred has not seen him for over a year. They were never friends in high school. As Floyd moved from success to success with easy grace, Fred stumbled an uneven path of mediocrity. All the old forgotten pangs of envy return as Floyd approaches their table to slap Ernie on the back.

"Ernie. Ernie Hanson, ya old sonovagun. Where you been keeping yourself?"

Floyd draws a chair from an empty table. He turns it around, and sits backwards on the chair next to Ernie.

"Hi, girls. Haven't seen you lovelies around town so I figure you're from somewhere else."

"We're at St. Joseph's Hospital," Joyce says.

"Patients or just visiting?" he laughs, slugging Ernie on the arm. He nods condescendingly to Fred.

"Neither. We're student nurses," Joyce says.

"Is that so," Floyd says without interest. "Ernie, Ernie. You old son of a gun." He slugs him again. "I haven't seen you for six months. Where have you been keeping yourself? We had some great times in the old days, eh, old buddy? What you been doing lately?"

"Nothing right now, helping Bud at the station."

"Listen, man, if you don't get yourself deferred some way or another, you're going to get yourself drafted. They've increased the quotas again."

"I'm already deferred, permanently."

"You 4-F?" Floyd asks.

"Yeah. I've got a heart murmur or something.."

"Is that right? I didn't know you could get deferred for that."

"Why not? You got deferred for going through the motions at the U."

"Hey, nix that motions stuff," Floyd says. "I'm taking it

serious. I've gone intellectual. Really hitting the books. No crap. Had a 3.2 grade point average last semester."

Ernie guffaws behind his hand and says,

"I heard from some of the boys that you'd gone queer. I didn't hear anything about intellectual."

"That's typical. That's typical of the whole stupid sophomoric mentality in America today. Once you get interested in ideas, everybody thinks you're a queer. We have the phoniest ideas about masculinity of any culture in the world today. I can tell you there are poets today right on the campus at the U. who are more masculine, tougher, more disciplined than any pro in the NFL."

Everyone is mildly stunned by his outburst. Fred doesn't know why but he feels like crying. Fred squirms in his chair. He was hungry a few minutes ago when they ordered, but now his throat is tightening, and he feels blocked emotion bloating his chest. He lights a cigarette. The waitress brings the drinks.

"What are you drinking, Floyd," Fred says. "Be glad to buy you one."

"No thanks. My drink is over at the bar."

"You better keep your eye on it; the bartender might clear it off."

Floyd doesn't answer.

"What are you drinking?" Floyd says and lifts Joyce's tall, frosted glass to eye level.

"A Tom Collins," she says.

"Ugh. A Tom Collins in November." He sets the drink down quickly as if it is contaminated. "That's a summer drink. No one drinks a collins after Labor Day."

"I do. I drink it because I like the taste," she says and takes a sip. But Floyd has already left her behind, narrowed his interest to Ernie.

They talk about the good old days in high school; they remind each other of the time they urinated on a hot radiator in the lavatory sending yellow steam billowing from the radiator and the stench down the senior hall as far as the auditorium. They had to evacuate the classrooms in the south wing and finally cancel the afternoon classes because the rooms, with open windows to ventilate the smell, were too cold to hold classes. "Jesus, was that ever funny," Floyd says. He laughs so hard that it seems tears form in his eyes and he must squint to clear the mist.

Except for an occasional outburst of gentle laughter, they are quiet for several moments.

Floyd, leans forward, his eyes sparkling with excitement. He flashes a gleaming white smile. Fred feels a bolt of rage tightening, lumping the organs of his chest and stomach.

"Hey, Ernie. Listen. I got to tell you about this novel I read this term in a lit class. You really ought to get hold of it. It's tremendous. In fact, you all ought to read it. It's one of the finest pieces of fiction in the last twenty years. It's got everything in it. Let me tell you about it."

"Oh, not now," Ernie says. "Save it 'til I'm really drunk some night."

But Floyd eager to perform before a captive audience proceeds anyhow.

"The name of it is *Look to the River, Oh, Lost Innocence.* It all begins with this guy, his name is Hal, with two broken legs telling this story to this psychiatrist in this mental rest home. Now you don't know why his legs are broken until the end, but I'll tell you now: it was a suicide attempt."

Floyd pauses while the shock of this revelation finds its mark, then he continues.

"It's really the story of his life from when he was a little kid until he grows up. This guy is real sensitive and he sees how phony everything is. His folks are phony, his teachers are phony. He's a regular archetypical American youth, a prototype. He gets into lots of trouble in high school and college because all of the phony authoritarians are always picking their noses and saying 'No' to him."

Fred interrupts.

"You say he is sitting telling all this to a nut doctor? How long is the book?"

"Three hundred pages," Floyd says dryly.

"Does he tell the whole story of his life in one sitting?"

"Yes, but Christ, Gerbracht, you don't get the point. It's only a device."

"But it's unrealistic. Somebody is going to get a sore tail sitting there listening to a couple of hundred pages of bull."

"I told you it's only a device. It's a symbolic framework for the revelation of the inner man."

"I think Fred has a point," Joyce says. "If he's going to use a device, it ought to be realistic or else he should just tell the story like other writers do."

Floyd avoids a direct answer.

"You're pretty conventional, aren't you." He leans his chair back, his enthusiasm ebbing.

"I suppose so," she says. "I just can't believe anyone would sit that long listening to a story."

"It's a psychiatrist's job to do that," Floyd says, conceding to their demand for realism. "But you still miss the whole point."

"If you don't let him tell us about this story, we're all gonna have sore tails from sitting here all night," Ernie says.

Floyd continues less enthusiastically.

"Well, he meets this guy in college who is quite a character, real witty and philosophical. This guy, his name is Jean Paul, is an existentialist, doesn't believe in God or anything. Then this one night they're out drinking and they have a car accident and Jean Paul gets killed. This is terrifically symbolic of the irrational universe we line in—a senseless death in a car accident."

Fred is bored but too timid to do anything about it. Ernie seems to be listening but Fred can tell he is just waiting till all of this is over. The girls sit politely sipping their drinks.

"During this summer vacation he meets this rich girl who goes to one of the Heavenly Seven back East. Well, her family is concerned with status seeking and she feels they have false values, so she has an affair with Hal because he's lower middle class, goes to a state university, and is Jewish. It's her form of rebellion against bourgeois morality and philistinism."

"Who's Jewish?" Fred asks.

"Hal is. He's half Jewish. I told you that at the beginning. Christ, if you don't want to listen, don't ask me stupid questions."

"You never told us he was Jewish," Francie says and Ernie nods in agreement. Floyd is mildly flustered.

"It doesn't make any difference anyhow. He could be Irish or Swedish. The main idea is he is from a minority group having this affair with a girl from the Establishment. Kind of like in Lady Chatterly's Lover."

"You haven't told us he was from a minority group either," Joyce says.

"Well, I have now." He barges on. "Anyhow, she knows her parents don't approve of Hal, so she has this affair with him all summer. They make love all over the house when her parents are gone. It's her way of flouting them symbolically, of course. They make love in her parents' bed, on the floor in the living room, in the recreation room on the ping-pong table, on the desk in her father's study. In fact, most of the novel has to do with this one summer vacation."

"Hey, now this is beginning to sound like great stuff," Ernie says. "On the desk in the study, huh? And the ping-pong table? When will it be out in paperback? I want to find out how he does that."

"Hey, I bet she does it on the ping-pong table because her old man used to beat her at ping pong all the time," Fred says with as much sarcasm as he can muster.

"Right, Gerbracht. Right. Now you're catching on."

Floyd has reached again the pitch of enthusiasm he had earlier. Fred thinks he would like to pound someone's head against the edge of the table.

"But that's nothing. Nothing at all. Wait until you hear the rest," Floyd says.

"Don't tell us the ending. Let us find out for ourselves. You'll spoil everything." Joyce says this and Fred thinks he senses mockery in her voice.

"Mature readers don't read fiction for the cheap shock value of the ending," says and proceeds to outline the ending.

"This girl, Cynthia, goes back to college in the East. Hal goes back to the State University. Then each returns home for Thanksgiving vacation. They spend one night together in a motel and she discovers that her love is cooling off. Hal leaves the motel first. After he has gone, she discovers he has left a package of rubbers behind. She doesn't know why she does it, but she keeps them and when she gets back East, she mails them to him with a note. There is nothing on the note but these lines from a Shakespeare sonnet. She knows that when he reads the poetry, he will know their affair is over. They're a pretty sophisticated pair." This last he adds parenthetically and pauses for effect.

"Now comes the best part. She makes a mistake in addressing the letter and because she used family stationery, the letter is returned to her home address with the statement on it that the person to whom it was addressed is unknown. Well, her mother opens the envelope and finds the contraceptives there and the lines from Shakespeare and she figures the whole thing out. She's no dummy. She was Phi Beta Kappa at Vassar. Well, she flies back East and she and her daughter get reconciled and come to an understanding of values."

Fred can't take it any more. He blurts out.

"Damn it all, Floyd. I find this whole thing unbelievable. You say she's in college and the dumb broad can't even put the right address on an envelope. Then to mail it in an envelope with a return address at home so her mother can get hold of it is just about the stupidest thing I ever heard of."

"You really are naive, Gerbracht," Floyd says with a sadness verging on compassion. "Really naive." Joyce puts her hand on Fred's arm to quiet him and explains.

"She never intended the letter to get to Hal. She wanted it to end up at home, indirectly."

"What in hell did she do that for?" Fred drinks off half of his whiskey and ginger ale.

"Right. Right. She wanted her mother to find out because she wanted her to pay attention to her, to love her again like when she was a little girl," Floyd says. "She was acting subconsciously and she was banking on her mother's intelligence to figure out the significance of the contraceptives and the Shakespeare poetry. Pretty subtle. Pretty damn subtle, I say."

"I thought you said this was a story. It's more like a stupid crossword puzzle," Fred says sullenly. Floyd leans back in his chair nodding and says to Joyce,

"You're pretty acute, pretty damned acute."

"Thanks. Five minutes ago I was conventional. But don't be so generous with your praise. I've read about two or three novels that have the same kind of plot, with variations, of course."

Fred stares at her in awe. She is intelligent, well read, and spunky as well.

"When Hal finally discovers his love affair with Cynthia is over," Floyd continues, "he goes completely to pieces. He turns negative, quits studying and drops out of school."

"I thought the story was all over," Ernie interrupts impatiently. Floyd senses that the charisma of his personality is fading. He hurries through the ending quickly.

"He wanders all over seeking escape, seeking a breakthrough to a higher reality. He goes from booze to marijuana to snow—there's a tremendous analysis of the psychology of the addict here. As Hal skids deeper into skid row the author really projects a vicious indictment of the economic establishment in America. Really vicious. Then he hits bottom and it's not until he purges his guilt with this homosexual relationship with this black that he starts back up again."

Fred figures he can't make a bigger fool of himself than he already has so he breaks in again.

"What does he do that for? Hasn't the white man done enough to the Negroes, we got to turn them all into queers to purge our guilt."

"Yeh," Ernie adds, "why didn't he just have regular sex with a good-looking colored girl?"

"Neither of you get the point," Floyd shakes his head. "The author has already described the sex act several times. What he wants is to reduce the whole of experience to literature. He wants to probe the psychology of the whole person including his perversions. Besides he makes some pretty devastating sociological comments in this section."

Fred shrugs, decides that if he shuts up, Floyd is bound to finish sooner. He derives some satisfaction from the fact that everyone is clearly bored. Fred hears Floyd's words but they have little meaning. He gulps down the rest of his drink and looks around for a waitress to order another round. He is depressed that even the whiskey seems to be failing him. He has had at least three drinks and he doesn't feel a thing.

Then the waitress arrives with the food. Fred feels a sense of relief. As she places the plates on the table, Floyd hurries his recapitulation of the final scene—the crowning epiphany of the novel. Hal is picked up by the men in the white coats at the cemetery where Jean Paul is buried. Fred has forgotten who Jean Paul was. He has apparently gone there in a mad attempt to evoke the spirit of his dead comrade and it is in this scene the reader discovers through the compassionate probing of the psychiatrist Hal's real problem: he feels guilty for Jean Paul's accidental death because he had willed it beforehand out of repressed jealousy.

Upon completion of his summary, Floyd picks a French fry from one of the steaming plates. He salts it, dangles it in the air, and nibbles at it like a fish until the last morsel between his fingers disappears into his mouth. Fred orders another round of drinks. He cannot touch his own food. Only Ernie seems eager to eat. Floyd eats another French fry and tells them about his paper, an exhaustive study he assures them, that he is currently finishing in his course on the modern novel. The title of his paper is, "The Symbolic and Rhetorical Function of Literary Sources and Parallels, Ancient and Modern: Hamlet, Huck, Holden, and Hal and the Problem of Evil." The girls begin to eat their shrimp.

When the waitress brings the drinks, Ernie raises his glass to Fred.

"Here's to you, old buddy."

"Good Luck ," Joyce mumbles hastily, her mouth full of shrimp. Francie almost spills her drink when she grasps for it.

"What is it, your birthday, Gerbracht?" Floyd asks indifferently.

"Naw," Ernie answers. "This is Fred's last night here. He's going in the service tomorrow."

"What did you do, enlist or something? The air force or the navy?" Floyd asks.

"Neither. I'm going in the army."

"The army!" Floyd cries. "The army! What did you join the army for?"

"I didn't join," Fred says. "I was drafted. It's only two years that way."

"Drafted?" Floyd is shocked. "Drafted. What in hell did you let them draft you for? Christ! That's the bottom. You'll end up carrying a stupid rifle in the infantry. Why didn't you enlist, get your own speciality guaranteed before you go in? Try for OCS! Be a conscientious objector first but don't let them draft you."

"What's wrong with being drafted," Fred asks. Floyd moves his chair back from the table and stands up.

"If you don't know the draft is designed to scoop up all the idiots and the animals, you really are naive. Hell, Gerbracht, everybody knows the draft is designed to protect the elite of America—the potential doctors, lawyers, and engineers. They don't want anybody with an I.Q. over 120 to get killed." Floyd turns away and swings his chair across the aisle. He is standing now over the table. "Christ, Gerbracht, only the draftees, the animals see action—the drop outs, the morons, and the lower class boobs."

Fred can contain himself no longer.

"I think you're full of it, Floyd. Right up to here. Really full of it." With his flattened, horizontal hand he marks the highwater mark at his hair line. "Right up to here," he repeats.

"You can think anything you want to, Gerbracht. All I know is when I go, it will be with a commission or I won't go. And you can bet I won't let them put me in the infantry. In fact, I've been thinking I'd do a little grad school work first, then maybe the Peace Corps for a few years. By then I'll be too old."

Fred is intimidated. He has no other recourse of action but a blind, savage, raging attack upon Floyd's person. But he holds his passion in check. He does not want to embarrass the girls. What good would it do? He would probably just get beat up anyhow. A fleeting image crosses his mind. Perhaps, he will learn judo or karate in the army and come back on leave and clobber the living hell out of Floyd Carlton.

Now Floyd delivers his final farewell to Ernie and the girls and departs across the floor. When Fred looks up to follow Floyd's retreat, he notices that the restaurant is almost empty. After a moment of silence to insure that Floyd is out of earshot, Francie drops all pretense of eating and turns angrily to Ernie.

"Well, I never!" she says.

"You never what?" Ernie says between his potatoes and his steak.

"Your friend, that conceited. Why didn't you say something? He was your friend. Fred at least tried to stand up to him."

"I couldn't help it," Ernie pleads afraid this excellent meal is about to be ruined. "Besides, Fred told him off three or four times and Floyd backed down every time."

Fred is surprised to hear that his pitiful challenge was interpreted as a kind of victory. Everyone eats in silence. Fred tries to eat. He cuts the steak into tiny pieces and chews the pieces thoroughly, but they seem to cling to the walls of his throat when he swallows. He forces the meat down with bread and potatoes and washes the food with his drink.

Suddenly a vision of hope springs from the depths of his gloom. He sees himself home on leave in the uniform of a paratrooper or a Ranger. He is standing over the prostrate form of Floyd Carlton who is writhing from the effects of two blows—chop, chop, karate chop—that Fred has reluctantly delivered after suffering with great restraint the unjustified provocations of his callous antagonist.

The vision fades as they get up to leave the table. He pays the bill and leaves a big tip; but not even this ostentatious generosity can lessen his humiliation. Floyd is right, Fred admits to himself grimly, absolutely right. And he perversely identifies with the rest of the misfits selected for military service: the blacks escaping the ghettos, the dropouts running from the terms of their defeat, and the restless purposeless young men like himself vaguely dissatisfied with they don't-know-what but certain that there must be more to life than the hollow opportunities they have been rather unevenly dealt.

CHAPTER TWELVE

Philosophically speaking, it is true: the best laid plans of mice and men often go awry. It is also true: the worst laid plans of mice and men often turn out quite nicely.

And he is bewildered when it all begins to happen.

As they drive back into town, Gerbracht mixes two more drinks in the ginger ale bottles and passes one forward to Ernie. He is taken back at first when she suddenly unfolds herself with a rush of words. He doesn't know how to respond. He wonders: Has the booze hit the mark? She sings along with the radio—a romantic love song from a Broadway musical comedy. She has a strong, church soprano. Between songs, she gushes her contempt for music without melodies or refinements of feeling. Her tastes run to musical comedy and light opera. She accepts Gerbracht's bottle and drinks daintily.

Between songs she talks, talks, talks, She talks about her father, and her mother, her older sister, and her younger brother. She talks about God, and the President, and about diseases, patients, and procedures at the hospital. She has opinions about civil rights and poverty and war in general and politics in particular. She ranges from birth control to underdeveloped nations to communism. Gerbracht is awash in the torrent of her words.

When they arrive at the Lookout, she is expounding on the spirit of renewal embodied in the documents approved by Vatican II. Most of her ideas can be traced to a young adult evening study and discussion group led by a progressive priest who was an observer at one of the sessions of the Council. When Gerbracht seems unimpressed by her enthusiasm for church renewal, she begins to explain the importance of the new accomplishments.

She tells him what things were like just ten years ago: how the church had become somehow irrelevant in the modern age, how it needed to be updated. He nods, pretends to affirm the importance of her enthusiasm, though he really understands little she is saying.

He offers her his whiskey and ginger ale and she drinks again pausing briefly between ideas to tilt her head and swallow. Off again, she pursues a new idea with a new stream of words on yet another level of generalization.

Ernie parks the car and sets the brake. Directly below them is the river, invisible in the darkness. To the right in the distance are the clustered lights of the city. Single ribbons of light lead out from the downtown area along the river and up the bluffs. Beyond are the regularly spaced lights of the stockyards which outline an enormous rectangle with uniform subdivisions.

As Ernie and Francie assume their practiced positions, Joyce grows philosophic. Gerbracht is afraid that all this talk is a screen to avert their intimacy. But he is struck by the sincerity in her voice. She tells about why she left home. It is necessary, she says, for some people to leave to grow, while others cannot grow away from their home environment. Her older sister is like that: she is married and has two children and has never been away from home for more than a week. Joyce admits she read the substance of this truth in a magazine, but it so reflected her identical feelings that she has made it her own. She, too, had to leave home to grow.

"Hey, I know the feeling," Gerbracht says.

"It's not selfishness," she asserts. "In many ways the provincialism of the home and the small town interfere with the true expression of charity."

Gerbracht is swept along by the force of her compassion.

Ernie breaks from a kiss and says, "If you two are going to talk all night, why don't you go for a walk. We can't concentrate."

Gerbracht offers to show Joyce the lower level, the terrace of benches below the parking lot. It was carved out of the steep bluff by the WPA in the thirties and dedicated to the memory of an obscure Indian battle. Ernie offers them the blanket covering the front seat and a flashlight.

As they step from the car to the uneven surface of the frozen gravel, Joyce grips his arm tightly. She clings to him for support as they make their way slowly down the winding steps. Gerbracht flashes the light occasionally from one side to the other, revealing the steep contour of the bluff they are descending. At last they arrive at one of the wooden benches on the lower terrace. A gust of cold wind blows sharply over the terrace and Joyce shivers. Gerbracht spreads the blanket out on the bench.

"I don't think that will keep us warm," she says. Then she wraps one end of the blanket around her shoulder. "Now, you put the other end of the blanket around your shoulder," she instructs. She then extends her inside free arm around Gerbracht and grips him just above the waist. "Now, you put your arm around me and hold the end of the blanket tight with your other hand."

As they sit on the bench wrapped as one, Gerbracht feels like shouting or singing. But instead he talks, a flood of words and feelings in response to her gentle probing. He is surprised to discover that he talks of his mother and father with kindness, even affection. His vision is so benign, so full of joy, he wonders for a moment why he wants to leave. In a while, he shifts the burden of conversation back to her. He is conscious of her body so close and yet so far; haunch to haunch they sit. He grips her tightly about the waist.

"And why do you want to be a nurse. I mean, there are a lot of other things a girl like you could do. Be an airline hostess or a model or something like that. Being a nurse means lots of dirty work and not much pay."

After a long pause, Joyce looks deeply into his darkened sockets and engages eyes she cannot see.

"I want to help my fellow man," she says with great sincerity.

Gerbracht is struck by the honesty in her voice. "I'm glad you told me," he says. "It's pretty hard to say anything like that to a stranger. I mean, everybody would make fun of you, would think you were phony. It shows you trust me."

"I wouldn't tell that to just anybody," she says. "You're right about people being so cynical. They don't believe anyone wants to do good in the world without selfish gain."

"And that's why you're studying to be a nurse?"

"Yes. I felt that was the most direct way to contribute to a successful fulfillment of the Vatican Council."

Gerbracht is swept along by her frankness.

"You know, I feel kind of like that about the service. Not serving humanity, but serving my country. I know that sounds corny, but I really feel I have a duty to do something for a few years. I don't mean I'm going to be a big hero or anything like that. I don't want to kill anybody or get killed."

He is surprised when he finishes this outburst of patriotism. He doesn't feel ashamed. She has made it all somehow clean, as if for once his words are adequate to the emotion he wishes to express. She slips a hand along his arm and entangles her fingers in his, and it seems to him that this slight enmeshing of their flesh has disengaged him from the harder boundaries of his spirit. He is encouraged to betray himself to her willing openness, her feminine receptivity.

"Do you know what I really would like to be, I mean if I could be anything I wanted to?" he says.

"I'm flattered that you want to tell me," she murmurs.

"It's not that I have the ability or anything like that. I mean, I don't want you to think I'm a phony or anything."

"I wouldn't believe that about you. To be completely honest, I think you're one of the few truly sincere boys I've ever met."

Gerbracht's apprehensions dissipate.

"I know I'm probably not good enough, but I thought that with a few years service and with growing up and practice." He stops. He cannot confess this all at once. It is too deep within him. "I realize I would have to get a lot better, but I'd give my left arm to be a professional bowler."

There. He has said it and no mocking laughter greets this outpouring of his deepest self.

"I mean, I know I would have to average way over two hundred to go on the tour, but I can't think of anything I'd like to do more than follow the PBA circuit."

"It sounds so adventuresome," she says.

"I mean, I don't expect or want to be a national champion. No Don Carter or anything like that, but if I could get good enough to place high in the money, maybe win a few over the years, get on T.V., you know, just get a reputation and then get my own alley back here somewhere and settle down in ten years or so." As he talks he is almost convinced, here in the distance from fulfillment, by the flow of his enthusiasm that all of this is possible, but the memory of his earlier miserable showing suddenly casts him into a gloom. He becomes apologetic.

"I know I didn't bowl good tonight," he says sullenly. He sees his ball breaking high in the pocket with unbearable consistency and the split leave. "But I didn't have my regular ball and even that is just one I picked up, not a fitted ball, not my own. I figure my own ball alone will add twenty pins to my average."

"That's probably true," she says, "and besides you have a good start already. You have a very good form."

She is looking up at him when she finishes this. He cannot restrain himself any longer. Out of gratitude and lust and happiness he bends to her lips and kisses her quickly. She is taken by surprise, but she acquiesces even responds though flatly. When they separate, he turns his head sideways. Instead of withdrawing, he leans his head against hers. They settle, temple to temple, and view the lights below them.

After a few minutes she says: "My feet are numb."

"We'd better go back to the car," he says.

They make their way back up the steps. When they arrive at the car, Gerbracht tries to open the back door. It is locked. He raps on the window and yells.

"Go away," a muffled voice responds.

"C'mon, open the door, Ernie. We're freezing."

"Walk around, jump up and down, stimulate the circulation."

Gerbracht stamps his feet up and down. When Ernie still does not open the door, he goes to the front of the car, climbs onto the bumper, and with his weight balanced, one hand on the hood, he begins to rock the car up and down.

"All right! All right," Ernie shouts. "You win."

The back door is unlocked. Gerbracht opens the door and he and Joyce climb in.

"Thanks a lot, old buddy," he says.

"Give me the stupid blanket," Ernie says. "I'm not going to sit here and listen to you two talk all night."

Gerbracht rolls the blanket into a ball and pushes it over the front seat. Ernie and Francie open the door and venture into the cold and darkness. Gerbracht and Joyce settle next to each other. She snuggles under his arm. After several moments she says:

"You know, Francie is in love with Ernie."

Gerbracht flinches when he hears the word 'love.' He is embarrassed but doesn't know why. The word seems all wrong, an exaggeration of the relationship.

"I wouldn't use that word. I mean, they haven't known each other very long." He tries to hear Ernie saying 'I love you' seriously, but he shakes his head at the improbability. No, no.

"I don't think he 'loves' her. I mean, I don't think the words mean anything at all," he says.

Now she seems to grow cold.

"It just doesn't happen that way in life," he says. "People don't run around saying 'I love you' even if they do. That only happens on television or in the movies." He can't express what he feels.

"I didn't say he said he is in love with her. I said she is in love with him," she says. "And I didn't say she said she loved him to him."

He is troubled. Whatever progress he has made seems to be slipping away.

"Oh, I didn't mean to accuse you of anything. I just think the word love is too high flown to use to describe their going together for a month or so."

"You can fall in love very quickly," she says looking away from him.

"I don't doubt it. I don't doubt it," he says wincing and yet retreating rapidly lest he close any doors on himself.

They are silent for some time. With his arm around her and the sides of their thighs and legs touching he begins to feel awkward. Their physical proximity is no longer an embodiment of their current emotion. He takes his arm from around her shoulder pretending he needs both hands to light a cigarette, and she rebuffed, leans forward, then resettles back on the seat leaving a larger gap between them.

Now he is angry at himself. He has cut her off and he doesn't know how to reopen negotiations. He sucks on his cigarette as though smoking were the reason they have separated.

But for tonight he is in luck. It is beyond his power to ruin this evening even though he seems to have a natural talent for that sort of thing.

"They are certainly strongly attracted to each other," she reluctantly compromises her romantic vocabulary. But this is worse yet. He recoils at 'attracted to each other.' He sees two circling, sniffing dogs. Her words reverberate. The dogs are certainly strongly attracted to each other. What now? He is dumb.

She tries again.

"I think they are serious," she says.

He seizes upon this compromise of words.

"I'd say that, too," he says eagerly. "All day he was a real joker—one laugh after another, but tonight I notice he settled down a lot—didn't crack too many jokes or anything. Seems awfully serious," he concludes.

This answer seems to satisfy her. She does not push for more information. She stretches her legs and back once more and resettles against him. He puts his arm around her, takes two or three quick sucks on his cigarette, opens the window an inch and flips the lighted cigarette into the night.

Now they kiss again. They press flat lips in a long embrace and breathe mistily against each other's cheeks. Gerbracht opens his eyes occasionally to look at her. Her eyelids are closed. They grip tightly with arms wrapped around each other, but the lower halves of their bodies remain side by side, hip to hip. Her breasts press against his chest but as a unit, a solid extension of the firmness of her body. There is no differentiation, no individualization of organs. Each conscientiously avoids embarrassing the other. He does not go too far, does not want to be rebuffed.

They break for air. She fluffs her hair. She raises her body slightly by pressing her arms against the seat. She loosens their closeness slightly without suggesting withdrawal. Apparently the trapped blood of pinched, tingling flesh has been released for she resettles comfortably on the seat.

She looks up at him and now she has something to say but she does not want to be misunderstood.

"Fred," she says. "Fred, do you have something in your pocket? I mean, something besides your wallet."

Gerbracht withdraws his arm from around her shoulder and slaps the front and side of his pocket. His left hand hits a hard protuberance. He smiles in recognition, rolls to the right, thrusts his hand into his tightened pocket and withdraws a bottle.

"I'm sorry. Was it pressing against you? I couldn't feel it. It was on the other side of my handkerchief." He holds it up before them, then places it in her hand.

"It's a goodbye present from my mother. She gave it to me along with a belt with a secret money compartment," he laughs.

"What is it?"

"A bottle of high-powered, super-duper vitamin pills." He takes his matches from his jacket pocket, strikes the paper wick, and holds the miniature torch to the label.

"See, it's a bottle of Super-Plenavites vitamin pills. Strongest pills on the market. My ma's afraid I might get meningitis or leprosy or something like that in basic training."

"Well, that's not so dumb. Contagious diseases strike most severely among populations with poor nutrition. Besides natural and acquired immunity, a good balanced diet is the best deterrent of disease known to man," she says seriously, paraphrasing one of her textbooks.

"Is that so? Is that so? You mean these will really help me?" He lights another match and reads the label closely. He examines the list of the percentages of minimum daily requirements in each pill.

"They'll keep your resistance up—not only against severe illness but also against virus colds," she says. "And if you do catch something, it won't be as severe." She is very reassuring.

Gerbracht shakes his head.

"I thought it was kind of stupid. I mean, that they wouldn't really do any good." She gives the bottle back to him and he places it in his jacket pocket.

"That's a very good brand," she says solemnly and Gerbracht feels a momentary sudden rush of warm affection for his mother.

He reaches to the floor, finds the whiskey and an unopened bottle of ginger ale.

"Want another drink?"

"No thank you. I plan to receive communion tomorrow morning."

She says that, right out of the blue, and snuggles in comfortably under his arm. Gerbracht doesn't get the connection at first, then he remembers something about fasting.

"Oh, yeah. I get it. You can't eat anything from midnight on."

"No, silly. The fasting laws have all been relaxed. We can eat up to within an hour of communion now."

"Well, have another drink then."

"No. You don't understand. It will be a sin if I have another drink."

"But you already had two Tom Collins and a seven and seven. I mean if you got anything against drinking like the Baptists, you already sinned plenty."

Gerbracht is now uneasy. What has drinking got to do with communion. He thought Catholics were all good boozers, that there was nothing wrong for a Catholic to drink. In fact, he has always felt the Catholics he has known were real hypocrites, drink all night, completely bombed, then off to church on Sunday with big hangovers.

"It's not a question of drinking per se." She is serious now as she echoes the words of her religion instructor. "It is a question of excess. Of drinking too much. Even a venial sin is to be avoided." She looks at Gerbracht. "You wouldn't invite God into a dirty house, would you?"

Gerbracht thinks: How in the world did she get there? God invited to a dirty house? What kind of weird Catholic logic is this?

"I wouldn't invite God into my house clean or dirty. You know, Lord, I am not worthy—and all that. But what is this 'venial sin' bit? I don't get you."

"A venial sin is a slight offense against the law of God. It's not real serious like a mortal sin which deprives one of the grace and presence of God."

"Well, if it's not serious, why worry about it? Have another swig." He offers her the seven-up bottle.

"No. You don't understand. If I drink any more, it will be to excess. I may lose control of my faculties or get sick, which is the sin of gluttony. Don't you see. Everyone's soul is like a house or a temple. Going to communion is like inviting Jesus to visit your house. If you commit a venial sin, it's like your house is dirty. If you commit a mortal sin, it's like closing the door on God."

Gerbracht gets her point but is not convinced by it.

"Well, to each his own. I don't see how one more swig is going to be a sin. I don't think I'm sinning at all and I've had twice as much to drink as you. I mean, why did God put booze on earth if he didn't want us to use it?"

She laughs. "If you keep talking like that, I'm going to have to avoid you. I'll have to move to the other side of the car. I mean, you'll become an occasion of sin."

"Occasion of sin! Holy Cripe. Venial sin, mortal sin, occasion of sin. I give up." He takes a drink from the bottle.

"An occasion of sin is any person, place, or thing which might lead one into sin."

"Like a temptation?" he suggests.

"Yes. And I've made a vow to avoid all occasions of sin. So if I don't avoid them, it will be a double sin."

"I won't tempt you anymore."

"Good. Then I won't have to avoid you."

Now he asks indirectly in an embarrassed, anxious voice. "How will I know if I'm an occasion of sin in other things? I mean, I don't want to get your house dirty by kissing you or anything."

As soon as he has blurted this, he is sorry, chides himself to shut his mouth. He finishes on a note of bitterness that surprises him. He sinks into himself sulking.

But she is tolerant, forgiving, compassionate.

"I'll let you know," she smiles and puts her arm over his shoulder and grips the back of his neck.

"How will you let me know?"

"I'll slap your face," she says ambiguously in a voice full of invitation.

She has him coming and going. He responds to her caresses now shyly, now aggressively, now with confidence, now with uncertainty, now with passion, now with restraint, but they sit rigidly hip to hip. He does not try to press beyond her subtle lead. He does not want to betray his hardened fullness. It is sufficient that she does not abhor his touch. With her restrained caress, she endows his flesh with all the meaning he can bear.

But there is a certain progress. Her lips are no longer flat. She has puckered them and rolls them back and forth against his lips. Although her lips are still tightly sealed, there is a deeper meaning and feeling in her kiss. Her head revolves slowly and her one hand seizes him by the nape of the neck and massages with quiet vigor an approval of his flesh.

When they break again for air, he kisses her openly, wetly on the neck below her ear and she in turn traces his features with her finger tips. They kiss again and he discovers she has licked her lips. The saliva lubricates the flow of feeling from soul to soul and in this salivary unity Gerbracht is delirious with escalating bliss.

And then, in their next separation he is transported beyond all pain and shame of flesh. He feels her darting tongue—her quick, shy, darting tongue—whispering gently to the lobe of his left ear: yes, yes, yes, yes, to everything on the pure side of venial sin.

CHAPTER THIRTEEN

PAIN. Deep as marrow but throbbing. Now when he moves his leg, it shoots, stabs. When the knife-slash, whip-lash edge subsides, then the dull, pervasive ache emanating from a core, pulses. He groans to himself. He begs under his breath: only quiet laughter, old buddy. No jokes. Take the corners slowly. Easy on the brake.

PAIN. All is stretched in sagging fullness. When the car parks in front of his house, he opens the door slowly and sets one foot down at a time carefully, so as not to quicken the knife edge. No sudden movements now. No jarring.

He measures each stride, plods up the sidewalk, labors each front step with arthritic caution. Ernie catches up to him at the door. Gerbracht kneels on the floor of the porch and feels for the key under the mat.

There it is. The cold brass seems harder, heavier. Still on his knees he fumbles, scratches, finds the mark, and clicks the latch open. He turns around and puts his finger to his lips.

"Sh-h-h. Quiet!"

He crawls through the entry into the living room and hits his head on the corner of the coffee table.

"Ouch! The coffee table. I remember. Just five more feet and I'll get the lamp."

"My God, you sure are crazy tonight. A real live wire. I thought you were going to eat that girl up alive or else talk her to death. I couldn't figure out which."

Gerbracht turns on the lamp and falls into the chair.

"I got it. Me after her? What are you talking about? She was after me. Where did you get her? I mean, she was really something."

Ernie stretches out on the sofa: "You like that stuff, huh? Well, any time you want more of that you just call your old pal, Ernie."

"I've known you for years, you bastard, and you never knew any girls like them. They were better than any we ever had before, I'll tell you. Talk about good looking and stacked." Gerbracht smiles. "You know what she did? She kept on kissing me on the ear. Right here. I almost went out of my mind."

"Did you get anything?"

"Naw, I didn't try. I didn't want to spoil a good thing. You know, they cool off real fast if they think you want to go too far."

"But what if she wanted to? Maybe you just lost the chance of a lifetime, old pal."

"Naw, she told me up-front just how far she could go. I don't have to grab it all in one night. Besides, she's Catholic. I'll be home on leave in a couple of months. I got a date set up with her."

"Yeah, if she ain't married by then. Them good lookers go fast around here once the word gets out."

"She isn't going to be hurried into anything. She's in control. I'm going to write to her and remind her about our date. You know there's something about a girl you never met before. Take Alice Burnhall, for example. She's about the best looking girl I know, but I would never go out with her. I remember her in the first grade. She was so nervous that she threw up all over the desk. I can't forget that. I don't care how good looking and available she is. I could be out necking with her and as I kissed her, I would think of the time she threw up. Naw, it just wouldn't work. What you don't know won't hurt you and that's what adds to strange women you've never seen before."

"You're getting to be a real philosopher. Don't let all that thinking get in the way of your love life." Ernie pauses. "How about something to eat?"

"There are sandwiches in the refrigerator. My ma made so many that even all our relatives combined couldn't eat 'em all."

Ernie goes to the kitchen. Gerbracht listens to the refrigerator door open and slam and then the footfalls as Ernie returns and settles down to eat.

Gerbracht breaks the silence: "You know something, Ernie?"

"You got more wisdom for me?" Ernie asks between bites.

"Naw. Nothing philosophic. Just my nuts are killing me."

Ernie jumps up: "You got the stone achers. The blue balls. We got to do something quick before they bust."

"Before what busts?" Gerbracht laughs.

"Your balls. All the blood goes there when you get hot and you've got to relieve the pressure or the blood vessels might bust. It'll make you sterile."

"Hey, that wouldn't be so bad, would it? Nothing to worry about then."

"I'll cure you. Old Doc Ernie knows the cure. You've got to lift something. I always lift the back bumper of the car. It draws the blood out of your balls to your legs."

"We ain't got no car in the living room, old buddy."

Ernie looks around. He goes to the coffee table, paces around it several times, looks at the sofa. He snaps his fingers.

"I got it!" he says. "I'll stand on the coffee table and you lift the edge."

He takes off his shoes and mounts the table, teetering. He balances his weight and spreads his arms.

"O.K. I'm ready," Ernie says.

Gerbracht grabs the front edge of the coffee table. Ernie directs him to open his grip and to spread his legs.

"You've got to get your legs and back into it."

"Are you sure you're ready now?" Gerbracht says.

"Let 'er rip, old buddy."

Gerbracht groans and grunts in exaggerated fashion. He lifts the coffee table slowly at first and then with accelerated force flips Ernie backwards toward the sofa.

"Whooeeee, I'm an airplane." As Ernie lands on the sofa, the springs complain the sudden lurch. He lies there laughing as if in a fit and then he begins to cough from the dust exploded from the cushions.

"I can't see that it did any good," Gerbracht says.

"You can't expect to be cured with one shot. Let's try again." Ernie scrambles back onto the coffee table.

"Can't you be like that ninety pound woman in the carnival last summer that even a weight lifter couldn't lift off the floor.?"

"O.K. I'll try real hard. I'll push down with my legs." Ernie grimaces as if there is a great weight on his shoulders.

"Ready?"

"Wait a second." Ernie balances his weight and checks the position of the sofa. Gerbracht lifts again slowly and then with a rush of power catapults Ernie into the air and he lands on the sofa.

"Whooeee! Off we go, into the wild blue yonder. Geronimo!"

"Hey, hey," Gerbracht says excitedly. "You do it to me once."

"No! No!" Ernie says pushing him away from the table. "You need the cure, not me. Besides, it's my game. I made it up."

"I won't lift you, then," Gerbracht says pouting. "You can jump on the couch if you want."

Ernie is standing on the table waiting to be thrown again.

"C'mon, Fred," he says. "C'mon. It'll cure you if you keep it up."

"I'll do it once more. Then it's my turn," he says smiling through his sulking.

"O.K., O.K. I'll lift you next, but you got to make this a good one."

Gerbracht throws Ernie back again and then takes off his shoes and climbs quickly onto the table. He waits a few moments until Ernie stops laughing.

"C'mon, old buddy. I'm waiting."

Ernie sets himself to lift the edge of the table.

"Now don't blame me if I throw you so far you land on the floor and break your bowling arm or something," Ernie says.

"Don't worry about me. I'll take care of myself. You just get me going."

As Ernie lifts, Gerbracht drives with his legs. He shoots through the air and lands high on the sofa back tipping it backwards precariously onto two legs. For a moment it appears that everything will tumble over backwards, but he drops to the cushions, redressing the force of his original thrust. The sofa slams violently to the floor, safely returned to equilibrium on its four stubby legs. Gerbracht lies there laughing.

"No more. No more," he says. "I'm cured. I'm cured."

A quiet, almost a gloom settles over them in the next few minutes. It is as though they have been suddenly drained of their reserves of energy. Gradually they recognize these moments are anticlimactic.

"Hey, Ernie. I got one question. How come you didn't leave the motor running and the heater on. I got colder than hell sitting in the back seat the last hour."

"I was going to start her up, but I remembered this story one of the truckers told me and Bud the other day," Ernie answers, his voice genuinely serious. "There was this kid, a senior in high school in some town in Wisconsin, who borrowed his buddy's car to take his girl out. Well, they went out to park and make love and he left the motor on and there was a leak in the muffler. When they finally found them, they were both dead."

"I wonder if a piece is worth all the trouble we go through to try and get," Gerbracht says reflectively.

Ernie gets up, picks up his jacket from the floor where he threw it and begins pulling the sleeves over his arms.

"You can have them. Women are all alike. They're all trying to save your soul or cure your neurosis. They all think they're ministers or nut doctors and that all you need to be cured of your problems is a night in bed with them. The only thing is it's got to be a holy and permanent setup."

"I'll bet you're married or engaged to Francie before I come home on my first leave. She's got you by the balls, old buddy." There is a gentle taunt in his voice.

"She ain't got that tight a grip, old buddy," Ernie says with bravado, but Gerbracht can sense his resolve is flawed. Ernie moves toward the front entry.

"And even if I do decide to marry her, it'll be a long way off." He smiles grimly. "In the meantime we'll keep going out and I'll have to keep getting blind dates for her girl friends. Next week, she'll want a blind date for Joyce and I'll tell her you ain't around and she'll wonder if maybe somebody else might be available."

"And then, Ernie continues, "when you're overseas somewhere getting your ass blown off in the mud and rain, I'll drop you a note giving you a round by round description of how somebody laid her in the back seat."

"You bastard, you wouldn't!"

Ernie opens the front door.

"Oh, I wouldn't, would I?" Ernie laughs, slugs him on the arm and without as much as a farewell, slips into the night.

After a moment's hesitation Gerbracht closes the door on the cold.

CHAPTER FOURTEEN

He has decided not to venture upstairs to bed, not yet anyhow. The whiskey is still with him but fading rapidly. He feels a faint afterglow of joy. The pain too is fading as the blood subsides from the swollen tissues. It is the too-soon surfeit-sign of a too-distant promise. But there is wisdom here, a consolation prize: the dull ache tells him of the flesh-bound price he must pay for the flesh-bound pleasure he receives. If he had a philosophic mind, he might conclude from this experience that there is a balance, a natural justice which abides even in the groin and the loins.

He sits on the sofa and lights a cigarette. He sees the magazine rack, gets up, and selects an old copy of the Reader's Digest. He does not want to go to sleep yet. He is beginning to dread the hangover which sleep will bring—headache and nausea from too many drinks and cigarettes and too little rest. In the morning hot coffee and aspirin will relieve his pain.

He tries to read. He makes his way through an article proving Red China is a worthless paper tiger. Poor transportation system. No navy. Weak air force. Undeveloped industrial base. Gerbracht decides the author must be an ex-Air Force officer. The article lists several targets to be bombed with conventional or nuclear weapons if necessary. "What are we afraid of?" the author asks. "Bomb! Bomb! Bomb!" the author answers. Gerbracht thinks of the hundred and fifty million people who might be killed the first night on each side. And there will be fallout for years. Escalation. Bomb. Escalation. Bomb, the author declares. Before it is too late, before Red China has a nuclear capacity.

This grand strategic musing is too much for him. It all seems too easy to be right. Another article brings the good news that medical science has achieved a startling breakthrough of curing a dread disease Gerbracht has never heard of and cannot pronounce. He thinks he has the symptoms, though, especially after he has had too much to drink.

He makes a mental note to avoid the dread Portuguese Man-O-War when he is swimming at the beaches in California, if he ever gets there, and after reading a glowing, enthusiastic description of an orderly and efficient life in a bee hive, he decides that if he is ever born again, he would like to come back as a honey bee and do nothing but fly from flower to flower and suck nectar all day. Only if he is ever born again, of course, but that's not part of the Christian faith so he dismisses it as an idle speculation.

He lies down on the sofa without turning off the light. He won't go to sleep; he thinks he will just lie there and rest. He closes his eyes and deepens the darkness by resting his bent forearm across the bridge of his nose. He sees a blue light, away in the distance, very tiny. It grows larger as it comes toward him until with sudden acceleration it bursts out of his vision. In its place another tiny blue ball, away off in the distance, begins to grow; it is as though someone is shooting balls of light at him from a Roman candle.

He turns on his stomach in hope that the direction of the meteors will reverse. Success. They disappear completely. All is quiet, peaceful for several moments and then slowly, gradually the room begins to turn. It continues to spin faster and faster until he feels he is the center of a tumbling ball. He jumps up quickly and spreads his arms. "Slow down there. Whoa," he commands. The room stops wheeling, but his head continues to spin. He feels dizzy, sick to his stomach.

He walks about the room. The nausea subsides. He goes into the kitchen and at the sink he rinses his mouth with water, squirting the fluid between the crevices of his teeth. In the refrigerator he finds a small bottle of ginger ale. He opens this and over the sink he washes his teeth and gargles and spits the foaming, carbonated sweetness into the sink.

He returns to the sofa, lies down again on his back and reaches up to extinguish the light. No blue spots, no rolling and turning, no nausea. He falls asleep.

In time he dreams. It is not much of a dream; though disjointed in sequence, it is realistic, comprehensible.

Gerbracht discovers himself walking along a crowded street in some large city. Although people meet and pass him, no-one seems aware of his existence, yet strangely enough each passerby seems to impinge silently upon his secret self. At his side is a girl, really a young woman, a transfigured composite of all the desirable girls he has ever known. She holds his hand tightly, and as they walk, she is looking up, worshipfully, into his eyes. He can see in her eyes, the windows of her soul, the signs of her submission to his will. He feels the urgency of her eager spirit, her fiery desire. He looks around for a shelter from the eyes around him. But where? Where can they go?

Suddenly, they are alone, mysteriously transported to a darkened room. She is standing, her back to one of the walls and he is leaning the full weight of his body against her. They can still hear the sounds of the street from which they have escaped.

When his eyes grow accustomed to the semi-darkness, he looks around the room for some furniture. There is neither chair nor bed; the room is empty. Then, oddly enough, he notices an open door across the room, through which pours a parallelogram of light. He turns away from the light to the waiting, eager arms of the girl. He is overwhelmed by desire and love, and he presses his body tightly against her. Now her arms are around him and he realizes that she is naked and he is naked. He bends his face to her lips and it seems in the gently rolling, rocking, pulsing fusion of their embrace that he is one with her.

BUT WAIT! HO! WHAT IS THIS? He hears footsteps, breaks his embrace, turns toward the door and catches with his eye an emerging shadow in the shaft of light.

SOMEONE IS COMING!

It is his mother, Good Lord, and there is a look of solicitude on her face. He knows immediately that she is looking for him. She appears worn and tired, as she squints trying to see into the far reaches of the darkened room.

In one hand she carries a pair of galoshes; over one arm is a raincoat and under the other is an umbrella. As Gerbracht walks toward his mother, the girl puts on her clothes and seeks feelingly, gropingly along the wall for some avenue of escape. Fortunately, she finds another door. She whispers a promise to meet him later and leaves quietly.

Gerbracht advances into the sunlight and confronts his mother. She is delighted to see him. She gives him the rain apparel and he puts it on to please her. He goes out through the light up a short flight of stairs and stands in an open field. It is a beautiful day. The sun floods the sky and the green earth. There are flowers everywhere. He turns to his mother who has followed him.

"Jeez, Ma," he says. "It isn't raining at all. It's a beautiful day."

"Well," she says. "Now it is clear, but it might rain any minute." She looks to the sky. "See, there's a cloud now," she says pointing into the distance. "You have to be prepared for any eventuality now that you are leaving home."

Gerbracht puts a hand into one of the pockets and withdraws a tube of Polygrip and a bottle of Geritol. "What do I need this stuff for, Ma? I'm only twenty-one years old. This is for old people. Why, I've only been out of high school for three years."

"Has it been that long already?" she says. "Three years and it only seems like yesterday." She considers Gerbracht seriously. "We grow old very quickly. Why, it seems like only yesterday that I graduated from high school. Those are the best years of your life."

"What years?" he asks.

"Your high school years, of course," she says.

"I hope not," he moans.

He plunges a hand into the other pocket of the raincoat and discovers a small box of Sominex. He hears,

> Take Sominex tonight and sleep
> Safe and restful sleep, sleep, sleep.

"*In case you can't sleep on the train,*" she sighs.

Still clad in his raincoat and using the umbrella as a cane, Gerbracht walks across the field and finds himself alone once again on a busy city street. Crowds are lining the curbs; children race for positions in the front rows. He is told that a parade is about to begin.

It is a Memorial Day parade. A thrill, a stirring urge catches him in the stomach as the American flag passes followed by a contingent of Marines. Gerbracht is told that they are actually Marines who were killed on Guadalcanal. He jokes out loud: "I hope they don't try to parade everybody who got killed in wars. We'll be here forever." But he is solemnly assured by several fellow onlookers that that is precisely the nature of this parade.

"My God," he says, "they must have started a long time ago."

"Two weeks ago in Los Angeles," somebody says. "That is where the American tour began."

Marching before Gerbracht now are the soldiers of the German Wehrmacht killed on the Eastern front. A tremor of terror and hatred passes through his chest as he watches them in full military regalia goose-stepping down the middle of the street. "We beat them," he says bravely and everyone nods assent.

Behind the Germans come the Russians. And behind them the Jews who were killed in concentration camps. They are the only group so far without uniforms. Gerbracht steps off the curb and looks up the street, trying to see the beginning of the parade. But there is no beginning. The lines of marching troops are endless.

Gerbracht says: "I hope they didn't let the Chinese in the parade. There's so many of them that they go around the world."

And soon before his eyes are the Chinese troops wearing the padded pajama style uniform of winter warfare on the Korean front. They carry sticks and pitchforks over their shoulders. All of the troops are young—whether they are Chinese, or German, or French, or British. Soon the Chinese have run out of uniforms and what is marching before him are young Chinese in traditional coolie style clothes with conical hats. There is no end to them. Gerbracht shakes his head.

"These are all the Chinese, not just the soldiers," he says sadly.

"There'll be no end now. They go around the world four abreast."

"I suppose we ought to just drop H-bombs on them right now while they're here," someone says gloomily. "Then there won't be any Red menace to plague our children."

"But they're already dead," Gerbracht argues. "There wouldn't be any point killing soldiers already killed would there?"

"What are you, a communist or something?" a voice challenges him angrily.

He is about to answer when from behind two soft, white arms fold about his neck and he turns to see his ideal girl smiling into his eyes.

"I've been looking all over for you," she says.

They are again hand in hand walking down a different crowded street. They are looking for a quiet, private room. They turn off the main thoroughfare and walk up a narrow, crooked street, but they have not gone fifty feet when they are accosted from behind by military policemen. Gerbracht thinks they are after him.

"I'm not a deserter," he says. "I don't even go in until tomorrow."

"We don't want you, Gerbracht," the officer-in-charge says scornfully. "We don't want you. We want her."

He takes an official document out of his pocket.

"We want her. It's a new law. All good-looking young women are to be conscripted to serve the future leaders of America as mistresses. What's good for the Pentagon is good for America," he says.

"Let's see that document," Gerbracht says angrily. He looks it over. There is the seal of the Secretary of Defense and there is the signature of the President. The girl looks over his shoulder and reads along with him.

"It's against my religion, Fred," she says sadly. "I'm a Catholic."

"You could be a conscientious objector," Gerbracht suggests. She thinks that over for a moment and then shakes her head.

"No, I couldn't do that. It is the law of the land. It is my duty. I must obey," she says with great sincerity.

"Goodbye then," Gerbracht says.

"Goodbye, Fred," she says. As she walks away with the mili-

tary police, Fred feels angry at himself." What did I let them do that for?" he says out loud to himself. "I shouldn't have let them take her." Just before she disappears around a corner, she stops and turns around toward Fred.

"Write to me while I am in basic training," she says.

"I'll be there, too," he says. "We'll write to each other."

Frederick Gerbracht wakes up.

And now his fallen nature dogs him to the end. When he sits up, a sharp pain breaks from the base of his brain near the neck and plunges through his head like a knife thrust to his forehead. He is momentarily dizzy. A fly lands on his cheek and as he brushes it away, it lands again quickly on his forehead. He feels a wild, violent compulsion to scratch his face all over.

He swings at the fly which has landed on the sofa. He misses, gets up, despite the pain, and finds a newspaper in the magazine rack. He folds it into a flat swatter and returns to the sofa to stalk his prey. After three swipes and misses, he discovers the fly on the coffee table. He moves slowly, quietly closer to the table and then with a lurch he delivers the final blow.

He sits back on the sofa and lights a cigarette. Through the window across the room he senses the morning light rising and he is moved to consider the prospects of the coming day. The bus will leave at ten. Then the train will leave at one. The moment of his delivery is only hours away. His world will open to a new world and new horizon to new horizon will follow in succession to his view.